# KING

KING SERIES BOOK ONE

# T.M. FRAZIER

*King*
Copyright © 2015 TM FRAZIER

All rights reserved.

ISBN-13: 978-1512038569
ISBN-10: 1512038563

This is a work of fiction. Names, characters, businesses, places, events and incidents are either the products of the author's imagination or used in a fictitious manner. Any resemblance to actual persons, living or dead, or actual events is purely coincidental.

Formatting: Champagne Formats

# ACKNOWLEDGMENTS

Thank you first and foremost to my readers for your patience. I love you all so very much. Thank you for making this dream of mine more wonderful than I could have ever imagined and thank you for sticking with me.

Thank you to Karla Nellenbach for making my words look pretty AND make some sort of sense.

Special thanks to Aurora Rose Reynolds for all of your encouragement and for taking the time to be an early reader for KING. I am honored to call you my friend.

To the blogs both big and small who have supported me since day one, thank you so very very much. I don't know where I would be without you. Aestas, TRSoR, LitSlave, and so many many more.

Special thanks to Milasy, my book soulmate. So much filth to read, so little time.

Thank you to Joanna Wylde for offering to help me and for all of your wisdom. I am forever grateful for your advice.

Thank you to my agent, Kimberly Brower, for believing in me and for being patient.

Thank you so much to Andree Katic for being a phenomenal King and cover model, and to Chocolate-Eye Photography for taking such a wonderful picture.

Thank you to my wonderful husband and beautiful baby girl. I couldn't do any of this without you and I wouldn't want to.

# DEDICATION

*For Charley & Logan*

# PROLOGUE

## KING
*Twelve years old*

"COME ON YOU FUCKING FAG! YOU'RE SUCH A LITTLE fag pussy!"

I'd seen some of the kids in my school bully other kids before, but I'd never felt like I should butt in. If a kid didn't have the balls to stand up for himself, then they deserved whatever they had coming to them.

But that morning I'd made the decision to leave home for good. Mom's current boyfriend had used her as a punching bag yet again. But this time, when I'd stepped in front of her, not only did she push me aside, but she defended the fucker.

She said she deserved it.

She even went as far as apologizing.

To *him*.

I hated her for that. For becoming weak. For letting him lay his hands on her like that. I wanted to wail on John's face so bad that I sat on the side of the school during recess clenching and unclenching my fists as I replayed that morning over and over again in my mind. I may not have been able to win in a fight against a grown man, but I was convinced I could have at least done some damage.

So when I heard those words shouted from across the playground it was like my anger had made the decision before I had a chance to really think about it. Before I knew it, I'd leapt across the sandbox and was on my way to a group of kids gathered in a circle on the far side of the yard next to the kickball field.

I towered over all the other kids in my grade and could easily see over their heads. In the center of the circle was a brute of a kid named Tyler, a dark-haired boy who always wore band logo t-shirts with the sleeves ripped off. He was holding this skinny kid by the collar of his shirt, punching him in the face over and over again with his closed fist. The littler kid grunted each time Tyler made contact. The boy's ripped shirt rose up over his pale stomach revealing bruises in varying shades of purple and yellow. His ribs were so visible I could count them. Blood dripped from his nose and fell to the ground. I pushed aside two little girls who were cheering on the beating.

Kids can be fucking cruel.

Adults can be crueler.

I jumped in front of Tyler and cocked back my fist. With one punch to the bully's pimpled jaw, I knocked him flat on his ass. The back of his head landed with a thunk against the pavement. Out cold.

I instantly felt better, although the need to inflict violence was always like a rat gnawing on my every thought and emotion, punching Tyler had temporarily dimmed the feeling from blaring spotlight to burning candle.

The skinny kid was on the ground holding his bloody nose. He moved his hands away from his face and looked up at me with the biggest most ridiculous smile, blood coating teeth that were too big for his mouth. Not what I expected from someone who'd just been beaten. "You didn't have to save me. I was just letting him get some punches in before I rained down the pain." His voice cracked on every other word of the lie. Tears ran out the sides of his eyes and down through the blood smeared across his lip. The circle of kids had broken up and gone back to their kickball game.

"I didn't save you," I said, stepping over him. I started walking away, but somewhere around the sandbox the kid had caught up with me.

"Of course you didn't. I could totally have taken him. But shit man, that fucking prick has a stick up his ass," the kid swore, throwing his hands up into the air as he jogged to try and keep up with my long strides.

"Oh yeah, and why is that?" I asked.

"Cause he wanted me to do his fucking math worksheet, and I'll tell you something. I'm no one's fucking bitch. So I told him to fuck off." His voice was muffled since he was still trying to stop the blood dripping from his nose by pinching his nostrils together.

"All you said to him was 'fuck no' and he started beating on you?" I asked, although I didn't find it hard to believe, aside from the bullshit with my mom and John it was mostly little things that had been making my fist ache for something to connect with.

The kid smirked.

"Well, there was that… and then there was how I told him how I thought it was cool that his dad didn't mind that his son was the spitting image of his mama's boss at the Price Mart." He brushed the dirt off the scrapes on his elbows, then dusted the palm of his hands off on his wrinkled khakis. "Name's Samuel Clearwater. What's yours?"

I stopped and turned to him. He extended his hand to me and I uncrossed my arms and shook it. For a gangly kid who was the same age as I was, he dressed and spoke like a foul-mouthed grandfather, someone too old to give a shit about filtering his words. And what eleven year old shook hands?

Samuel Clearwater, that's who.

"Brantley King," I answered.

"You got a lot of friends, Brantley King?" Samuel's unruly sandy blonde hair fell forward into his eyes, and he brushed it away with dirt caked fingernails.

"Nope." None of the kids in school were like me. I'd felt alone since my very first day in Kindergarten. While everyone else was learning the words to Old McDonald, I was worried about how long I was going to have to wait until after dark to go home. Too early and whatever guy my mom let move in that month would be ready to brawl.

Being on my own was natural to me. As time went on, it became something I liked. Although I was the biggest kid in school, I'd always managed to move around like a ghost.

Until I started getting in trouble.

Then WE started getting into trouble together. Preppy and I. Two peas in a juvenile delinquent pod.

"Me neither. Way more trouble than their fucking worth," Samuel said, almost convincingly. He re-tucked his too-large plaid shirt into his khaki pants, righting his suspenders that fell off his shoulders every few seconds. He straightened his yellow polka-dotted bow-tie.

"What's up with the bruises?" I asked, pointing to his ribs.

"You saw those, huh?" Sadness crossed over his face, but he fought back whatever he was thinking about and pursed his lips. "Step-daddy from hell with issues, ever since my mom died. Actually, he's got only two issues. Beer and me. Beer he likes though. Me? Not so much."

I could relate. Although I didn't have one stepdad, more like a constant parade of men. They all had different names, different faces, but essentially they were all the same.

"Well, kid, I don't think Tyler is going to bug you again." I started walking again, heading back to my spot on the side of the building where I could be alone. In the corner of my eye I saw Tyler hobbling up the steps into the school, clutching his jaw.

*Pussy.*

"That's it?" Samuel followed close behind me, knocking into my heels.

"What else is there?" I ducked under the branch of a low hanging tree. Samuel was easily a foot shorter than me and scooted under it without any problems. When we got far enough away from the other kids I lit the half-cigarette I'd been saving in my back pocket with the last match from the book I'd been hiding in my shoe.

"Can I try?" Samuel asked, startling me. I hadn't realized he was still there.

I passed him the cigarette, and he inhaled deeply. He then spent the next five minutes choking. I put the cigarette out on the sole of my sneaker while his face turned a weird shade of purple before going back to pale smeared with freckles and blood. "That's really fucking good, but I'm a menthol man myself."

A burst of laughter escaped me, and I bent over, hugging myself at the waist. Samuel ignored my outburst and continued talking. "Where do you live?"

"Here and there." Nowhere was the truth. I wasn't ever going back home again. School would now become just a place to go during the day so I could sneak into the locker room before class to shower and for the free breakfast program. Everything I owned was in my backpack.

And it was light.

"I'm over in Sunny Isles Park. It's a fucking shithole. When I grow up, I'm going to have one of those big places on the water on the other side of the causeway with the long legs that look like they're from Star Wars."

"Like one of them stilt homes?"

"Yeah man, a fucking Star Wars stilt home, right on the bay." This boy lived in a trailer park where he was beaten up by his stepdad, and here he was dreaming about his future. I couldn't see my way past next week, never mind to the next ten years. "What about you, man?"

"What about me?" I unhooked my pocket knife from the waistband of my jeans and used it to pick at the falling stucco on the side of the building.

"What are you gonna do when you grow up?"

The only thing I really knew was what I didn't want. "Not sure. I just know that I don't want to work for anyone. Never liked being told what to do all that much. I'd like to be my own boss, run my own shit."

"Yeah, man. That's fucking amazing. Yes, that. I'll help you. We can do it together. You run the shit. I'll help you run the shit. Then, we'll buy a big 'ole Star Wars stilt home and live there, and no one will be able tell us what to fucking do ever again!"

Samuel removed a composition notebook from his backpack and turned to a blank page. "Let's make a mother fucking plan."

The idea seemed silly, sitting down with a kid I didn't know and making a plan for a future I'd never thought of, but for some reason the thought of hurting his feelings made my chest feel stabby, a feeling I was very unfamiliar with. Unsure of what to do next I gave in. I sat down next to him in the grass and sighed. He smiled up at me like just me being there meant we were halfway there.

"We can't be pussy's about this," he continued. "We aren't going to get the Star Wars house by getting jobs in a shitty hotel or factory, and I never been much of a fisherman. So this shit starts now. Pussies get pushed over and stepped on. My uncle, who's a total fucking asshole douche-bag, sells weed. We could steal some from him and sell it. Then, we can use that money to buy our own to sell."

Using a black marker from his bag, Samuel began to draw on the page. The top read GOAL and he drew a house with legs underneath that did look like a stick figure version of the whatever-you-call-it-thing in Star Wars. I didn't know the name of it because I'd never seen the movies, just the previews. Then, he drew what looked like it was supposed to be us, him much smaller than me. With a green marker, he drew dollar bill signs all around us floating in the air.

"So what? We friends now, Preppy?"

I'd never had a friend before, but there was something about this boy with the foul mouth that got my attention. I plucked the marker from his hand and took over his drawing. I was never good at much in school, except for art. Just drawing really.

Drawing was my jam.

"Fuck yeah!" Preppy said, watching me add on to his stilt home. He'd also drawn a picture of what I assumed was his uncle because he'd written douche-bag over the top. "You're fucking good at that. Man, we've got to have you do that, too. Art shit. Write that down in the plan. We gotta have hobbies, too."

"Then what's your hobby?" I asked.

"My hobby?" He smiled and wiped his nose, which had just started dripping blood again, a single drop fell to the page and splattered on stick figure Preppy. He nodded slyly and purses his lips, hooking his thumbs under his suspenders. "Bitches."

I think I laughed more that day then I ever did in my whole life. I also learned that 'bitches' could be a hobby.

"So what happens if we get caught?" I asked, pausing the marker over the page.

"We won't. We're too fucking smart for that shit. We'll be careful. We'll make plans and stick to the plans. Nobody will get in our fucking way. Nobody. Not my step-dad, not my uncle, not teachers, and especially not bitch-ass bullies like Tyler. I ain't ever getting married. I ain't ever having a girlfriend. This is just about Preppy and King crawling out of the shit instead of rotting in it."

"But really, what if we get caught?" I asked. "I'm not talking about by the cops. I'm talking about by your uncle, or anyone else that does the kind of shit we're talking about doing here. These are rough people. Bad people. They don't like being messed with." I knew these kinds of people first hand. More than one dealer had come to our house armed with guns, demanding payment. Mom would settle her debt by taking them into her bedroom and closing the door.

This kid may have just been screwing around, but the more I thought about it the better it all sounded. Living a life without answering to anyone. A life without fear of what someone could do to me or to this little preppy kid, who by the looks of it had enough bullying to last him his whole life.

The idea of growing up and being my own man, the kind of man people didn't mess with, the kind of man who didn't take shit from anyone, became more and more appealing as it rolled around in my brain and latched on, taking up residence where I was missing other things the guidance counselors said I was lacking, like a 'firm sense of right and wrong'. But they were the ones who were wrong. It's not that I didn't know the difference.

It's that I just didn't care.

Because that's what happens when you've never had anything to care about.

If I was going to take this kid seriously, I needed to know that he wasn't going to bitch out on me if it all went south. I needed to know he was as serious about the plan as I was getting, so I had to ask, "What really happens if someone gets in our way? In the way of our business? In the way of our plan?"

Preppy held the end of a marker to the corner of his mouth where blood had begun to dry and crust over. For a moment, he stared over my head, deep in thought. Then, he shrugged and locked his eyes onto mine.

"We kill them."

## KING

O N THE DAY I WAS RELEASED FROM PRISON I FOUND
myself tattooing a pussy on a pussy. The animal onto
the female part.

A cat on a cunt.

*Fucking ridiculous.*

The walls of my makeshift tattoo shop pulsed with the
heavy beat of the music coming from my homecoming party
raging on the floor below. It shook the door as if someone were
rhythmically trying to beat it down. Spray paint and posters
covered the walls from floor to ceiling, casting a layer of false
light over everything within.

The little dark haired bitch I worked on was moaning like

1

she was getting off. I'm sure she was rollin' because there was no way a tattoo directly above her clit could be anything other than fucking painful.

Back in the day, I could zone out for hours while tattooing, finding that little corner of my life that didn't involve all the bullshit I had to deal with on a daily basis.

In the past when I'd been locked up, albeit for much shorter periods of time, the first thing on my mind was pussy and a party. But this time the first thing I did when I walked through the door was pick up my tattoo gun, but it wasn't the same. I couldn't reach that place of temporary reprieve no matter how hard I tried. It didn't help that the tattoos people requested were getting dumber and fucking dumber.

Football team logos, quotes from books you know they've never read, and wannabe gangsters wanting teardrops on their faces. In prison, the teardrop tattoo represented taking a life. Some of the little bitches who wanted them looked like they couldn't step on a roach without cowering in the corner and crying for their mamas.

But since the majority of time my clients paid in favors and consisted mostly of bikers, strippers, and the occasional rich kid who found himself on the wrong side of the causeway, I should've lowered the bar on my expectations.

But then again it was good to be home. Actually, it was good to be anywhere that didn't smell like vomit and wasted lives.

My own life had been moving forward at nothing short of full fucking speed ahead ever since the day I'd met Preppy. I'd loved living outside the law. I fed off the fear in the eyes of those who crossed me. The only thing I'd ever regretted was getting caught.

When I wasn't locked up, I'd spent almost every single day of the twenty-seven years I'd been on the earth in Logan's Beach, a little shit town on the gulf coast of Florida. A place where the residents on one side of the causeway lived solely to cater to the rich who lived on the other side, in high-rise beachfront condos and mansions. Trailer parks and run down houses less than a mile from the kind of wealth it takes more than one generation to accumulate.

On my eighteenth birthday, I bought a run-down stilt home hidden behind a wall of thick trees, on three acres of land that practically sat under the bridge. In cash. And along with my best friend Preppy, we moved on up to the rich side of town like the white trash version of the motherfucking Jeffersons.

True to our words, we became our own men and answered to no one. We did what we wanted. I turned my drawing into tattooing.

Preppy got bitches.

I fucked. I fought. I partied. I got wasted. I stole. I fucked. I tattooed. I sold dope. I sold guns. I stole. I fucked. I made fucking money.

And I fucked.

There wasn't a party I didn't like or that didn't like me. There wasn't a chick who didn't give me the go-ahead move, lifting her hips so I could slide off her panties. I got that shit every single fucking time.

Life wasn't just good. Life was fucking great. I was on top of the fucking world and no one fucked with me or mine.

No one.

And then it all changed and I spent three years in a tiny windowless cell, studying the changing cracks in the concrete block walls.

When I was done with the purple cartoon cat, I applied salve, covered it with wrap, and disposed of my gloves. Did this girl think that guys would be turned on by this thing? It was good work, especially since I'd been out of commission for three years, but it was covering up my favorite part of a woman. If I undressed her and saw it, I would flip her over.

Which sounded like a good idea. Getting laid would help shake this post prison haze and I could get back to the things that used to be important to me without this lingering sense of dread looming in my conscious.

Instead of sending the girl back out to the party I roughly grabbed her and yanked her down the table toward me. I stood, flipping her over onto her stomach. With one hand on the back of her neck, I pushed her head down onto the table, releasing my belt buckle with the other. I grabbed a condom from the open drawer.

She knew beforehand that money wasn't the type of currency I was looking for, and I didn't do free. So I lined up the head of my cock and took her pussy as payment for her new tattoo. Of a pussy.

*Fuck my life.*

The girl had a great body, but after a few minutes of irritating over-the-top moaning, she wasn't doing anything for me. I could feel my cock going soft inside her. This wasn't supposed to be happening, especially not even after years of my right hand and my imagination being my only sexual partners.

*What the fuck is wrong with me?*

I grabbed her throat with both hands and squeezed, picking up my pace, taking out my frustrations with each rough thrust in rhythm with the heavy beat from the other room.

Nothing.

I was about to pull out and give up.

I almost didn't notice the door opening.

*Almost.*

Staring up from my doorway was a vacant pair of doll-like blue eyes framed by long icy-blonde hair, a small dimple in the middle of her chin, a frown on her full pink lips. A girl, no older than seventeen or eighteen, a bit skinny.

A bit haunted.

My cock stirred to life, dragging my attention back to the fact that I was still pumping into the brunette. My orgasm hit me hard, spiraling up my spine and taking me by complete surprise. I closed my eyes, blowing my load into pussy tattoo, collapsing onto her back.

*What the fuck?*

By the time I opened my eyes again, the door was closed and girl with the sad eyes was gone.

*I'm fucking losing my mind.*

I rolled out of and off the brunette who was luckily still breathing, although unconscious from either strangulation or the dope that had made her pupils as big as her fucking eye sockets.

I sat back on my rolling stool and dropped my head into my hands.

I had a massive fucking headache.

Preppy had organized this party for me, and the pre-prison me would've already been snorting blow off the tits of strippers. But post-prison me just wanted some food, a good night's sleep, and these fucking people to get the hell out of my house.

"You okay, boss-man?" Preppy asked, peeking his head into the room.

I pointed to the unconscious girl in the chair. "Come get

this bitch out of here." I ran my hand through my hair, the pulsing of the music making the pounding in my head grow stronger. "And for fucks sake, turn that shit down!" Preppy didn't deserve my rage, but I was too fucked up in the head to dial down my orders.

"You've got it," he said, without hesitation.

Preppy slid past me and didn't question the half-naked girl on the table. He hoisted her limp body over his shoulder in one easy movement. The unconscious girl's arms flailed around on his back, smacking against his back with each step. Before he could get too far, he turned back to me.

"You done with this?" he asked. I could barely hear him over the music. He gestured with his chin to the brunette on his shoulder, a childlike grin on his face.

I nodded, and Preppy smiled like I'd just told him he could have a puppy.

*Sick fuck.*

I loved that kid.

I closed the door, grabbing my gun and knife from the bottom drawer of the tool box I kept my tattoo equipment in. I sheathed my knife in my boot, and my gun in the waistband of my jeans.

I shook my head from side to side to clear away the haze. Prison will do that to you. Three fucking years sleeping with one eye open in a prison full of people with whom I've made both friends and enemies.

It was time to keep some of those friends and call in some of those favors, because there was something more important than my own selfish shit that I needed to take care of.

*Someone* more important.

Sleep could wait. It was time to go down stairs and make

nice with the bikers. I'd avoided doing business with them in any capacity for years even though their VP, Bear, is like a brother to me. Bear tried to get me to join his MC a hundred times, but I'd always said no. I was a criminal who liked my crimes straight up, without a side of organized. But now I needed connections the bikers could provide as well as access to shady politicians whose decisions and opinions could be swayed for a price.

I never cared about money before. It used to be something disposable for me, something I used to fund my *I don't give a fuck* lifestyle. But now?

Payoffs to politicians didn't come cheap, and I was going to need a lot of cash and very fucking soon.

Or I was never going to see Max again.

## Doe

NIKKI WAS MY ONE AND ONLY FRIEND IN THE ENTIRE world.

And I kind of fucking hated her.

Nikki was a hooker who'd found me sleeping under a bench. I'd unsuccessfully avoided the previous night's downpour and had just shivered and chattered myself to sleep. I'd already been living on the streets for several weeks at that point and hadn't had a real meal since running away from Camp Touchy-Feely, a nickname I gave the group home I'd been left to rot in. I'm pretty sure Nikki was trying to rob me—or what she thought was a corpse—when she just happened to have noticed I was still breathing.

Frankly, I'm surprised she even bothered with me after realizing I was very much alive.

Not so much living, but alive.

Nikki snorted the last of her blow through a rolled up post-it-note off a yellowed sink that was days away from falling free from the wall. The floor was littered with toilet paper, and all three toilets were on the verge of overflowing with brown sludge. The overwhelming scent of bleach singed my nose hairs like someone doused the room with chemicals to lessen the smell but hadn't bothered with any actual cleaning.

Nikki tilted her chin up toward the moldy ceiling tiles and pinched her nostrils together. A single fluorescent light flickered and buzzed above us, casting a greenish hue over the gas station bathroom.

"Fuck, that's good shit," she said, tossing the empty baggie onto the floor. Using the wand from an almost empty tube of lip-gloss, she fished out whatever was left and applied it to her thin cracked lips. She then smudged the thick liner under her eyes with her pinky until she nodded in satisfaction into the mirror at her racoon-esque smoky look.

I stretched my sleeve of my sweater down over the heel of my hand and wiped the filth off the mirror in front of me, exposing two things: a spider web crack in the corner and the reflection of a girl I didn't recognize.

Light blonde hair. Sunken cheeks. Bloodshot blue eyes. Dimple chin.

Nothing.

I knew the girl was me, but who the fuck was I?

Two months ago, a garbage man discovered me in an alley where I had been literally thrown out with the trash, found lying in my own blood amongst a heap of garbage bags beside a dumpster. When I woke in the hospital, with the biggest fucking headache in the history of headaches, the police and doctors dismissed me as a runaway. Or a hooker. Or some hybrid combo of the two. The policeman asking me questions at my bedside didn't bother to hide his disgust when he informed me that what probably happened was a simple case of a John getting rough with me. I'd opened my mouth to argue but stopped.

He could've been right.

Nothing else made any sort of sense.

No wallet. No ID. No money. No possessions of any kind.

No fucking memory.

When someone goes missing on the news, teams of people gather together and form a search party. Police reports are filed and and sometimes candlelight vigils are held in hopes the missing would soon return home. What they don't ever show you is what happens when no one looks. When the *loved ones* either don't know, don't exist…or just don't care.

The police searched the missing persons reports throughout the state and then the country with no luck. My fingerprints didn't match any on record, and neither did my picture.

I learned then that being labeled a missing person didn't necessarily mean I was missed. At least not enough to require any of the theatrics. No newspaper articles. No channel-six news. No plea from family members for my safe return.

Maybe, it was my fault no one had bothered to look for me. Maybe, I was an asshole and people celebrated the day I went away.

Or ran away.

Or was shipped down river in a fucking Moses basket.

I don't fucking know. Anything was possible.

I don't know where I came from.

I don't know how old I am.

I don't know my real name.

All I had in the world was reflected back at me in the bathroom mirror of that gas station, and I had no fucking clue who she was.

Without knowing if I was a minor or not, I was sent to live at Camp Touchy-Feely, where I only lasted a couple of weeks among the serial masturbators and juvenile delinquents. On the night I woke up to find one of the older boys standing at the foot of my bed with his fly unzipped, his dick in his hand, I escaped through a bathroom window. The only thing I left with was the donated clothes on my back, and a nickname.

They called me Doe.

As in Jane Doe.

The only difference between me and a real Jane Doe was a toe-tag because what I was doing sure as shit wasn't living. Stealing to eat. Sleeping wherever I could find cover from the elements. Begging on the side of freeway off-ramps. Scrounging through restaurant dumpsters.

Nikki ran her chewed-off fingernails through her greasy red hair. "You ready?" she asked. Sniffling, she hopped on the balls of her feet like she was an athlete amping up for the big game.

Though it was the furthest thing from the truth, I nodded. I wasn't ready, never would be, but I'd run out of options. It wasn't safe on the streets, each night in the open was a literal gamble with my life. And not to mention that if I lost any more weight, I wouldn't have the strength to fight off any threats. Either way I needed protection from both the elements and the people who lurked around at night before I ended up a real

Jane Doe.

I don't think Nikki was capable of registering the feeling of hunger. Given the option, she chose a quick high over a full stomach. Every single time. A sad fact made obvious by her sharp cheekbones and dark circles under her eyes. In the short time I'd known her, I'd never seen her ingest anything but coke.

I judge her and I feel shitty about it. But something inside me tells me that she's better than the thing she does. When I'm not extremely irritated with her I feel almost protective of her. I was fighting for my own survival and I wanted to fight for hers, but the problem was, she didn't want to fight for herself.

I opened my mouth to lecture her. I was about to tell her that she should lay off the dope and change her main priority to food and her overall health, when she turned toward me. There I was, my mouth agape, ready to rain down judgment on her regarding like I was better than her. The truth was that I could've been knee deep involved in the same shit before I lost my memory.

I closed my judgmental mouth.

Nikki eyed me up and down, appraising my appearance. "I guess you'll do," she said, blatant dissatisfaction in her tone. I refused to cake on makeup or pluck out all of my eyebrows just to draw a thin line in their place like she did. Instead, I'd washed my hair in the sink and used the hand dryer to speed along the drying process. My face was makeup free, but it would have to do, because if I was going to do this, I was determined to do it my way and without looking like Nikki.

*Yep, I am a judgmental asshole.*

"How is this going to work again?" I asked. She'd already told me ten times, but she could tell me ten thousand times and I still wouldn't feel comfortable.

Nikki fluffed out her limp hair. "Seriously, Doe, do you ever listen?" She sighed in annoyance but continued on. "When we get to the party all you have to do is cuddle up to one of the bikers. If he likes you there is a good chance he might want to take you in, keep you around for a while, and all you have to do is keep his bed warm and a smile on his face."

"I don't know if I can do it." I said meekly.

"You can do it, and you will do it. And don't be all shy like that around them, they won't like that. Besides, you're not the shy type, that's just your nerves talking. You're all rough edges, especially with that horrible case of foot-in-mouth syndrome."

"It's eerie how you have me pegged in the short time you've known me," I said.

Nikki shrugged. "I'm a people reader, and believe it or not, you are very easy to read. Like for example, right now you're super tense. I know this because your shoulders are all hunched over." She presses my shoulders back. "Better. Stick out your chest. You don't have much to work with up top but without a bra, if you keep your shoulders back, they can catch a glimpse of a little nip, and guys love the nips."

That was it. I could get a biker to like me, he would protect me, hopefully long enough for me to figure out plan B. "Worst case scenario is that he's only looking for a quick one-time thing and he'll throw you a few bucks and send you on your way." Nikki made it sound more like a vacation than prostitution.

I could fool myself into thinking that if I wasn't soliciting on the street then I wasn't like Nikki, but the truth was no matter which way I twisted the facts, this plan would turn me into a whore.

*Judgey McJudgerpants.*

When I wracked my brain for other options, I'd come up

as empty as my stomach.

Nikki pushed open the door, and sunlight invaded the dark space as it swung back and forth. With one last glance at the plain-faced girl in the mirror, I whispered, "I'm sorry."

It was a comfort knowing that whoever I was before my slate was wiped clean didn't know what I was about to do.

Because I was about to sell her body.

And whatever soul I still had.

## Doe

I SAT IN THE BACK SEAT OF SOME BALD GUY'S ANCIENT Subaru, willing myself to become temporarily deaf so I wouldn't be forced to listen to Nikki suck off the driver. He was taking us to the party, which was in a house in Logan's Beach. When we finally came to a stop, I leapt out of the car like it was on fire.

"Bye, baby," Nikki said sweetly, wiping the corner of her mouth with one hand and waving with the other as our ride pulled away. When he was out of sight, she rolled her eyes and spit onto the ground.

"I think I'm going to be sick," I said, trying not to gag.

"Well, I didn't see you offering to suck his cock for a ride," Nikki snapped. "So shut the fuck up about it. Besides, I got us here didn't I?"

*Here* was on a dirt road at the edge of a property over-grown with trees and hedges. A small gap in the brush allowed room for a narrow driveway. It was dark and there were no street lights to guide our way up the to the house, the path seemed to go on forever. A mild fish odor permeated the air. My empty stomach rolled, and I covered my mouth and nose with my hand to keep from getting sick.

Flickering lights appeared in the distance. As we approached the house I realized what we were seeing weren't lights at all, but plastic torches stuck into the ground at awkward angles, creating a makeshift path through the grass around to the back of the house.

The house itself was three stories and built on a foundation of pilings. The majority of the bottom floor under the house was open area, filled with shiny motorcycles and cars parked in every inch of available space. Two doors took up the far wall, one with a deadbolt and a metal bar across it and another a few feet off the ground with two concrete steps leading up to it. Wrap around balconies made up the second two stories and lights flashed through every window, revealing shadows of the people within. The music vibrated off the wet ground, shaking the water off the tall blades of grass onto my legs.

"Do the bikers live here?" I asked Nikki.

"No, this house belongs to the guy they're throwing the party for."

"And who is that?" I asked. Nikki shrugged.

"Beats me. All I know is that Skinny said it was a coming home party." Skinny was Nikki's sometime boyfriend, sometime pimp.

When we reached the back of the house, I got my first glimpse of the bikers and my stomach rolled again. I stopped dead in my tracks.

There they were, surrounding a fire pit in the center of the massive yard, flames and billowing smoke shot up as high as the house. I was so caught up in what I was going to have to do I'd forgotten to stop and think of who I was going to have to do it with. There were seven or eight men, some sitting in lawn chairs, some standing with a beer in their hands. They all wore leather vests with varying amounts of patches adorning them. Some wore long sleeved button down shirts under their vests; others wore nothing at all. Women who looked like they took their fashion cues from Nikki laughed and danced around the fire. One girl was on her knees, bobbing her head up and down on the lap of a man who casually talked on his phone while guiding her head with his hand.

*This is just a means to an end.*

I turned to tell Nikki that maybe we should reconsider the plan, but she was already gone. Scanning the yard, I spotted her with an arm already draped over a tall guy with a red braided beard. An American flag bandana tied around his forehead.

Strong arms wrapped around my waist from behind and hauled me hard against a wall of muscle. My immediate reaction was to shake him off, but when I struggled to break free he held me tighter. His hot breath smelled of garlic and liquor, assaulting my senses when he spoke with his lips pressed against my neck. "Hey, baby girl. I'm ready to party. How 'bout you?" Grabbing my wrist he forcefully wrenched it behind my back until I was sure my shoulder had dislocated. He shoved my hand down the front of his jeans, rubbing my clenched fist up and down the length of his erection. "Feels good, don't it, baby girl?"

I opened my fist and grabbed his balls, squeezing them with all the strength I could manage.

"You bitch!" he yelled out.

Releasing me, he dropped to his knees in the grass. Hands cupped over his privates, he fell onto his side and raised his thighs to his chest. I raced up the steps that led into the house.

"You fucking bitch! You're going to fucking pay for that!" he called as I disappeared into the house sliding past a ton of party-goers. I took the first set of stairs I came across and ran all the way up to the third story. I tried the handle of several closed doors down a narrow hallway, but they were all locked. It wasn't until I was almost to the end of the hall when one finally gave.

I hadn't even taken a step inside when I quickly realized the room may have been dark, but it wasn't empty.

A smattering of neon paint on the walls made the room look like as if it were glowing. I couldn't see much in the way of features, but I could make out two bodies in the center of the room. At first glance it looked as if someone was standing be-hind another person who was lying down. It took me a second to register it, but after I did, there was no mistaking what it was I'd walked in on.

Skin slapping against skin. Moaning. The smell of sweat and something else I couldn't quite place. It seemed like hours I'd been standing there, but in reality it wasn't more than a few seconds. I should've turned around and closed the door the instant I realized the room was occupied, but I couldn't tear myself away from the scene playing out in front of me.

A magnetic pair of eyes locked onto mine. Under the

artificial lights, they glowed bright green. The man stared right through me and much to my surprise he didn't blink or look away. Faster and faster, his hips slammed against hers. His eyes bore into mine as he thrust over and over again. When he closed his eyes and threw back his head with a long throaty groan, our connection was severed.

The man collapsed onto the girl's back and released his grip from her throat. He'd been strangling her? She was moaning when I first walked in on them, and then she had fallen silent.

Dead silent.

I quickly remembered I had feet and closed the door, fleeing back down the stairs. I hid beside the water heater under the house, beside all the cars and bikes, where I sat for over an hour, running the gravel through my hands and hoping to come to terms with the shitty direction my life was heading in. As much as I wanted to take off into the night and run I couldn't go far, my overwhelming fear of the dark held me captive at the house where I may have just witnessed a murder, but it least I could find light.

*Fear had seriously fucked with my priorities.*

It was that fear, as well as my growling stomach and light-headedness that reminded me of why I was there in the first place.

Basic survival.

*I am desperate, and desperate people don't have the luxury of options.*

I sucked in a deep breath. I had to do what I had to do, even if I didn't exactly know what that was. I mean, I knew the mechanics of it. But my brain was like a car with the mileage turned back to zero. A clean slate that I was about to make filthy dirty.

I may have been homeless and starving, but I was determined to get myself off of the streets and into a real life someday. A life with a soft bed and clean sheets. Once I didn't have to worry about my safety or my stomach, I could focus on finding out the truth about who I really was.

I made a promise to push through the here and now and do what needed to be done, then I would never think about this time ever again. It would be a small spot on the radar of my life that I vowed I would never dwell on.

I stood up and brushed myself off and began my internal pep talk. I was going to do this. I was going to make it. I was going to have to fake like I knew what I was doing, like I wasn't afraid, but pretending like I wasn't scared shitless wasn't something new for me, I'd done it every single day since I woke up with no idea of who I was.

I would be a biker whore because it was what I needed to be. I would be a tightrope walker if that's what it took to stay alive.

With newfound determination, I walked back around to the bonfire, grabbed a beer out of the cooler, and cracked it open. The cool liquid lubricated my dry scratchy throat. I darted around from biker to biker and the girls who had their attention. I found myself particularly interested in a girl straddling the lap of a biker who must have outweighed her by at least a hundred pounds.

It was the look on her face I was intrigued by. The smile she wore that said *your dick would feel great jammed down my throat.* I mimicked her demeanor, and hoped it was enough to get the attention of someone who would take an interest in me.

Someone who could help me survive.

"Hey there," a deep voice rumbled against my ear.

When I turned around, I was eye level with a wall of leather with white patches sewn into it. One read VICE PRESIDENT and the other, BEACH BASTARDS. The man wearing the vest had long blonde hair that draped over to one side of his head, revealing the shaved area beneath. He had a beard, not stubble, a full-on beard that was a few inches long and very well groomed. He stood well over six feet, his frame lean yet very cut and muscular. I couldn't tell what color his eyes were because his lids hung heavy and were slightly reddened. His entire neck was covered with colorful tattoos and when he went to light a cigarette I noticed that the backs of both of his hands and were covered in ink as well.

"Hey," I answered back, trying to assert my newly found false confidence.

He was beyond attractive. He was gorgeous. If I had to end up in someone's bed, I imagined that being in his wouldn't be half-bad. He sniffled, drawing attention to the light dusting of white powder trapped in his nostrils.

"They call me Bear. You belong to anyone?" he asked seductively, leaning in toward me.

"Maybe…you?" I winced at my choice of words. Of all the fucking things I could have said, THAT was what came to mind? Stupid fucking mouth. Nikki was right. I spoke first and thought second.

Bear chuckled. "I'd love that, beautiful, but I've got something else in mind."

"Oh, yeah? What would that be?" I asked, trying to keep

my tone light although my mind and heart were racing.

"This party? It's for my buddy. And he was down here for a total of thirty minutes before he hightailed it upstairs to drown himself in a bottle of Jack. He's like a cat in a tree, can't seem to talk him down. It's understandable, seeing as he's been away a while, but I figure you can help me out."

He hooked his finger into the front of my skirt and slowly dragged me toward him until my nipples were flush up against his chest. He pressed his fingers into the skin right above my pubic bone and I resisted the urge to jump back by biting down on my bottom lip.

"The BBB's have never really been his thing." He paused when he saw the confused look on my face at his abbreviation. "Beach Bastard Bitches." He explained. "But you? You're new. You're different. You've got this cute little innocent thing going on, but I know you're not or you wouldn't be at this kind of party if that was your deal. I'm thinking he'll like you." Bear brushed his lips against the side of my neck. "So maybe you go up there. Make him happy for me. Make little him happy by wrapping those gorgeous lips around his cock for a while. Then when you're done, bring him back down here to civilization. And maybe later, if you're a good girl and do what you're told, we can go back to the clubhouse and have some real fun." He grazed his teeth along my earlobe. "Think you can you do that for me?"

"Yeah, yeah I can do that," I said. My skin prickling from his touch. And I could do it.

*I think.*

"What's your name anyway?" Bear's hand slowly traveled up the back of my leg, pushing up my skirt, it came to rest on my ass cheek, which was then exposed to anyone who might have been looking in our direction.

"Doe. My name is Doe," I breathed.

"Fitting," He said with a chuckle. "Well, my innocent look-ing little Doe." Bear leaned in close and surprised me by plant-ing a soft kiss on the corner of my mouth. His lips were soft, and he smelled like laundry detergent mixed with liquor and cigarettes. I was just beginning to think that the kiss meant that he'd changed his mind and didn't want to send me away to his friend, but no such luck. He pulled away abruptly and turned me around by my shoulders so that I was facing the stairs. He swatted me on my ass, propelling me forward. "Up the stairs you go, sweetheart. Last room at the end of the hall-way. Be good to my boy, and me and you will get to play later." He sealed his words with a wink and as I made my way up the stairs I turned back and flashed him a fake smile. I hoped the guy at the end of the hallway was like Bear, because then maybe it wouldn't be so bad.

Then a thought hit me that had me fighting back the tears that sprung from my eyes with a sudden force that almost took me to my knees.

I'd officially sold myself, and the price was far more than any dollar amount.

## Doe

Boom. Boom. Boom. Ba-boom.

It was hard to tell where the bass ended and my pulse began.

I wiped my palms on the tattered skirt I'd lifted from the Goodwill donation bin and maneuvered through a sea of bodies rhythmically writhing up against one another. A thick layer of smoke lay trapped under the low ceiling. Hauntingly robotic party goers danced and gyrated under the flickering lights on every available inch of floor space.

In the dark, with only the pulsing of the lights to guide me, I made my way up the stairs, and as Bear instructed, to the door at the very end of the hallway.

The door to my salvation.

The door to my hell.

I turned the handle, and the hinges shrieked. The only light in the room was courtesy of the dim and muted TV on the far wall. The heavy scent of pot wafted from the room.

"Hello?" I squeaked into the darkness, trying as hard as I could to make my voice sound as sexy as possible, but failing miserably.

A voice, deep and rough, broke through the silence, his words vibrating through to my very core. "Shut the fucking door."

Snaking its way into every crevice of my already fragile mind and body, an entirely new feeling enveloped me, causing the hairs on the back of my neck to stand on end. I'd expected to feel hesitant, nervous, and even anxious.

But what I felt was far more than that.

It was fear.

Heart racing. Pulse pounding. Red alert. Fear.

The impulse to turn and run as fast as my trembling legs could carry me was overwhelming, but any thoughts of immediate escape were interrupted.

"Door," the voice commanded again. I hadn't moved an inch. As much as I wanted to run, my desperation propelled me forward.

I closed the door behind me and the chaos downstairs disappeared with a click of the latch, shutting out the noise as well as the possibility of anyone hearing my cries for help.

"Where are you?" I asked hesitantly.

"I'm here," the voice said, offering no indication of where *here* really was. I took a deep, steadying breath and then a few steps toward the TV until I was close enough to make out the outline of a bed in the middle of the small room and a pair of long legs hanging over the edge.

"Ummm, welcome home? Bear sent me." Maybe, talking would give my heart time to get a grip inside my body. But the realization of what I was about to do struck me stupid and left me standing paralyzed in front of the shadow.

Ignoring my pitiful attempt at conversation, he shuffled to the edge of the bed. Although I couldn't make out his features, his shadowy frame was massive.

He sat up and reached out, I braced myself for his touch, but there was no contact. Instead, he grabbed a bottle off of the nightstand behind me. He tilted it up to his mouth, taking a long, slow pull. His swallows were loud in the silence of the little room.

Again, I wiped my palms on my skirt, hoping the darkness cloaked my nerves better than the perspiration on my hands.

"Do I make you nervous?" he asked, as if reading my mind. I could smell the fresh whiskey on his breath.

"No," I answered breathlessly, the lie getting caught in my throat. A large hand grabbed my waist roughly, tugging me into the space between his legs. His fingers dug into my hips and I squealed in surprise.

"Don't you lie to me, girl," he growled, without a hint of playfulness. My blood ran cold. My heart raced. He took another swig from the bottle, reaching behind me again to set it down. This time when he trailed back, he did it slowly, rubbing his cheek against mine, his facial hair not long enough to be considered a beard but longer than stubble. Unexpected tingles danced down my spine, and I fought the urge to touch his face. "Do you always ignore people when they ask you a question?"

Yes, yes he made me nervous. He made me so fucking nervous I couldn't find my tongue. I didn't expect this. I expected to spread my legs for some drunk horny asshole so he could have his way with me in a room that was too bright.

Instead, I stood in the dark, pressed between the thighs of a man I could barely see, but the feel of him alone sent shivers up my spine.

"I'll take your silence to mean you want to skip the small talk." He grabbed hold of my shoulders and shoved me down hard. I reached out to brace myself, my hands landing on rock hard thighs as my knees hit the carpet. "That's better."

*You can do this. You can do this. You can do this.*

"Suck me," he ordered, leaning back on the bed, propping himself up on his elbows.

I ran my trembling hands up his thighs until I found his belt. I slowly unbuckled it, my fingertips brushed the heated skin of his stomach. His ab muscles clenched under my touch and he sucked in a breath through his teeth. I shook out my trembling hands, trying to regain some control. When I reached for his zipper, I hesitated.

*Desperate people.*

*Desperate things.*

I steadied my hands as much as possible and slowly I dragged his zipper down. I closed my eyes in an effort to calm my erratic breathing, fearful that I was going to pass out and fall into his lap. I was hoping that closing my eyes was going to bring me some sort of comfort knowing I could remove myself from what I was about to do.

I'd just gotten his zipper down and was reaching into his jeans when his voice boomed over me like a cannon shot at close range. I jumped back in surprise, falling ass first onto the carpet.

"What the FUCK?" he roared. With my eyes closed, I hadn't seen him turn on the side lamp, but when I looked up from the floor, I found myself staring into a beautiful pair of hate-filled green eyes, boring into me like I was the reason for everything wrong with the world.

Familiar eyes.

He pushed my hands away from his fly and grabbed me by the wrists. He stood and yanked me up to my feet, his hard chest pressed up against mine. "I walked in on you earlier, you were having sex with some girl," I blurted, instantly regretting it. Fuck me and my speak-before-I-think disease.

His tight black wife-beater showcased the ripples of his impressive muscular frame. A myriad of colorful tattoos decorated one side of his neck, chest and shoulders, continuing all the way down both arms to the backs of his hands and knuckles. He wore bracelets that weren't actually bracelets at all, but leather belts with metal studs wrapped around his wrists and forearms. Dark hair cropped close to his head, a black stud in each ear. A white scar through his right eyebrow. Stubble on his square jaw that was more than a few days past needing a shave.

I thought he was large when he was relentlessly pounding into the girl on the table. Even when he was only a shadow I knew he was big, but in all reality I'd had no concept of the wall of man who stood before me.

This guy didn't look like he hung with the wrong crowd.

This guy was the wrong crowd.

"You?" he asked. His nostrils flaring as he glared down at me. I don't know what I did to make him so angry, but getting a look at him in the light made me more fearful than I ever was of him in the dark, and I wished I'd just listened to my instincts earlier and ran when I had the chance.

"Obviously you don't know shit because if you did you would know that what you saw wasn't sex."

"I know what I saw," I argued.

"No, you don't because you would know that I wasn't having sex with her. I was *fucking* her." The way he said the word fucking sent a flush of wetness into my panties.

*You stupid girl. Your brain must really be damaged, because this is not someone who warrants that type of reaction.* "Who are you?" he demanded.

"I'm no one," I answered, truthfully. My heart ached at hearing the words spoken out loud from my own mouth.

"You're no fucking biker whore," he stated flatly. He cocked his head to the side as he stared down at me. Running over my features as if he were trying to figure me out. His gaze lingering on my lips, his tongue darted out to wet his own.

"You don't know who I am," I spat. I tried to take a step back but he held me firmly in place.

"No, but biker whores typically don't tremble and practically hyperventilate when they're about to suck cock." He squeezed my wrists tightly and pain shot up my arms.

"Let me go!" I jerked my wrists unsuccessfully from his grip. I needed to get out of there, but he held me even tighter, forcing me backwards until the back of my head hit a wall.

"So you're saying you do this all the time then? That you know what a guy like me wants? That you know how to suck and fuck like a pro?" He ran his index finger down the side of my cheek and I tried to ignore the heat that lingered in their wake. "You think you can take care of me, little pup? Fine. We can start back up right where we left off." He guided one of my hands to the front of his pants and held my open palm to the bulging erection threatening to spring from his open jeans. The hairs on the back of my neck stood on end. "Aren't you going to show me how you can make me come?" he taunted, his words a warm whisper against my ear, although the words themselves were cold. Terrifying. I could hear my blood coursing through my veins as my heart beat faster and faster. "You already made me come once tonight." I looked at him and furrowed my brows.

"That's a lie. I barely touched you."

"No, not now. When you saw me earlier, with that girl. You stood in the doorway and you watched us. Did you like what you saw? Did you like watching me come for you?"

"You give yourself way too much credit. I didn't stay to watch you. I was just surprised. You were practically strangling her, why would I stay to watch that?"

He moved his hands to my throat and squeezed hard, leaving me with just enough airway so I could still breathe. "You mean like this?" He asked, looking into my eyes as I tried to hide the terror alarms going off in my body. He was feeding off my fear.

"Fuck you," I spat, mustering all the courage I could manage. He was toying with me, and I may have been afraid, but I was no fucking pushover.

"I know that you wanted to be that girl. You wanted it to be you who my cock was slamming into. I saw the way you looked at me and it made me explode. I see the way you look at me now and behind the fear you want me, maybe even because of it."

"You're wrong. That's not how I'm looking at you."

"No? Then tell me what you are really thinking when you look at me. Right now. What's going through that pretty head of yours?"

"I was thinking about what a shame it was that good looks are wasted on someone like you." He smiled out of the corner of his mouth and squeezed my throat tighter, leaning in so that his cheek was flush with mine and I could hear his words vibrate off my skin.

"How old are you, Pup?"

"What the hell is it to you?" I seethed through gritted teeth.

"I just want to know if you're illegal." He pulled back and his gaze roamed over my body with one long slow sweep. He released my throat and pinned both my wrists above my head with one hand. He dipped a calloused finger into the low neckline of my tank top, slowly tracing the rounded flesh of my breasts. Goosebumps rose on the flesh of my arms.

I inhaled sharply.

"I've seen all the shit going on out there," I said, tilting my head toward the door. "Like you really give a shit about illegal." My breaths shallow and quick.

"I don't give a shit," he said with a deep chuckle, "As a matter of fact, I'm hoping you *are* illegal." He pressed his forearms against the wall on both sides of my head, caging me in with his massive frame, pressing his erection up against my stomach. "Cause I do illegal real fucking well."

I gasped and my lungs felt heavy in my chest. I squirmed in his grip and couldn't decide if I wanted to rub up against him to find the friction I now craved or slap the living shit out of him. He must have sensed my indecision because he looked me in the eyes and shook his head.

"Go ahead, Pup. But I wouldn't if I were you." His expression stern, his eyes dark and dangerous, glimmering with a trace of amusement. He pressed his forehead to mine and sighed. "You and I could've had a lot of fun, Pup." He shook his head and for the first time I noticed the dark circles under his eyes and the redness of his eye lids.

He looked tired. And not the kind of tired you feel after a long day, but the kind of tired that lingers no matter how much sleep you get or how much coffee you ingest. The kind of tired that is less about rest and more about unrest.

I knew this because I was the same kind of tired.

He released me and stepped back. The second his intimidating presence was gone from my personal space I felt the coldness of his absence.

He grabbed the bottle from the nightstand and headed for the door.

I was still frozen to the wall. My jaw firmly affixed to the floor.

*What the hell just happened?*

"You're leaving?" I asked. My relief warring with some fucked-up misplaced sense of disappointment.

He cracked the door open and paused with his hand on the handle. The music filtered in through the opening, penetrating the silence, each heavy beat taking another footstep inside. "It's been a long fucking day and you've caught me at a really weird time. As much as the innocent thing you've got going on makes my cock hard, I don't do gentle, so you should be happy I'm walking away." He took a swig from the bottle and cast one last confused glance toward me, taking in my body that was still pressed up against the wall. "Three years ago I would have fucked you into the middle of next week without thinking twice."

Then he was gone.

*What the fuck did that mean?*

My stomach interrupted my thought by growling loudly. The twisting pain threatening to topple me over. I hugged myself in an attempt to soothe the ache. I'd looked around for some sort of food when I'd first arrived, but all the tables downstairs were covered with beer and liquor bottles. The coffee table had nothing on it but a mirror and a mound of blow, which was being cut into lines with a credit card by a man who looked old enough to be a grandfather.

A knock at the window made me jump. "Let me in, bitch!" Came a high-pitched voice from outside.

*Nikki.*

I scrambled over to the window to lift the latch. Nikki leapt up and stumbled into the room, falling onto the floor. Her greasy red hair was plastered to her forehead with sweat, her old faux-fur shawl that may have once been white, but was now an off gray color, was draped haphazardly over one shoulder.

"How did you know where I was?" I asked. I hadn't seen Nikki since she took off on me hours ago when we first got to the party.

"That Bear guy told me. I totally wanted to sit on his face but he just took off on his bike with some Tyra Banks looking chick."

*There goes that option.*

I helped Nikki up off the floor. "So how was it? How was he? I saw him downstairs earlier and holy hot man." She adjusted the strap of her bag across her shoulder. "Did you do that thing with your tongue I told you to do?" She asked me with the same excitement as if she was asking if I rode the Ferris wheel at the carnival. "Did you make him come? Did he make you come? Tell me everything."

I sighed, both defeated and relieved. "No. No one made

anyone do anything. He just…left."

Nikki looked me up and down, her expression turned from elation to annoyance. "No wonder he left. Have you seen what the fuck you look like? I should've never let you come up here looking like that."

I looked down at the plain gray tank top that I'd tied in the back to make it appear more form fitting and the tattered, sequined skirt that was missing most of the sequins. I knew I didn't look great, but I didn't have the resources to look great.

Or even good.

Nikki shook her head, gesturing wildly with her hands up and down at my body. "You look like a kid fresh off the playground who's been playing with her mama's old clothes."

She sniffled and adjusted her own denim skirt that barely covered her ass cheeks. Her green tank top had a bleach stain over her right boob.

"It doesn't matter now. He's gone," I said bitterly. "Let's get out of here." I had to clear my head and come up with a new plan.

Which included getting away from Nikki.

"Not so fast, little one. What's your hurry?" Nikki took a turn around the room and when she reached the door she turned the lock. "Let's see what we can find in here," she said playfully, opening the drawers of a dresser one by one, searching the contents, pushing aside socks and t-shirts.

"What the hell are you doing?" I asked. "We need to leave and leave now. You didn't see the look on the guys face before, because if you did we would already be halfway across the state by now."

"Oh shush, you're so fucking dramatic. What's your hurry? Besides, this place has air conditioning," Nikki said, fanning her pits. She picked up a photo with a thin plastic frame and turned it to me. "Sweet looking kid huh?" She ran her fingers over the picture of a little blond girl with curls smiling into the camera. For the first time since I'd met Nikki I saw her smile, although there was a lingering sadness behind it. She shook her head, set down the picture, and opened the bottom drawer, shuffling through some paperwork.

"Motherfucking BINGO!" She shouted. When she lifted her hand from the drawer, she produced a huge stack of bills tied together with purple bands. She waved it in the air and my stomach flipped at the sight. That money could buy a lot of food.

*It could buy the start of a whole new life.*

The thought went out just as fast as it had come in, because there was no fucking way I was about to steal it.

*There is no way I am stealing from HIM.*

I was desperate, not suicidal.

There was a loud bang followed by the rattling of the door-knob. "What the fuck?" A voice on the other end of the door shouted. "Why is this locked?"

"We gotta go!" I shouted. Nikki grabbed another stack of bills from the drawer and darted for the window, shoving me aside before I could offer for her to go first, losing a few bills along the way.

Nikki barely had one leg out the window when the door flew off its hinges, sending the door frame splintering into a million little wooden pieces throughout the room. Bear, the man who'd sent me up here, stood in the doorway. We locked eyes for a split-second before he noticed the empty drawer, the loose bills on the floor, and the open window where Nikki was already halfway out.

Bear took one step into the room. Nikki reached into her purse and produced a small handgun I didn't know she had.

"Stay where you are!" she shouted, aiming the gun at his chest. He stopped, raising an eyebrow at Nikki.

"Are you sure you want to do that?" he asked with no sign of fear in his voice, if anything he sounded like he was taunting her. Teasing her. He made it seem as if it was old hat to him to have a gun pointed directly at him.

The green-eyed shadow man appeared in the doorway and instantly my heart restricted in my chest. When he saw Nikki and the state of the room his lip curled up on one side. He took slow confident steps toward her, passing Bear. "Don't fucking move, or I'll fucking shoot!" Her voice wavered as he approached.

"So shoot," he dared, each step toward her a challenge.

Nikki turned toward me, the gun shaking in her hand, an unreadable emotion flashing in her teary eyes. "I'm so sorry," she said.

She squeezed the trigger.

There was a loud echoing crack in my left ear, like a pik being hammered into a block of ice, followed by a disorienting ringing sensation.

I don't know how I ended up on the ground, but I found myself lying on the carpet on my side, holding my knees up to my chest. My eyes closed. My hands covered my ears, and I just laid their willing the ringing to stop. Just as it had started to subside, strong hands flipped me flat onto my back. My head thunked against the ground like a dead weight.

"Redhead's gone," Bear said, tapping the screen of his phone with his thumb. "I sent Cash and Tank to find her and put the word out to the locals. Town's too small for her to get too far without someone noticing. We'll catch up to her sooner or later."

The green eyed man glowered down at me from only inches above my face. A vein pulsed in his neck. "Seems I was wrong. You are a whore. A thieving little whore," He must have taken my confused look for not being able to hear because he ripped my hands away from my ears. "Listen you little cunt bitch…" He paused mid sentence and looked down to where his hands held mine, and my gaze followed. Sticky red coated my palms. He grabbed my chin, turning my head one way and then the other. When he touched a spot over my ear, pain sliced down my neck, and I cried out.

"Fuck," he said, his fingers were now coated in the same red as my hand.

*Is that blood?*

Bear stood off to the side with his arms folded across his chest. I opened my mouth to ask him what had happened, but nothing came out.

The two men exchanged some words I couldn't make sense of. A black halo formed around the room and it's contents, and as the seconds ticked by everything faded further and further into the expanding dark tunnel. My fear of the dark caused my pulse to race, but a sudden eerie sense of calm took over and I concentrated on the beautiful face of the angry man hovering above me.

"I don't even know your name," I whispered.

I managed to stay conscious long enough to hear his answer.

"They call me King."

Then the blackness surrounded me and swallowed me whole.

## KING

I'D NEVER BEEN SO ANGRY IN MY ENTIRE FUCKING LIFE. And in the past twenty-seven years I'd been alive more than a few people had felt the wrath of Brantley King.

Few had lived to tell about it.

How old was this girl anyway? Seventeen? Eighteen?

I didn't know her long enough to hate her, yet I had the overwhelming urge to wrap my hands around her throat and strangle her. Better yet I wanted to unravel one of the belts from my forearm and tighten it around her neck. I wanted her to feel every bit of my fury as I squeezed the life from her bony body.

I wanted to take out all of my frustration on her, but it wasn't just her I was angry with. I was also pissed-off at myself.

I've always been nothing short of meticulous about security, but I'd haphazardly tossed the stack of cash Preppy had
given me that day into a drawer.

*A fucking drawer.*

The old me from three years ago would've placed it in my
attic safe and changed the combination three times already.

*How did I go from being overly careful to dangerously
careless?*

I should've had security guarding the doors. I had enemies
going into prison, and I came out with a few more. Instead,
I forgot all my past protocol and left a girl I didn't know shit
about, alone in my fucking room, when I should've tossed her
out on her ass the second I decided I wasn't going to fuck her.

Which wasn't me either.

I didn't fuck her because she was afraid of me? Because she
seemed innocent and naive? Not to say that she didn't get my
dick hard, because she did. I nearly came in my pants when her
hands shook as she undid my belt. I told myself that I couldn't
go through with it because what I needed was a girl who could
work me like a pro so I could rid myself of the pent up aggres-
sion that was turning me stupid.

But that was a lie.

Something inside me, something I could almost mistake
for a conscious, told me not to take advantage of the situation.
No, it told me not to take advantage of *her*. Walking away while
her cheeks were still flushed from fear, embarrassment, anger,
and if I was reading her right, a little bit of desire, was torture
on my straining cock. It took a lot of control not to march back
and take her up against that wall.

But that was before. Any feelings of doing right by her flew
out the window with her friend and my money. The six grand

the redhead managed to steal wasn't enough to scratch the surface on the amount I would need for a payoff, but the amount didn't matter. Two fucking cents would have been too much.

One way or another, the girl passed out in my bed was going to pay.

I sat down on the mattress and peeled back the covers. Her skirt, which was much too large for her little frame was rolled up at the waistband so it wouldn't fall off her hips. The material, which was missing most of the sparkly things hanging off of it, had ridden up to her waist in her sleep, her white cotton panties exposed to me. I trailed my fingertips up the outside of her leg from her ankles to her thighs. The simple contact caused my body to shudder and my dick twitched to life.

She was too skinny. Her cheeks were sunken. She had dark circles under her huge eyes. Her elbows were sharp and her ribs reminded me of how Preppy looked when I first met him. She wasn't the usual kind of girl I went for. I liked tits, ass. Something to play with while my cock took care of business.

So why couldn't I stop myself from touching her?

I peeled off her tank top and tossed it to the floor.

No Bra.

Small but perfectly round tits. Tits that made me wonder how much more perfect they would be with some meat on her bones. Tits I wanted to watch bounce in my face while she rode me.

The girl sighed heavily but didn't wake. When her breathing had again leveled out I traced lazy circles onto the smooth skin of her stomach, around her belly button and then around her little pink nipples. It took a fuck of a lot of restraint not to lean over and suck them into my mouth. I wanted to bite them until I drew blood. I wanted to lick the blood off of her pale white skin.

I'd never both hated and wanted something so much in my entire life.

A quick hate fuck might wipe away the unfamiliar senti-mental feelings rolling around in my twisted brain, but the girl was injured and passed out in my bed.

Technically, you can say that I was caring for her.

Technically, I wanted to face fuck her until she gagged.

My conflicted feelings were giving me a fucking migraine.

I had to get out of there. There was no good that could come of me touching her while she slept, but I couldn't bring myself to get off the bed. Then she stirred. Just a little, just enough to remind me that I was crossing into Preppy territory. But I couldn't leave just yet. What if she woke up and tried to escape? Then, I would really never know where the redhead went with my money.

I ignored the fact that it was impossible for her to escape, especially since I had her handcuffed to my headboard. Instead of getting up and walking out the fucking door like I should have, I stripped down to my boxer-briefs and got in bed beside her. Hauling her back against my chest, I covered us both with the blanket.

It was a first for me. I'd never been underneath the covers in my bed with a woman before. I'd never let anyone stay long enough to sleep before.

I splayed out a hand on her concave stomach, the heat from her core radiating onto my thigh making my dick even harder. I propped my head up on my elbow and found myself fascinated at the contrast between us, her pale and perfect, to my tanned and heavily tattooed.

Now I was painfully hard.

The thought of tearing off those innocent little school girl panties and defiling her pussy with my cock right then and there sent spasms up my spine. The only reason I came back to the room earlier was because I'd changed my mind. As innocent as she appeared, she was the one who'd offered herself to me, and who the fuck was I to say no to that?

Maybe prison had changed me, but I wasn't ready to accept that change. I had been downstairs for only ten minutes when I turned on my heel and headed back upstairs to strip her down, bend her over, and show her what the fuck she'd gotten herself into.

I twisted a lock of her white-blonde hair in my fingers. Over and over again, I reminded myself that the girl was a thief and a whore and that I had every right to take payment for what she stole from me and then some.

I owned this bitch.

She was mine to take.

Only as much as I wanted to roll on top of her and sink deep down inside, I couldn't bring myself to do it.

There was more to this girl's story than what was obvious on the outside. Her friend was obviously a junkie with her humungous pupils and shiny red nose. This girl didn't act like a junkie, but her clothes and rail thin frame had me thinking that dope could be the only reason she'd be hanging around with Bear and his crew.

I was going to pry her story from her when she woke up. Then I was going to decide what my plans were for her which would preferably consist of naked and on her knees.

She let out a deep sigh, and I stilled, fearing she might wake before I had the chance to get out of bed, but oddly enough her entire body relaxed back into me. Her ass pressed against my straining erection.

I stifled a groan.

Only my boxers and her panties separated us. I wanted to rock against her, alleviate the pressure building in my balls, but I stopped myself and just as quickly as I'd gotten into bed, I got back out.

I picked my jeans up from the floor. Before I left the room I glanced back at the girl sleeping in my bed. The moonlight shone through the window making her blonde hair appear even lighter, her skin even paler.

More haunted.

I didn't know whether I wanted to kill her or fuck her.

Maybe both, but one thing was for sure.

One way or another, I was going to make her scream.

I was finally starting to feel like my old self again.

## Doe

I awoke groggy and confused. My skull felt like it was going to crack open against the pressure of my aching head. The mattress underneath me was soft, the sheets cool against my skin. A much better alternative to the park benches or pavement where I usually made my bed.

I stretched out my legs one by one, then raised my arms to do the same. Except my left arm wouldn't cooperate, it was stuck. My eyes sprang open when I heard a rattling. My wrist was bound to the headboard.

By handcuffs.

*Fuck.*

I sat up quickly and glanced around in a panic. Sharp scratching pain assaulted the side of my head when my shoulder brushed my ear. Feeling around, I realized my left ear had been covered in some sort of bandage. Then, I remembered the events of the night before.

I'd been shot.

*Nikki* had shot me.

I was in the same room as the previous night, but in the light of morning the details that the darkness had hid were now on full display. At the foot of the bed a wooden dresser that was splintering at the corners sat below a huge flat screen TV. A bi-fold closet took up the entire wall on the right side. The room was only large enough to fit one nightstand beside the bed. It wasn't huge, but it was comfortable with a plush navy blue comforter and simple wrought iron headboard—the one I was cuffed to.

*Where are my clothes?*

I was completely naked from the waist up, but thankfully, my panties remained.

*I had to get the fuck out of here.*

My stomach twisted. I let out an agonized moan and clenched my hands over my belly. The door opened, and the man from the night before appeared.

*They call me King*

He stepped into the room like he was stepping out of the gates of hell and onto earth where the very presence of us mere mortals pissed him off. He held my gaze with a steady glare that shook me to my very core.

"Name," he demanded, closing the door behind him, stopping at foot of the bed. He folded his muscular arms over his chest. On the right side of his neck a vein pulsed beneath the ink of his tattoos.

His eyes darted down to my chest and I crossed my free arm over my breasts the best I could to cover myself.

"What's it to you?" I quipped. King wore the same dark clothes as the night before, same belts around his forearms. The only difference was the addition of a dark grey skullcap. In the light of day I noticed that the tattoos I'd caught a glimpse of the night before were very intricate. If you took the scary out of the equation, King was drop dead gorgeous. His eyes were so dark green they almost looked black. His lips were full and slightly pink.

"I figured we might start with your fucking name and then move on to you telling me where the fuck that bitch went with my money." He seethed.

He was the most terrifyingly beautiful thing I'd ever laid eyes on. With my fear of the dark, things always seemed scarier at night when my mind had a tendency to exaggerate the situation. But in the daylight King was more everything. More intimidating, more scary, more angry…more beautiful.

"You stole from me, Pup. This is your one and only chance to tell me where the redheaded bitch went. You will pay one way or another, but if you tell me right now, you might just get out of paying with your life."

My head was fuzzy and starting to spin. My life was on the line, but I could only seem to focus on trivial things. "Where are my clothes?" I asked.

"You stole six fucking grand from me, your fucking clothes should be the least of your concern."

*Holy shit! Six grand?*

*Fucking Nikki.*

"Don't play with me girl." King wrapped his hands around

my ankles and yanked, sliding me forward until I landed flat on my back. My arm stretched as far as it could without tearing out of the socket, held captive by the handcuffs. My other hand was braced on the bed, my breasts were again exposed. "Are you worried I copped a feel while you slept? Maybe I did. Because what you are going to learn is that I can do whatever I want with you, whenever I want. Because right now, I fucking own you."

In all the time I'd been living on the streets, I've had some close calls, some serious gut check moments. I've seen things that have made my skin crawl and my heart race. I was very familiar with feeling afraid.

Fear had nothing on King.

"Don't keep trying to cover those pretty tits of yours. Last night, you were about to wrap those pretty lips around my cock, so don't suddenly feel the need to cover up now. Even though, those little girl panties of yours have kept me hard since I stripped you down." King leaned forward, bracing a knee on the mattress on each side of my hips. He cupped my cheek in his hands. I tried to turn away from him and he dug his fingers into my jaw and yanked me back to face him. "Do you want to know what exactly it is that I do to people who steal from me, who take what's mine?"

"No," I panted. And I didn't want to know.

"I'd refer you to someone who could tell you firsthand, little girl, but none of them are breathing right now."

*Shit.*

"I don't know where she is, I swear. Please, just let me go," I pled as I squirmed underneath him. I didn't want to die because of Nikki's stupidity. "We can work something out," I said. I have no idea what exactly I meant by that, but I would've said anything to get the hell out of those cuffs and out of that house.

King looked me up and down. "I'm not interested. That ship has sailed," he said, coming close enough to me to run a finger along my protruding collarbone. "You may be pretty, Pup, and those eyes of yours get my cock hard, but you're all skin and bones. Besides, I don't fuck junkies."

"I'm not a fucking junkie!" I screamed wildly. Being called a junkie when in the time I'd been living on the street I hadn't touched a single drug, set me off like a lighter to a fuse.

"Bullshit! There is no other reason you could possibly be stupid enough to steal from me besides needing a fix. And I know you're not from around here, because if you were you wouldn't have even thought about taking what's mine." His voice grew louder, his glare ice cold. He thought I was just like Nikki. A junkie. He expected me to cower.

He expected wrong.

"I don't give a fuck who you are, asshole," I seethed. "And you're not as smart as you seem to think you are. Tell me something, who exactly was it who appointed you judge of all people?"

I thought my words would start an all out war but instead King didn't look angrier, he looked only mildly amused. "Well you are partially right. Because when it comes to me and mine, I am the judge. I am the jury. And if need be, I am the mother-fucking executioner."

His words hadn't yet had the chance to marinate in my brain when my stomach took the opportunity to interrupt by growling loudly. King's gaze followed the sound to where I hugged myself with my free arm around my mid section in an effort to steady the ever-growing ache. The dizziness again threatened to take me under, but I fought it back.

King was still sitting upright on his knees, straddling me. I sat up as far as the handcuffs would allow until my face was only inches from his. "Nikki is the junkie. I'm just hungry you fucking asshole!" I spat.

King fists clenched at his sides. He raised his hand. I ducked and covered my face the best I could, bracing myself for the strike.

But it never came.

After a moment I opened my eyes. King was staring down at me, his hand raised, but not in anger, he was rubbing his palm over his short hair. His eyebrows furrowed in confusion.

I was bound in his bed with no way out and no way of knowing what was going to happen to me. It was a bad time for my foot-in-mouth syndrome to be acting up. "I'm sorry. I didn't mean it. I mean, I just—"

"Shut up," He said with a new calm control.

"I don't do drugs. I never have. I mean, not that I know of. You see, the thing is—"

"Shut up."

My stomach growled again, it twisted so hard I saw stars in front of my eyes. I needed to eat. I needed to escape. I needed to be anywhere else, but in his bed. "I swear I didn't take your money. It wasn't me. That wasn't the plan. I was just supposed to get a biker to—"

"Shut the fuck up!" he roared, his explosive rage effectively silencing my scrambled monologue.

My stomach twisted and turned again. This time I closed my eyes until the pain passed. I tried to wet my cracked lips with my tongue, but it was also dry and hung heavy in my mouth. King reached down and touched my cheek with the pad of his thumb. I was so involved in trying not to pass out that I barely registered that he was touching me. After a few moments with nothing but the sound of my heart beating in my ears, King abruptly stood up and walked out, slamming the door behind him.

I was his prisoner.

I was either going to die of hunger, fear, or at the hands of King. But the how wasn't important. It was the when I was waiting for, because I was certain I wasn't ever going to leave that house again.

At least not alive.

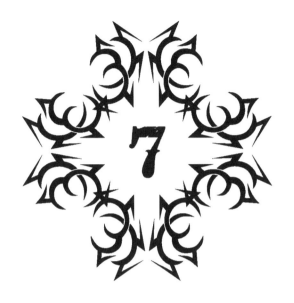

## Doe

I WAS DRIFTING SOMEWHERE BETWEEN AWAKE AND unconscious when the door opened and heavy footsteps approached the bed. Something metal was set on the nightstand, clanking and rattling as it settled. It was the smell that brought me back to the land of the living as abruptly as if smelling salts had been waved under my nose.

*Food.*

The metal of the cuffs bit into my wrist as I lunged for the tray that was set just beyond my reach. I let out a frustrated shrill-sounding scream.

"Easy now, killer," a voice said. I hadn't noticed the guy

leaning on the dresser at the foot of the bed, his arms and legs crossed in front of him. I recognized him from the party the night before. Only when his eyes traveled down to my bare breasts, I remembered that I was still nude from the waist up. I quickly covered myself by balling up as small as I could, huddling close to the metal headboard.

He smiled and slowly approached me.

"No!" I shouted when he got close enough to extend his hand out to me.

"No?" he asked. "So you don't want this?" He picked up the tray and set it on the bed in front of me.

"No, no, I do. I do want it," I assured him. I sat up again and winced when my injured ear accidentally rubbed against the metal headboard. If it was food he was offering, my modesty was going to have to wait until after my belly was full. I removed my arm from my breasts and reached out to slide the tray closer to me. When I saw what was on it, I paused.

*What the hell?*

There were two plates. One held a sandwich of some sort, wrapped in white paper, a sticker with the name of the deli held the wrapping together. The other plate was not really a plate but a mirror. On it, white powder, cut into three lines along with a rolled up dollar bill. Next to it was a plastic Ziploc bag containing a needle, spoon, lighter, and another smaller baggie filled with another type of darker looking powder.

"What is all this?" I asked.

"Breakfast," he said straight-faced. "You get to choose one item from the tray and one only." He sat down across from me on the bed.

"Is this a joke?" Who the hell would choose drugs for breakfast?

*Nikki*, I thought.

"Choose wisely, girl." He pointed to the tray.

I grabbed the sandwich and tore off the wrapper before he could finish his sentence. I took a monster bite that contained both sandwich and paper.

"Slow down," he warned. I detected amusement in his warning. I ignored him, choking when I tried to swallow down half-chewed bites, but the feeling of chewing and swallowing was euphoric. I kept going until the sandwich was completely in my stomach.

I didn't need drugs. I was high on food.

I wiped at the mess I made on my face and licked my fingers clean. He handed me a glass of water, and I downed it in three big gulps. I sat back on the bed and patted my bare stomach, no longer caring that I was practically naked in front of this stranger. I opened my mouth to speak when a sudden wave of nausea washed over me. I sat up and held a hand over my mouth.

"What's wrong?" he asked, as I frantically looked around for something I could throw up in. I didn't see anything within arm's reach, but it only took him a second to realize what it was I needed. He leapt up and grabbed a metal wastebasket from the corner of the room and ran back, just in time for me to empty the entire breakfast into the basket. Every little bit of barely-chewed, undigested sandwich came back up in waves until once again my stomach was completely empty.

"I told you to slow the fuck down." He walked to the far side of the room and opened the window, tossing the entire basket out. "I'll hose that out later."

I never cried when I woke up in the hospital and couldn't even recall my name. I didn't cry when I was told I might never regain my memory. I didn't cry when I was thrown into a group home full of perverts. I didn't cry when I ran away and had to live on the streets. I didn't cry when I came to the realization that using my body was the only way I was going to be able to survive. I didn't cry when a bullet grazed my ear. I didn't cry when I was handcuffed to a bed by a tattooed psychopath who I was certain was going to kill me.

But losing the first full stomach I had in weeks?

I cried.

Not just a few little tears. I sobbed. Loud and long. Shoulders shaking. No end in sight.

*Ugly* cry.

Hope. It's something I hadn't yet given up, but right then and there, I was ready to throw in the towel. I didn't care if I stayed attached to that bed until I died and the skin rotted away from my bones.

I was done.

I'd been dealt all I could handle, and I was more than fucking over it.

Over being afraid. Over being hungry. Over redheaded hookers. Over being shot at.

Over this sorry excuse for a life.

I sat back on the bed and rested my head against my arm, which hung at an awkward angle. I let my body go limp. Looking out the window, I noticed the sun was out. I didn't even know what time it was. I didn't care.

No one looked for me when I might have been someone, so no one would be looking for me now that I was absolutely no one.

It's ironic really. I'd been wishing for a bed and a roof over my head and in a really fucked up way, for however long they kept me alive, I had it.

The guy whose name I didn't know left the room but left the tray on the bed. How much of that stuff did I have to take for it to be lethal? Half? All of it? Maybe, King's plan was to inject me with the drugs himself. Or maybe he was a coward and would order his friend to do his dirty work for him.

Maybe, if I was lucky, my death would be quick. Just a nice bullet to the head.

Either way, it didn't matter how I was going to go. I just knew it was the end, and oddly enough, it was comforting to come to terms with it instead of spending my remaining hours fighting it.

I was beyond exhausted.

Maybe, King thought I would make things easy on him and off myself with the drugs. I huffed. I wasn't about to give him that satisfaction. If he wanted me dead, he was going to man-up and do it himself. I used every ounce of strength I had and kicked the tray off the bed. The mirror bounced off the carpet. The coke billowed into the air in a white cloud of fine powder.

And I laughed.

I laughed so hard my entire body shook and tears ran down my face. I laughed so hard that the sound of my laughter got caught in my throat. There I was. Half-naked. Handcuffed to a bed. Puke on my face. A tray of drugs scattered on the floor.

Maniacally laughing like a schizophrenic who'd skipped out on her meds.

The door opened again and in walked the same guy from earlier. I didn't acknowledge him, just continued to stare out the window as the sun began to set.

"Do you know how much that shit is worth?" he asked with his eyes wide.

"Nope. And don't know why you would bother bringing it to me since I already told your friend that I'm no fucking junkie." I rolled onto my side, turning my back to him. "Why don't you just kill me, and get it over with."

"It was a test," he said, rounding the bed. He propped himself up next to me, his back against the headboard, a steaming ceramic bowl in his hands. "You passed."

"A what? What the hell does that mean?"

"King. He wanted to know if you were telling the truth, so he tested you. A junkie would've said 'fuck the food' and dove nose-first into the dope." He extended the bowl out to me. "Here. I'm Preppy, by the way."

Odd name for an odd guy. He looked like a cross between a thug, a teacher, and a surfer.

I'd seen him briefly the night before, but I didn't take the time to really look at him. Preppy was close to six feet tall. He wore light jeans and a short sleeved yellow collared shirt with a white bow tie. His sandy blonde hair was tied back into a wild ponytail on the top of his head, but beneath it his head was shaved clean on both sides above his ears, revealing intricate vine tattoos that started at his temples and circled around his head. His arms, hands, and knuckles were also covered with ink. He had a dark beard that didn't match his hair color. At first glance, you'd think he was much older than he was, but it was his eyes that gave away his youth.

"What is it?" I asked, staring into the steaming bowl.

"Chicken broth. Drink it slowly so you can keep it down. How long has it been since you ate?" He crossed his legs at the ankles and rested his hands behind his head.

"Not sure." I don't know why but saying the words out loud made me feel ashamed in a way I hadn't thought about before. "Days, I think."

Hesitantly, I took the bowl from his hands. It was warm on my palms and instantly made the ache in my weak hands subside. I lifted it to my mouth slowly, relishing the feeling of the steam against my cheeks and the warmth of the liquid as it spread down my throat.

"Why are you even bothering with feeding me?"

"You say you're not a junkie, but your fucking ribs are practically poking through your skin, and I could sharpen my knife on that collarbone of yours. King's not the kind of guy who starves someone to death."

"So, he's not going to kill me?" I asked, hopefully.

"Didn't say that. Just said he wouldn't starve you to death. Bears crew has a lead on the redhead. If we catch up to her and we find out you weren't in on it, he might let you go."

"Might?"

"He's not the most predictable guy, and he's been away for a few years. Hasn't been acting like himself, so there's no telling what's running through his head right now."

"Years?" That's when I remembered that the party last night was supposed to be a coming home party. "Where was he?"

"State."

"College?"

"Prison."

Prison made much more sense than college.

"What did he do?" I was pushing my luck by even asking. But I thought that maybe, if I knew more about King— knew what made him tick—I would have more of a chance of convincing him to let me go.

"You sure ask a lot of questions, little girl. Why do you want to know?"

I shrugged and sipped more of my broth. "Just curious, I guess."

"He killed someone, got caught," he said casually. I swallowed a huge mouthful of broth in one tight gulp.

"Who?" My curiosity made my mouth run faster than the speed of my usual word vomit.

Preppy smiled. His dark brown eyes glistened with excitement. I knew then that there was a lot more to him than what I saw on the surface. Something sinister was lying just beneath the tattoos and bow tie.

Something that made the hair on my arms stand on end.

Preppy leaned forward, resting his chin on the back of his folded hands.

"His mom."

## Doe

THERE WAS NO DOUBT IN MY MIND THAT KING WAS capable of the kind of things most normal people couldn't fathom, but what kind of person kills their own mother?

Preppy asked me the same questions King had about who I was, and I told him my story. The difference between Preppy and King is that Preppy actually listened to me.

I gave him the short version.

*No memory.*

*Group home.*

*Living on the streets.*

*Nikki.*

*Attempting to sell myself for protection and shelter.*

Also unlike King, Preppy seemed to actually believe me.

I drank every last bit of broth, and Preppy changed the bandage on my ear. It was already starting to itch as it scabbed over.

"Why don't you let me go?" I asked, bunching the waistband of the sweatpants he'd given me to wear in my hand so they wouldn't fall down. "You can just tell King that I escaped."

Preppy shook his head from side to side. "That's not going to happen," he scoffed, like there was something wrong with my question, not the fact that his friend had a girl handcuffed to his bed against her will.

Preppy uncuffed me. Temporarily, he made sure to tell me, and led me to one of the doors in the room I'd assumed was a closet but turned out to be a small but clean bathroom.

I hadn't realized how bad I had to pee before then. I let the sweatpants fall to the floor and was about to push down my underwear when I noticed the door still stood open and Preppy watched my every move.

"Can you please close the door?"

"Sure." Preppy took a step inside and shut the door behind him.

"Not exactly what I meant."

"Sorry, kid. Boss-man told me not to let you out of my sight."

"Do you always do what he tells you to?" I asked, bitterly.

"For the most part." Unable to wait a second longer, I pushed down my underwear and sat on the toilet.

Nothing came out.

"Don't have to go anymore?" He asked.

"I do, but I can't pee with you staring at me like that. Just turn around. It's not like I'm going anywhere. This room doesn't even have a window."

"I'm sorry. I wasn't aware that your highness had stage fright," Preppy said sarcastically, rolling his eyes.

He opened the bathroom door again and this time he turned his back to me. The second I knew he wasn't looking, my body was able to relax and let go. The relief felt so amazing I moaned out loud.

"I may appear nice, kid, but don't get it twisted. King and I are cut from the same cloth."

"If he asked you to kill me, would you do it?" I asked, needing to know if he would be the one to possibly end my life.

"Yes," he answered. No hesitation.

When I was done, Preppy led me back to the bed and secured my cuff around my wrist. This time, he connected it to a lower rung on the headboard so I wouldn't have to sit with my arm raised above my head.

"Prep," King's deep voice boomed from the doorway, startling me. He motioned to Preppy with a lift of his chin. Preppy tightened the cuff around my wrist and left the room. King glanced at me for a brief second, then followed Preppy out, closing the door behind them.

Did they find Nikki? Did she tell them I didn't have anything to do with stealing from him? Or maybe, she turned on me and told them it was all my idea. Nikki was oddly overprotective of me when she was sober, but when she was high she was unpredictable, and if her life or her drugs were on the line, there was no doubt in my mind that she would throw me to the wolves.

I heard a door slam, and then their muffled voices rose up

to the window from outside. I strained my neck and peered out. King and Preppy were on the lawn, just beyond the deck. The sun was just setting; the sky glowed orange.

I stretched out my leg and slid the window open a crack with my bare foot.

"Found the redhead," King said. He lit a cigarette.

"Where?" Preppy asked.

"Andrews' place up the highway. That old motel with the pool in the parking lot."

"You get the cash?" Preppy asked. He leaned back against the railing and crossed his arms over his chest.

King shook his head and blew out the smoke.

"I think she's telling the truth, man," Preppy said, gesturing up to my window with his hands. I ducked in reaction although from that angle there was no way they could see me. "I think you know I'm pretty good at detecting a liar, and this girl doesn't scream thief to me. What did the redhead say about her?"

"She didn't say shit."

"How come?"

"'Cause she's fucking dead."

Nikki was dead.

I couldn't catch my breath.

My head spun.

King had said that anyone who stole from him would have to pay a price, and Nikki had paid it.

*With her life.*

There was no doubt, that without King being able to ask

Nikki about my involvement, that I was next.

Thunderclouds clapped overhead. King and Preppy walked back toward the house, but I could no longer make out what they were saying. I closed the window and propped myself on the bed just as they'd left me.

The first chance I got I was going to make a run for it. There was no time to wait and plan. This was going to have to be quick and on-the-fly.

After a few minutes, Preppy came back into the room and uncuffed me. "Let's go," he said. Yanking me into an upright position, he dragged me toward the door.

"Where are we going?" I asked frantically. Then, it came to me. This was King's house. His bedroom. He wouldn't carry out killing me in his own home, so it was very likely they would take me somewhere else first. This was my only shot, and I was going to have to take it.

"Not far," Preppy said.

It was getting dark, and it was about to storm. Couldn't they at least wait until morning? I could think better when I wasn't being choked by my own fear of the dark.

"Why?"

"Come on. You'll see."

We walked down the narrow hallway and down the stairs to the main living area of the house. King was nowhere in sight. Figures he would ask Preppy to do his dirty work for him. A part of me wanted King to do it.

I wanted him to see the look in my eyes as he killed an innocent person.

But it didn't look like I was going to get that chance.

Preppy led me out onto the balcony, and I stopped short when we reached the stairs. Preppy was already a few steps below me, his grip on my wrist still tight. He turned around when he felt me come to a stop. This was my only chance to escape with my life. I didn't think. I just acted.

I reared my foot back and kicked him in the balls. HARD. He released my wrist to grab his crotch and I shoved on his shoulders with all my might, sending him tumbling backwards down the steep staircase.

I ran down the steps and jumped over Preppy who was curled up at the bottom of the stairs groaning obscenities face-first into the grass.

I took off as fast as my bare feet and weak legs would take me. Clutching the sweats with one hand, I ran down the dirt driveway, but when I reached the road, there was nothing but more trees in every direction. I didn't remember which way we'd come from the night before, and there was nothing telling me which way would bring me toward people.

Toward help.

A door slammed somewhere behind me. Heavy boots against the wooden deck echoed over my head. The wind carried the shouts of a very deep and very unhappy voice.

*Shit.*

The sun had almost fully sunk into the horizon. Although I couldn't see in the dark, I had to get off the open road where I was a sitting duck.

I took off across the road. Pushing some brush aside, I jumped through the opening I created, stumbling over twisting roots and cypress knees. Finding my footing on the soft wet ground was almost impossible.

So was running straight.

Vines and brush blocked my every move. Spider webs stretched over my face as I tried to clear a path. Just a little further in, and I would be able to hide within the thick brush.

My foot landed on something sharp and I hissed, tumbling forward onto a narrow path. I leapt across the mud and used all my weight to flatten a bush. I'd just lifted my leg as high as it could go so I could step over it when I was tackled from behind, landing hard on my side. The wind left my lungs with a whooshing sound.

No matter how hard I tried to suck air back in, I couldn't. Over and over again, I opened my mouth to breathe, and over and over again, my lungs failed me.

I was still gasping for air when strong arms flipped me onto my back. Massive, hard thighs held me like a vice on each side of my ribcage, threatening to snap them with one twist of his knees.

King leaned over me, his grip tight on my wrists, which he held together and raised above my head. I tried to gain control of my lungs. When I was finally able to pull in some air, my chest rose and fell in quick pants. My breasts brushed up against King's hard chest.

The wind howled. The sky answered with a thunderclap that I felt in my bones. The rain started slow. Icy drops caused my skin to prickle. I was suddenly hyper-aware of the man lying on top of me. The rain quickly turned from drops to sheets. Water poured down King's face and into his dark demon-like eyes, but he didn't look possessed.

He looked like the devil himself.

"I thought I made it clear that I owned you," he growled. His nostrils flared. "Your debt has yet to be paid, Pup."

"So, kill me already, and get it over with," I said hoarsely, in the loudest voice I could muster, which was barely a whisper. "Either let me go, or just fucking kill me!"

King scoffed. "That would be too easy."

"What then? What do you want from me? I heard you. Nikki's dead. Your money is gone, and I can't pay you back. I don't have anything you want." I struggled to throw him off, but I was as effective as a gnat to a tiger.

"Oh, but I think you can pay me back, Pup. You do have something I want," he said, running his fingers up my arm to my shoulder. He grabbed hold of my throat in his large palm and squeezed with calloused fingers, not enough to choke me, but just enough to remind me he could.

"Please, just let me go! I'm nothing! I'm no one! You don't want me. Last night, you walked out of that room because you didn't want me. Remember? So just let me go. Please. I'm begging you."

I'd stopped struggling because it was pointless, the only thing I had that could possibly get to him were my words.

And I was failing miserably.

"But that's where you're wrong. Last night, I thought you were a scared little girl, unable to handle what I want, what I can do, what I need. But that doesn't matter anymore. Because now you're my property, and I can do what the fuck I want with what's mine." He emphasized this by squeezing harder on my throat.

I opened my mouth to protest, to tell him that I wasn't his and never would be when suddenly King's lips came crashing down over mine with such force that the back of my head was pushed down further into the mud. There was nowhere for me to go, nowhere to get away. His full lips were soft, but his kiss was anything but. He sucked my lower lip into his mouth and licked at the seam of my lips with his tongue.

King was hard and scary as hell, so was his kiss. And if his words weren't getting his point across, his kiss told me that he owned me. It made me forget for just a second that the man behind those lips was a raging psychopath.

The rain continued to assault us. For once it wasn't my mouth speaking before my brain. It was my body. Because as much as I told myself that I didn't want his kiss, my body was very much saying that it wanted it. Wanted him.

I opened my mouth to protest, but the second I did, his tongue touched mine, and he groaned. The contact produced a spark, an energy that radiated through my entire body, pooling between my legs.

King used a knee to spread my legs apart, then settled between them. Not once did he take his lips from mine as he rocked his erection against my core. My body hummed at the friction, and I moaned into his mouth. His hands flew to the back of my neck, pressing me up against him as he kissed me until I was dizzy.

It was an entirely new type of hunger.

With a deep, throaty growl, King abruptly ended the kiss. Sitting back on his knees, he reached down and ran the pad of his thumb across my cheek. He looked down at me as if he were seeing me for the very first time. His expression soft. His lips swollen from our kiss.

My chest heaved as I again tried to catch my breath. Without King lying on top of me to shield me from the cold rain, a chill ran down my body. My teeth began to chatter. His eyes drank me in as they skimmed over my face, then down the rest of my body. I could swear that it felt as if he were actually touching me, not just looking at me.

"Go," King snapped, jumping to his feet like he'd been electrocuted.

"What?" I asked. I somehow managed to get to my knees, still holding up the now wet and heavy sweatpants, the drawstring already pulled as tight as it would go.

"Just fucking go!" he roared, standing up fully.

He took a menacing step toward me. His sudden proximity forced me backwards. I stumbled over a rock and fell back onto my ass.

"That path will take you to the highway," he said, pointing to the ground behind me. I turned and found the path, but when I turned back around, he was gone. The crunch of the brush under his boots faded quickly, swallowed by the sounds of the storm.

I was free.

But I was also truly alone. In the dark. And that clouded over the elation I should have felt.

My chest grew tight. I pressed my hands against my heart to try and physically tame it from leaping out of my body. Faster and faster it beat until I thought it would come to a screeching halt. Again, I couldn't catch my breath.

Panic set in.

My vision blurred. The forest around me spun and spun until the foliage blended together into one big green and brown vortex, like staring up into the eye of a tornado.

I'd felt safer minutes earlier, staring into King's hate-filled eyes.

I tried to get up. I sat up on my knees, but I slipped in the mud and fell forward onto my forearms. Unable to find the courage to try again, I turned onto my side and pressed my cheek into the mud, holding a hand over my exposed ear.

I needed to be invisible. I needed to disappear into the dark, and then just maybe the dark would disappear around me. I hugged my knees to my chest.

Twenty-four hours ago, I thought I would be set up in some biker's bed by now, basking in the comfort of a roof over my head and food in my stomach. I wouldn't have my dignity, but I hadn't had the luxury of dignity since I woke up in the hospital. Instead, I was barefoot and cold in the middle of the woods. And as the moon disappeared behind dark storm clouds, I was enveloped in complete blackness.

I tucked my bare feet as close to my body as I could to keep the chill off my toes. My chattering teeth turned into a full body shake as the rain pummeled me. Each icy drop felt like a pin-prick into my skin.

*Why the hell did he kiss me? Why the hell did I let him?*

I was mad at myself. For not fighting him off, for liking it.

I'd done a lot of fucked up things in the last few months. Eating out of dumpsters. Sleeping in abandoned cars. But nothing I'd done left me more disgusted with myself then yielding to his kiss.

What was even more fucked up was, that more than anything, I'd hoped at any second the tall grass would rustle and he'd appear out of the brush to rescue me from the dark.

King wasn't the rescuing type, I reminded myself.

*He was the killing type.*

My body shuddered. Still angry. Still scared. Still really fucking cold.

Still turned on.

In the light of day, it was easy to push things aside with the distraction of survival to keep me busy. But alone with only my own thoughts in the dark, I became more aware that without memories of the past, lessons lived and learned, I was a mere shell of a person.

I was a stranger to myself.

I was an alien, invading the body of a girl I didn't know. I stole it from her, entirely by accident, a byproduct of a tragic event that wiped her from the earth and set me up in her place.

On nights like these, when the panic threatened to consume me, I talked to her out loud.

*I know it's weird But in an odd way, I miss you. I know I tell you this all the time, but I'm so sorry. I'm sorry if what I'm doing isn't what you would do. I wish you were here and that I wasn't, because starving on the streets isn't a life I want for you or for me. I am so sorry that I'm failing you.*

*I hope every day that when I wake up that you will be back. And I'm so sorry about earlier, about trying to sell my body for protection. It was a moment of weakness, but I'm over it now. I can do this on my own. I can protect myself. And I'm sorry about what just happened with King. I don't know how far I was going to take it, but I promise I wasn't going to let him fuck me.*

*Or fuck you. Fuck us both?*

*Weirdest fucking threesome ever.*

I laughed manically into the mud, accidentally sucking some into my mouth. I coughed and gagged until it dislodged from my throat, spitting onto the ground.

*I'll try harder. I promise. I can survive...for you.*

## Doe

THE MOMENT THE SUN MADE AN APPEARANCE, I started walking.

I made my way to a road with more potholes than asphalt, and for hours and hours I trudged on, covered in dirt that grew tight around my skin as the sun baked it onto my body and it hardened like clay.

Each step through the hot grass lining the side of the road was nothing short of complete agony. They call them *blades* of grass for a reason, as each one felt like a tiny knife against my already bare, bloodied, and battered feet.

I was limping my way to nowhere when I finally came

across the first sign of civilization: a one-story apartment complex.

I needed to get to a phone, or a police station, or a church. Anyone who could help me, but I didn't have the energy to look any further and needed a place to sit and regain my wits because my mind was a cloud of confusion, exhaustion, and dehydration.

*Why did King let me go?*

There was something unsettling about his indecision that nipped at my nerves. I half-expected him to pull up along the side of the road at any second and drag me into the car. Maybe, it was the kiss that changed his mind. He thought he could use me for whatever perversion he had in mind, but when he kissed me, he must have realized he'd only be disappointed. So, he'd let me go.

That had to be it. But why, if he killed Nikki, wasn't I dead as well? Why did he spare me and not her?

Nothing made any fucking sense.

After thinking I was seconds away from death more than once in the past thirty six hours, freedom was something I never thought I'd have again.

But being back on the streets was a captivity of another sort. Freedom meant you had choices.

I still had none.

I stumbled into the apartment complex. Old and unkempt, the building had about ten units and a dark shaker style roof. Half the shingles had been replaced with mismatched plywood. Knee-high weeds grew through cracks in the concrete walkways.

Unable to take another step, I collapsed against the wall of the breezeway and slid down until my butt hit the sidewalk.

Finally sheltered from the blistering sun that still felt as if it were searing into my scalp through the center part in my hair.

I just needed to sit a while, catch my breath, and collect my thoughts.

"You can't stay here, girl. Move along." A husky man appeared, wearing a t-shirt three sizes too small that depicted a unicorn jumping over a rainbow. He stood over me and folded his arms across his chest. "You some kind of deaf, girl? You can't stay here. I can't be having the riff-raff lingrin' about." He nudged my thigh with his sneaker like he was trying to rouse a lazy dog. "Move along, now."

"Please. I just need to use your phone. Please?" I begged, my voice dry and scratchy. I didn't even care about the fact that when I called the police they would probably throw me into another group home.

I thought about one thing and one thing only.

I had a murder to report. Nikki may have been a whore and a thief, but she didn't deserve to die for it. Somedays, I didn't think she even liked me all that much, but she was all I had.

If there was such a thing.

The man sighed, clearly annoyed. "What you need it for?" He dug into the party-sized bag of Cheetos he'd been holding. After shoving a handful into his mouth, he sucked his fingers clean of orange powder.

"Please. You have to help me. I'd been kidnapped. I was locked in a room, handcuffed to a bed. I escaped and I spent the night in the woods. I've been walking all day. I'm thirsty and sunburnt and tired, and this is the first place I came across. Please, I have to call the police. My friend, my friend Nikki was murdered by the same man who held me captive."

He shoved another handful of Cheetos in his mouth and wiped his hand across the unicorn. "Oh yeah? Well, you're in luck, I'm the deputy in these parts. Name's Crestor. So, you can report it to me." He lifted the fat of his stomach and pointed to a previously hidden badge attached to his belt. Cheese sprayed from his mouth when he spoke. "And who is it that you're thinkn' killed your friend?"

"I don't think he killed her. I know he did. I heard him confess. And I don't know his full name, or even if it's his name at all. I only know what they call him."

"And what would that be?" He leaned up against the wall, focusing on a light bulb in the ceiling that turned off and on every few seconds on its own, completely disinterested in my story.

"They call him King."

His eyes went wide and his fingers loosened around the bag. He dropped the Cheetos to the ground.

Within a second, he'd bent over and grabbed me under my arms, yanking me to my feet. "Wait, what are you doing?" I asked as he shoved me toward the parking lot. My right foot twisted when I stepped on an uneven section of pavement, and I fell forward onto the road, skinning my hands and wrists.

"Go on and get! And don't you ever fucking come back here!" he shouted. With his hands on his head, he spun around and waved his arms in the air in frustration. "I don't need that kind of trouble here. Go, girl! If I see you again, next time it'll be my shot gun escorting you out."

He left me on the road and hustled back to the building, his back fat bouncing up and down as he disappeared behind a door with a window marked OFFICE. He drew the shade the instant he stepped inside.

I stood on shaky legs and wiped gravel from the wounds on my hands onto my t-shirt. The bottoms of my feet stung. My twisted ankle sent sharp pains through my shin with each step. My already bad limp became much more severe.

King apparently had reach. But how far? If I had any chance of seeking help for myself, or for Nikki, I had to get the hell out of Logan's Beach, but I didn't even know if I was going the right way.

My foot dragged behind me as if it were no longer attached to my body, but hanging on, like cans tied to the bumper of a car.

Hours passed, and although I'd been walking the entire time, I don't think I'd gone very far. I could still see the apartment complex in the distance behind me.

Not a single car had passed me all day. My stomach was again protesting its emptiness, twisting and groaning. My face and ears were hot to the touch. The soles of my feet were thick and swollen, thankfully becoming numb to the constant scraping.

I trudged on.

For every inch the sun sank into the horizon, my anxiety increased. A brutally sunny day was again about to be cloaked in the darkness of night.

I came upon an old, abandoned bank with boarded up windows just as thunder rolled in the distance. The sky flashed as lightning jumped from cloud to cloud. I smelled the rain before I felt the first drop splatter on the tip of my nose.

I hobbled toward the covered awning of the drive-through, but I didn't make it. The sky poured itself over me before I could reach shelter. By the time I took cover, I was sopping wet from head to toe, the blacktop underneath me turning brown as the water rinsed off the mud from the night before. I settled against the out of order ATM machine and sat down on the curb, resting my forehead against my knees.

I felt defeated. And somewhere in the back of my mind, I wished for one of the bolts of lightning to jump from the clouds and reach under the awning to strike me dead. Dead was better than unwanted.

*Dead had to be better than this.*

"Why hello there." A voice said from out of nowhere.

Chills spread from my spine to my neck. Goosebumps broke out on my forearms. I looked up to find a man with a dirty grey beard standing over me. The wrinkles around his eyes spread over to his cheeks. Some of his front teeth were missing, and his chin was covered in red sores.

"You lost or something?" He smelled of rotten milk, his clothes were torn and tattered.

"Or something," I muttered.

"I'm Ed," he said, extending a hand. His fingernails each about an inch long and yellowed.

Realizing I wasn't going to take his hand, he kneeled down to me, and my heart sped. Ed reached out a filthy hand and attempted to run a knuckle down my cheek. I shuddered and pulled away, jumping to my feet. I swayed unsteadily. Spots danced in front of my eyes. I grabbed the ATM on the wall to steady myself.

"Now don't be rude to ole Ed. What's your name?" he asked, licking his lips and adjusting the stained crotch of his once khaki pants.

"Um…nice meeting you, Ed," I said as confidently as I could. "But I gotta go." I tried to sidestep him, but he stepped in front of me, blocking my only exit.

"Why don't you stay here and dry off for a while." His eyes roamed down my body. His toothless smile grew bolder. "Although I like a woman who's all wet." He clucked his tongue against the roof of his mouth.

"Um, no thanks. I'm just waiting for my friend to pick me up," I lied, wishing it were true. I made a move to side-step him again, but this time he grabbed my arm. I tried to shake him loose, but even a child was stronger than me at that point. "Get off me!"

"Now, you listen here. You came into my house. Now, you're going to stay and see how hospitable I can be."

Ed yanked my wrist, turning me around until my back was flush up against him. He held my hands captive in front of me. His cock twitched against my thigh, and I gagged. If I'd had anything in my stomach, it would have come up right there.

I stomped on Ed's booted foot with my bare one, sharp pain exploding in from my foot to my hip, hurting me more than him, but it was just enough to momentarily stun him. I broke free from his grip.

I'd only made it a few steps when I was yanked backwards by my hair, sending me flying onto my back, smashing the back of my head into the concrete. For the second time in twenty-four hours, the wind was knocked out of me. My windpipe wouldn't open. My lungs struggled inside of my body, painfully asking for air. My vision became hazier and hazier.

This was the very reason why I was seeking protection from a biker. At that moment I wished that Bear had just taken me to his place instead of sending me to King.

But then, I remembered my renewed promise to her.

I had to protect her. At all costs.

And I wasn't going down without one hell of a fight.

When Ed tried to drag my legs down and pry them apart, I kicked out wildly until my foot connected with his face. Blood spurted from his nose, and the heel of my foot felt like it was on fire.

"You're gonna pay for that, bitch!" Ed hissed.

Rearing back, he punched me square in the jaw. My head twisted to the side and fell onto the concrete with a thud. My mouth filled with warm coppery liquid.

Ed held something cold and sharp at the base of my throat. "Try to fight me, cunt, and I'll slit your fucking throat," he warned through tight lips.

With an unsteady hand holding the knife, he ripped down my sweats and panties in one forceful yank. Each of my gasps elicited another sting from his knife.

I closed my eyes. This is what happens when you wish for death, right?

Sometimes, wishes come true.

I only hoped that he would kill me when he was done so I didn't have to relive this moment for the rest of my life.

Not even a day had passed since I made my promise to protect her and I'd already failed.

Ed shuffled around with his pants, and I braced myself, coming to terms with the fact that I was going to die under a bank awning in a little town in the middle of nowhere.

As no one.

Then, Ed was gone. His weight suddenly disappeared.

There was a shuffle, then a loud explosion that echoed through my ears. A familiar sound.

I wanted to lift my head to see what was happening, but my neck wouldn't cooperate, and my head felt like it weighed a thousand pounds.

Strong arms reached around my back and under my knees, lifting me effortlessly into the air, cradling me against a hard chest. I tried to fight off whoever it was, but I couldn't manage anything more than a wiggle.

"I've got you," a familiar deep voice murmured into my hair.

*King.*

"I thought you were letting me go," I said, my thoughts all swimming around each other in my head, smashing into one another.

"I changed my mind." King's muscles barely tensed under my weight. He covered me with a leather jacket and wasn't the least bit strained when he walked out into the rain.

The world around me grew fuzzy. "I thought my life was supposed to flash in front of my eyes?"

"Why would you think that?" he asked. In my weakened state, I didn't know if the concern in his voice was genuine or something I was making up.

"Because that's what happens when you're dying," I answered.

"You're not dying."

"Oh, good. Because I don't have a life to flash in front of my eyes. I thought whatever higher power exists up there was just showing me you instead."

"Why would you see me if you were dying?" he asked. When I didn't answer immediately King shook me and said something about trying to stay awake, but I couldn't listen. I believe what I said next was very similar to, "'Cause you might be all angry and stuff, but you're really pretty to look at." I yawned. "Why did you come back for me?"

I used all the energy I had left to open an eye and glance

around King's shoulder. Ed was slumped against the ATM, staring blankly ahead.

A bullet hole between his eyes.

King held me tighter and lowered his mouth to my ear.

"Because you're mine."

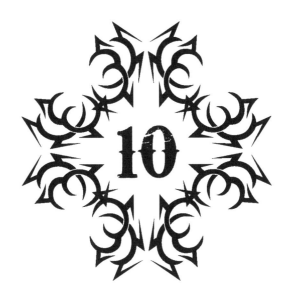

## Doe

I awoke submerged in warm water. Every ache and bruise and sore throbbed in the healing heat. When I opened my eyes, King was hovering over the edge of the tub, washcloth in hand.

I gasped and sat up quickly, sloshing water over the side and onto the floor. I scooted to the far edge, crossing my arms over my breasts. King forcefully grabbed my wrist and pulled, removing the only protection I had against his gaze. With his other hand, he trailed his calloused fingertips from my collarbone to my breast. When he made it to my nipple, he pinched.

HARD.

I yelped.

"I've already seen them, Pup. No need to hide them from me now." King was shirtless, his ab muscles rippled and his tattoos became animated with his every movement.

"You killed Ed," I blurted out. The events from the night before tumbled over each other into my mind, one horrific detail after another.

"Ed?" King asked, cocking an eyebrow.

"The guy last night," I clarified. "The one you..."

"Killed," King finished. "I didn't realize you two had gotten to know one another." King raised the washcloth. I flinched. "I'm just wiping off the mud."

"You don't sound very remorseful. You seem fully convinced that you have the right to be judge, jury, and executioner," I said.

"A simple 'Thank you, King, for saving my life.' would do," King said. "But what you should know, and what Ed found out, is that if you fuck with me and what's mine then yes, I am the judge. I am the jury. And sometimes, when the situation calls for it, I am the motherfucking executioner." My stomach flipped.

"But why do you give a shit if he hurt me or not?"

"Because you're mine."

"Why do you keep saying that?"

"Because it's true."

"I never agreed to be yours, whatever that means."

"It's not something you need to agree to. This isn't a negotiation. Would you rather I'd let Ed do whatever it is he planned to do to you?"

"No, that's not what I'm saying." Even in the warm water, my skin turned to gooseflesh when I thought of what would have happened if King hadn't saved me.

I would be dead.

Was I upset that Ed was dead? No. It was a him or me situation, and I was glad I'd come out on the other side with my life.

"This is why I needed a biker," I mumbled.

"What was that?" King asked.

"Nothing," I said. Not realizing I'd said that last part out loud.

"No, you said that's why you needed a biker. What the fuck exactly does that mean?"

"For protection!" I snapped. "You don't know what it's like out there on the streets. There is an Ed on every fucking corner just waiting for you to fall asleep or not pay attention or wander into the wrong alleyway. It's not like it was my first choice, but I didn't know what else to do. Nikki said there would be bikers at your party. That if one liked me that he could protect me."

"You came to the party to whore yourself out to a biker?" He sounded angry and disappointed and for some stupid reason, I really hated the idea that I'd somehow disappointed him. Almost as much as I hated the fact that I'd disappointed myself.

Or *her*.

"Yes," I answered honestly. "At least for a little while. But I realize now how stupid that idea was. That's not what I want anymore." I didn't realize how embarrassed I was until I spoke the words out loud.

"At least, it all makes a lot more sense now. Here lean back," King ordered.

I tilted my chin back and he supported my neck with one hand. He grabbed a cup off the floor and scooped up water, slowly pouring it over my hair.

"You killed your mom," I whispered. As nice as the bath was, I was still completely unable to get a hold of my mouth and stop the words before they poured out like water from King's cup.

"Fucking Preppy." King shook his head. "He shouldn't have said anything. It's none of your fucking business," he spat. I'd hit a nerve. "It's none of anyone's fucking business." After a moment or two of silence, his breathing again evened out and the vein in his neck stopped pulsing. He finished rinsing my hair. "You know I was in prison then, yeah?"

"Yeah."

"Do you know how long I was locked up for?"

"Three years," I said, recalling what Preppy had told me.

"Yeah, three years. You know anyone that gets three years for murder?"

I don't know why I didn't think of it before. It didn't make any sense. I shook my head.

"There's a lot more to that story. But, I'm not in a storytelling mood tonight."

"But you killed Nikki," I cursed myself for not being able to keep my trap shut. Much to my surprise, King laughed. An actual laugh as if I told a joke. I didn't think the man was capable.

"No," he countered. "I didn't."

"Yes, you did," I argued. "I heard you tell Preppy you killed her. Why would you deny it?"

"Think about it. Did you actually hear me say that I killed her?"

He was right. I didn't hear him say the actual words.

"I only said she was dead. I'm sorry, Pup, but she is. I found her with a needle in her arm in a shitty motel a town over."

King wiped a wayward tear from under my eye with the

pad of his thumb.

"She shot you. Does she really deserve that tear?" He surprised me by sucking it off his thumb.

"She didn't shoot me," I defended. "She was trying to escape. She shot me by accident. She was aiming at you. She was desperate. We both were. Desperate people do desperate things."

It was then I realized that I missed her. As fucked up as our relationship was, she was all I had.

And now she was gone.

"Pup, on purpose or not, the bitch shot you. To be honest, if I'd found her alive and she drew that gun again, she'd be dead now anyway."

"My life seems to be a bunch of questions piled on top of a bunch of questions, and frankly, I'm ready to add some fucking answers into the mix before my brain explodes and leaks out of my ears."

"How...graphic of you."

"I'm serious. Why did you look for me? Why did you even bother bringing me back here?"

"When I let you go, it was a momentary lapse in judgment. The reason why I let you go doesn't matter. The fact is that your friend is dead, and you still owe me. You're my property, and you will be mine until I decide otherwise."

He ran the washcloth down my legs and brushed over the wound on my foot. I cried out, and he scowled. "You're pretty banged up."

"I guess that's what happens when you're left in the woods to rot and then walk miles barefoot in the blazing sun," I spat. I expected him to argue with me, fight with me, but he surprised me.

"I'm sorry about that. As I said, momentary lapse in judgment."

"Did you just apologize to me?"

"No, I said I was sorry about having a momentary lapse in judgment. I didn't say I was sorry to you."

"How exactly am I supposed to pay you?" I asked hesitantly. "We've been through this. I don't have anything to give you," I sighed. "I don't have anything at all."

"In whatever way I want, Pup."

"What if I don't want to be yours?"

King didn't hesitate. "Then, I'll let Preppy have his way with you. He may seem nice, but you'll learn that kid is a sick fuck who will smash your back door in without warning. He likes it when they scream. He likes it when they're passed out. He likes it even better when they say no. Or maybe, I'll loan you out to Bear's crew. I hear Harris and Mono have a fetish for knife play."

There was no humor in his voice.

"But if you cooperate, you'll be mine and mine alone. You'll be under my protection. When I'm tired of you and I feel your debt has been paid, you will be free to go."

"Protection," I repeated. The very thing I'd been looking for. "What happens if you don't get tired of me?"

King chuckled. "Oh, It will happen. Always does. But until then, you'll do what I say. You'll live in my house." His eyes narrowed to the space between my legs. "You'll sleep in my bed."

"You're going to rape me?" My heart hammered in my chest. "Because it's one thing to sell myself. It's another thing entirely to have the decision taken from me. If that's your plan, you can just shove my head under the water and get this over with now."

"You may be weak in body, but it doesn't seem that mouth of yours got the message." Adrenaline sprung to life inside me, coursing through my veins, readying my body for another fight for my life.

I stood up, splashing more water onto the tile floor, my nakedness on full display. I didn't bother to cover myself.

King surprised me by standing up and stepping into the tub, soaking his jeans up to his shins. I held my clenched fists out in front of me like I was going to box him. He laughed and wrapped both arms around my waist, hauling me into his colorful, bare chest.

"You'll find out that I'm a lot of things, but I'm no fucking rapist. Before I fuck you—and I will fuck you, Pup—you'll be begging me for it," he whispered against my neck.

I clenched my thighs together to try and ease the ache he created there. The adrenaline surge I was ready to use for combat changed into something else entirely. I was still ready for him. Only in a completely different way.

*Traitorous body.*

"But first, you need to heal. Your feet are all sliced up and your ear is bleeding again." King stepped from the tub and lifted me out with him, setting me onto the cold tile my teeth started to chatter. He opened the cabinet under the sink and wrapped me in a soft towel large enough to double as a blanket. "And there are a few other things I need you to tell me."

"Like what?"

"Preppy told me what you'd told him, what happened to you. But how is it that someone like you is missing in the world?"

"Someone like me?"

"There has got to be someone out there who misses these

beautiful eyes." He locked his fingers into my wet hair and tilted my head back.

"I tried to find someone who knows me," I said with my teeth still clacking together. King dried me with the towel, treading carefully over my injuries. "The police tried, too, but there was no missing persons report that matched my description. My fingerprints aren't on file anywhere. No paper trail."

King unbuttoned his jeans and stripped them off, hanging the wet fabric off of the shower rod to dry. All that was left of his clothes were his black boxer briefs, his enormous erection straining against the stretchy fabric. He noticed me looking and made no move to make an excuse for his arousal. He didn't make any move to cover himself. He smiled out of the corner of his mouth, took a few steps toward me. He lifted me up into his arms as if he were cradling a baby and carried me out into his bedroom where he set me on the bed.

The cuffs from the night before still hung from the headboard.

"So that's it? I'm your prisoner? You're just going to keep me cuffed to the bed?"

King shook his head. "No, Pup. You're not my prisoner. I don't think we need these anymore." He gestured to the cuffs. His well-built, highly-tattooed, muscular physique gleamed under the light of the moon shining through the window. My mouth went dry, and I again had to press my thighs together to quell the building ache that was starting to overshadow my other injuries.

He may have been the devil, but his body was sculpted like a god.

I scrambled to form my question. "Then, what am I?" I whispered. My exhaustion beginning to take hold.

# KING

"I told you before." King leaned in close stripped the towel away, letting his gaze linger on my body before covering me with the bed sheets. With one knee on the mattress, King leaned over and sucked my bottom lip into his mouth. A tingling sensation started in my belly. He released my lip with a pop. "You're not my prisoner. You're mine."

## KING

AGAINST MY BETTER JUDGMENT, I'D BROUGHT HER back to my house. I fed her. I bathed her. I put her to bed, and she didn't bother to fight me off when I climbed in beside her and held her close while she cried herself to sleep. She was here against her will and I was one fucked up motherfucker.

Because I'd never been happier.

It was the kiss that fucked everything up. I hadn't meant to kiss her in the woods, but I couldn't ignore the overwhelming urge to take her mouth. At first, I thought it was just a sick part of me that needed to kiss a girl who was struggling underneath me. But then, she opened her mouth to me, and all the sense I'd ever had was lost in that kiss.

Her taste, her tongue, the pull I'd felt toward her when she was first in my bed had exploded into something I couldn't reign in. I lost myself in her for a good minute before I came to my senses. Stopping was the hardest thing I'd ever done even though the idea of taking my revenge out on her body made every part of me turn rock hard.

I wasn't going to go after her. But the entire night I lay awake and stared at the ceiling fan. I didn't even fucking know the girl and I was worried about her. What was she doing? Did she make it out of the woods? Then, I spent hours hoping she went in the right direction, because if she went toward Coral Pines, she wouldn't find any sort of civilization for over ten miles.

I wrestled with the idea of going after her all day. Then, Preppy had filled me in on what she'd told him about not having a memory.

So I did something. Something that made the decision to go after her an easy one. A decision that would forever change the lives of everyone around me.

Some for the good.

Some for the bad.

Some for the dead.

I found out who Doe really was.

## Doe

**A**LTHOUGH MY EYES ARE OPEN, THERE IS A DARKNESS *surrounding me that is about to open the flood gates of my panic. A pair of heavily-lidded chestnut brown eyes loom over me and remind me I'm not alone, and my fear is momentarily suppressed. The look of raw desire reflected in his gaze sends a flush of wetness between my legs. The heat of his naked chest radiates against mine, and I am lost in sensations of skin against skin.*

*Slowly, he drags his fingers up my thigh, touching every part of my body except the one place burning for his touch, aching and pulsing with a need I'd never known. His touch is soft but nervous, like he doesn't know where to place his hands next. I shift in an effort to send him where I crave his touch the most.*

*"Ssshhhh," a deep voice whispers into my neck, causing the hair on my arms to stand on end and my stomach to flip flop with anticipation. "Is this where you need me to touch you?"*

*His hand comes to rest on my breast, rolling my already sensitive nipple between his fingers. I arch my back and groan from deep within my throat.*

*"No," I say. It comes out as barely a breath. I need him lower. Much lower.*

*He releases my nipple and a soft hand cups my breast and squeezes lightly. "Is this where you need me?" the voice asks, teasing me with his words as well as his touch.*

*"No," I moan again, the agonizing torture of waiting for him to make contact is too much to bear.*

*I kick out my legs impatiently.*

*"Sssshhhhh. Behave, and you'll get what you want," the voice whispers, trailing his tongue down the side of my neck at the same time working his hands between my legs. Slowly, two fingers brush over my clit, lingering there without any movement. An almost touch.*

*His body stills.*

*I writhe beneath him, seeking the release he is denying me. "Please," I beg.*

*No answer.*

*"Please," I say again.*

*Still no answer.*

*I look up into the eyes that held the promise of pleasure just a moment before, but they are slowly fading away. I reach for him, but I grasp only the night air. Even though I can still feel the places where he touched me as if he'd burned my skin, I can no longer feel him on me.*

*Then, he is gone altogether, and I am left alone in the dark.*

*Before I can panic, what I'd felt on top of me is now behind me, but the feeling isn't quite the same. The person isn't the same. This body is warmer, harder, and much, much larger. The hand rubbing my thigh isn't soft and gentle; it's rough and callused. The erection prodding against my lower back is thick and long, rubbing against the slit in my ass, into my wet folds and back again.*

*"Please," I beg. Release. There must be some sort of release at the end of all this. I craved it, needed it, and I knew he could give it to me.*

*These new fingers don't linger, and I almost fall apart when they find the wetness between my legs, spreading it over my clit until I am writhing against the thickness behind me, begging for it with my body, needing to be filled with it until the pure pleasure of it all splits me in two.*

Two fingers penetrated me.

My eyes flew open. It was then that I realized I was no longer dreaming. I lay on my side, facing the wall. In a bed.

In King's bed.

WITH KING.

It was his fingers filling me, stretching me. He curled them inside me, and they brushed against a spot that caused me to buck up against him and arch my back. I gasped and tried to tear away when King tucked me under his forearm, wrapping it tightly across my chest, holding me against him.

"I've got you, Pup," he growled, his breath teasing a spot behind my ear, sending shivers down my spine.

I knew I should argue, or at the very least push him away, but I couldn't think. Right or wrong and good or bad escaped me because his fingers started pumping while the pad of his

# KING

thumb circled my clit, faster and faster until I was panting into the pillow, throwing myself back against his hard body, chasing the release that I craved more than my next breath.

"I've got you," King said again. His voice was strained and thick. I lost myself in a fog of sensation.

"What are you—" I started to ask, but I couldn't form the words because my body clamped down on King's fingers, causing me to gasp.

"I'm going to make you come, Pup. I'm going to make you come real hard," he promised. When it felt like I was reaching the edge, King held me tighter and pressed down on my clit. I hung on, afraid to fall from the heights he'd brought me to.

"It's okay, baby. I want to make you feel good. Don't be afraid to come for me."

With one final stroke of his fingers, I saw stars. Then, I plummeted, crashing down in the most amazing free-fall I never knew existed, off of a place that I never wanted to leave. Screaming into the pillow, fisting it into my hands, my orgasm tore through me from my chest to my toes and back again. My core continued to pulse around King's fingers as I fluttered back down to earth.

"You're gonna fucking kill me, Pup," King groaned. He removed his fingers and then sucked them into his mouth. "Ahhhh fuck."

*What the hell had just happened?*

King sat up against the headboard. As much as I wanted to move, I was frozen to the mattress. "Something you need to know right now. Next time you're having dreams that make you moan and touch yourself in my bed, I'm not going to be responsible for what happens. That's on you. Because next time, I'm not going to be a nice guy and use my fingers to solve your

95

little problem."

"Who said I needed you to solve anything? I don't remember asking for your help," I snapped. Blood rushed to my cheeks, burning me with embarrassment.

"Shit, anyone within ten miles knew what you wanted, but next time, you're going to wake up with something much larger than my fingers inside that pussy of yours. And when that happens, you're going to come so fucking hard you'll think what you had tonight was nothing more than a fucking hiccup. And I'll remind you that this is my bed. This is where I sleep, and now it's where you sleep. So, tread carefully."

"I…"

"And I don't need you dreaming about some guy while you're sleeping next to me in MY FUCKING BED." The sudden anger lacing his voice confused me.

And pissed me off.

"One, I don't see why, what or who I dream about is ANY of your fucking business, and secondly—" I held up two fingers. "I don't want to sleep in bed with you. It's you who carried me here. And three, how do you know it WASN'T you I was dreaming about?" I'd hoped to take some of the embarrassment off of me, but with every word I spoke, it built and built until I felt everything from my eyelids to my ear lobes burning red hot.

"You weren't dreaming about me," he said confidently, crossing his arms. Suddenly, I was aware of something.

"Did I call out someone's name? Whose name?"

"No, Pup. You didn't call out anyone's name. Although I can't wait until I'm making you call out mine."

"You weren't in my head so there is NO WAY you could know who or what I was dreaming about," I argued, my voice getting louder with each sentence. Disappointed that I'd gotten my hopes up over a name. Angry with myself for enjoying the mind-blowing orgasm he'd given me.

"Pup, do you want to know how it is I knew you weren't dreaming about me when you were about to come in your sleep?"

"Yes," I whispered.

The anger faded from his eyes for a brief moment. He fixed a cocky smile on his perfect lips and rolled over on top of me, forcing me to lie back against the pillows as he caged me in. He lowered his face to mine, his breath cool against my heated skin.

"Cause, baby, if it were me you were dreaming about, you'd been screaming a fuck of a lot louder than that," King growled.

"You cocky son of a fucking bitch!" I shouted, but he'd already leapt off the bed and left the room. My shouts reaching no one but the already closed door.

As much as my body responded to him, as great as I knew he could make me feel—and I had no doubt he could fulfill every promise he made about making me come—I had to stay away from him and keep my renewed promise to *her*.

Which was going to be very hard, since I was going to be sleeping in his bed.

The dream I was having before King interrupted me was too real, too vivid. I had an underlying sense that it was more than just a dream. Maybe, if I was lucky, it was a glimpse into my past.

The chestnut brown eyes just might be the key to unlocking the truth about who I really was and what had happened to me.

I went back to sleep that night dreaming that the boy with

the chestnut colored eyes came and rescued me, taking me back to a life filled with family and friends, and everything that had happened in the past few days was nothing more than a quickly forgotten nightmare. I dreamed there were really people out there who were sick with worry, who wouldn't rest until they found me.

I ran this scenario through my mind over and over again until I almost believed it.

*Almost.*

King was smart, calculating, and cunning. Worst of all, he had the power to make my knees both tremble in fear and weak with desire. He was someone I had to stay away from, but according to him, that wasn't about to happen.

I didn't dream about him; he was right about that. Because King wasn't a dream.

He was a nightmare.

## Doe

KING NEVER CAME BACK TO BED, AND I WAS RELIEVED. As much as I didn't want to be the property of someone who ran hot and cold faster than a faucet, I decided to focus on what was in front of me. Or rather, what was under me.

And over me.

And around me.

And inside me.

A bed. A roof. Walls. Food.

The sun beamed through the windows. I stretched out my arms and legs and took a deep breath. My situation may not be as good as I'd hoped it would be, but it certainly had some perks.

At least, my hands weren't cuffed.

"Rise and Shine!" Preppy shouted, flinging open the door and tossing some clothes on top of my head. "We've got shit to do, and I hate fucking waiting, especially for chicks."

I pulled the clothes away from my face and onto my lap. "Why are you so chipper? Don't you hate me for what I did to you?" I asked, referring to the not so pleasant kick to the nuts that sent him down a flight of steps.

"Nah, I was kind of impressed, actually. Don't get me wrong. It was fucking stupid. You should have seen the look on boss-man's face. He looked like he was about to bust an artery or something. And if Little Preppy and the boys weren't working properly, you would be singing a different tune, but thankfully the boys know how to take a hit. Sometimes, they like it. But they're good, so no foul. Now, let's fucking go!"

"Where are we going?" I pulled the shirt on over my head. Preppy jumped on top of the bed and bounced up and down like a little kid. I couldn't help but react to his infectious enthusiasm.

"Holy shit, she smiles!" Preppy beamed, jumping harder until I had no choice but to get off the bed or end up on my ass on the floor. "It's a nice smile. Doesn't make you look like such a crack-head."

"Excuse me?"

"Crack. Head," Preppy said, enunciating each word like I hadn't heard him.

"I know what you said. Is that really what I look like?" Suddenly self-conscious of my waif-thin frame, crazy bed head and raspberry colored sunburnt skin.

"No?" Preppy asked, smiling awkwardly. I eyed him skeptically and crossed my arms protectively over my chest. He jumped down from the bed and clasped my elbows in his hands. "We can fix that. Don't you worry. We can fatten you up and put some tits and ass on that boney body of yours in no time."

I suddenly remembered what King had said about Preppy, the things he liked to do with women. I tore my elbows from his grip and took a step back. If King wasn't around, would Preppy hurt me? I swallowed hard, and the look on my face must have given away my thoughts.

"Ah, I see. Boss-man threatened you with me, didn't he?"

I nodded reluctantly. "Is it true?"

Preppy took a step toward me and again grabbed me. This time, he yanked me forward until I had to tilt my head up to look him in the eyes.

"Yes, it's true."

He tucked a strand of hair behind my ear. Surprisingly, his touch didn't make me shudder. The man standing in front of me was capable of the same brutality as King and did things that made my skin crawl, but Preppy himself didn't. I felt oddly comfortable in his presence.

"I'm not sorry for it, either. I've had some shit happen to me you don't want to ever fucking know about. I'm not making excuses. Shit is the way it is. I am the way I am. That's all there is to it. That's all there is to me. However, I'm concerned why King felt he had to threaten little ol' you, with crazy ol' me."

"Maybe, he's losing his touch," I whispered.

"Ah, she makes jokes, too." He smiled. "What is it about you?" Cupping my face in his hands, he searched my eyes as if he was looking for an answer my words couldn't provide. He pursed his lips and raised his eyebrows.

"I keep asking myself the very same thing."

Preppy suddenly took a step back and shook his head as if he was clearing his thoughts. He smiled again, this time a full toothed, ear-to-ear smile. I was fast becoming familiar with this being his patented look. He clapped his hands together and rested his chin on the backs of his interlocked fingers.

For some reason, Preppy started talking in a fake Spanish accent. "Boss-man has informed me that you are now our slave, and since he's got important shit to do today, I am to take you with me on my run. So, get fucking dressed, slave, and let's get this fucking show on de road!"

Preppy pointed a finger into the air and snapped his heels together.

"Those should fit," Preppy said, pointing to the clothes on the bed. "Put them on, and let's roll. Time's a motherfucking wasting."

"We're going somewhere? Whose clothes are those? Where are we going?" I asked without stopping to take a breath between questions.

"I know you said you lost your memory, kid, but is your short-term still intact? Because I'd hate to have to repeat myself like this all the fucking time." He spoke mockingly slow. "Yes. *We* are going somewhere. Clothes are on the bed. Get dressed. Meet me in the kitchen in five minutes." He resumed normal conversational speed. "And stop asking so many fucking questions, or it's going to be a long, *looooong* day."

"You're leaving me alone?" I picked up the clothes and held them to my chest. "The other day you had to watch me pee, and today you are just leaving me?"

"You would rather I watch?" Preppy said with a wink.

"'Cause we can make that happen, although I'm under strict orders—and I quote—'not to fucking touch you.'" He punctuated each of his words while making air quotes with his fingers.

"No, I'm just confused is all. About Nikki. About King. About you. About everything." I bit my lip.

"Me, too, kid. Me, too, but I'm just following boss-man's orders," Preppy said. "But let's just fucking roll with it, and maybe, we can have some fun in the meantime—the boring PG kind—that is, when King isn't around to be the fun police. Now, hurry the fuck up!"

Preppy left the room without closing the door, whistling as he walked down the hall. The whistle faded, along with his footsteps, as he got further and further away, disappearing altogether when he turned and bounced down the stairs.

The clothes Preppy had given me were simple. A pair of jeans, a black tank top, and flat black sandals. The sandals fit like they were made for me. The clothes were all two sizes too big, but soft and comfortable. He'd also left me a new toothbrush and a pair of bright red lace panties with the tag still on it. I spent four out of the five minutes it took me to get dressed on just brushing my teeth.

I'd gone to bed with my hair wet from the bath, so it was a bit crinkly, I did the best I could taming it with a brush I'd found in the bathroom.

I was wearing real clothes and real shoes.

It was heavenly.

The bath had done wonders for my wounds. I found what I needed in the bathroom and changed the bandages on my ear and foot. Then I applied aloe onto my sun burnt skin, which looked a lot less red than it had the day before.

When I found my way downstairs and to the kitchen, I

stopped dead in my tracks. In the middle of a small yellow kitchen with avocado green appliances was an old, faded table completely covered from top to legs with carvings and little drawings. People's names, pictures of penises, quotes, and a lot of INSERT NAME was here's. But that wasn't what caught my attention. It was what was in the center of the table that had me drooling.

Pancakes.

Stacks upon stacks of mouthwatering, buttery, perfectly round pancakes.

Preppy stood at the stove with a spatula in hand, flipping pancakes on a griddle pan. He wore a lacy red apron over his red short-sleeved dress shirt and faded jeans. His yellow checkered bow tie peeked over the top. His white sneakers were scuff-free and matched his white suspenders.

But *pancakes*.

Before he was done telling me to help myself, I'd already shoved two so far in my throat I might choke, but I didn't care. They could be fucking poisoned, I didn't care. If I died with a mouthful of pancakes while the poison ate out my insides, it would be a fate I'd surrender to willingly.

Because *pancakes*.

Preppy turned the burner off and flopped another stack down on the plate in the center of the table.

"Slow. Remember?" he reminded me. He poured me some orange juice into a red plastic cup, and I managed to swallow down the pancake that was threatening my life. After that, I made a half-assed attempt to take smaller bites and chew slower.

"So, what exactly are we doing today?" I asked.

"Errands," Preppy answered vaguely. "Business."

"Why can't I just stay here?"

"Oh you can, but I would have to cuff you to the bed again. I'll be a while. So eating, peeing, or anything other than laying there is kind of off the table."

I rolled my shoulder, which was still sore from being tethered to the bed. "Business it is then. What kind of business?"

As with most of my words lately, as soon as they were out, I wished I could suck them back in.

*Something you probably shouldn't be asking about, you idiot.*

Preppy didn't seem to mind my stupid question, but he didn't answer. "Shut up and finish your food, so we can get out the door this fucking century."

Preppy had a way of talking that was different than anyone else. His demeanor was light, but his words and language were crude.

But then I shut up, and I did what I was told.

Because *pancakes.*

I followed Preppy out to a large garage on the back corner of the property. I moved slow and still limped. Although my feet were much better than they were the previous day, each step was still more painful than the next.

I'd never really seen King and Preppy's house during the daytime. Now, I took a good long look around.

It sat directly on the back bay. The house itself was huge, and so was the property, at least an acre. Parts of it looked like it had been under renovation at one point, but whoever was doing it had given up. Rusted scaffolding lined one entire side of the house. Blue siding sat under plastic at the bottom, covered in dirt. Weeds had grown around it on all sides. Rusted buckets of paint and miscellaneous tools lay, strewn around in the grass. The back of the house was partially painted a dove gray. THE KING OF THE CAUSEWAY was written in graffiti onto a high peak of the house with black spray paint. It looked as if someone had tried to paint over it at some point, but the bold lettering was still clearly visible through the thin attempt.

"Are you my babysitter now?" I asked as we rounded the house.

"I guess I am," Preppy said. "I've done a lot of shit for King, but this is kind of new for me. I've never taken anyone on a run before. But he's also never taken in a stray either."

"Stray?"

"Well, you're kind of like a stray dog, without the mange. Cute, but too skinny, and kinds of scraggly."

"Okay, I guess, but I wasn't taken in. I'm here against my will," I corrected.

"When King saved you from that bum the other night, was that against your will?"

"No, that guy was going to kill me."

"Okay. So here is another question: you got somewhere else to be?"

I shook my head.

"See? He took you in. Just like a stray."

That was the first time I considered being there as anything other than a violation of my free will, and Preppy made me see that.

"I mean, yeah, he saved me," I conceded. "But on the other hand, he also expects me to pay off a debt that isn't mine by bending to his psychotic will."

"There are two sides to every argument. Two ways to be wrong. Two ways to be right," he sang as we passed the fire pit in the back yard. It wasn't just a hole in the ground as I'd previously thought, but a large brick circle built a few feet off the ground. Beyond the pit, at the end of the huge yard, was a wooden dock with mangroves threatening to swallow it on either side. From the dock was the mirror calm waters of the bay surrounded by nothing but nature.

No other houses. No other docks.

A bird took off from a nearby tree, shaking the branches. It hovered just inches above the glassy water. A small black snake dangled from its beak.

This place was as confusing as King. Hard edges, unfinished and unrefined, yet mysterious and beautiful in it's own way.

A tattered frat house in some ways and a complete paradise in others.

"Who else lives here?" I asked as we entered a side door to the detached garage. Tarps at different stages of fading covered rows of what I assumed were cars and bikes. They hung thick with dust, like everything was wrapped a dirty fog. Specs of debris came alive in the one ray of sun that invaded the otherwise dark garage, through the corner of a broken window.

"It's just the two of us in the main house," Preppy said, lifting the tarp off of a shiny black sedan that looked like something right out of a movie from the fifties. "But Bear keeps an apartment here in the garage. He crashes here when he doesn't feel like being at the clubhouse, which is a lot lately." He gestured to the door at the far end of the wall that was covered from top to bottom with random bumper stickers.

Preppy started the car then ran to open the garage door.

He drove the car out of the garage and put it in park so he could repeat the garage door routine except this time he closed it.

He rolled us down the driveway at an extremely slow pace. "Don't want to kick mud up onto Busty Betty," Preppy informed me, lightly smacking the steering wheel.

"You named your car?"

"Um…yeah, of course. Everything important should have a name."

"Isn't that the truth," I said, no longer referring to the car.

"Oh come on. You are important. And you do have a name. We just don't know it yet. Maybe, your name totally sucks. Like it could be Petunia Peoplebeater or something. You should be grateful that you are possibly avoiding a total name tragedy," Preppy joked.

"I guess Doe is better than Petunia Peoplebeater," I agreed with a laugh.

"Damn right it is." Preppy accelerated once we reached the end of the driveway and turned onto the road.

The only town I'd been to before Logan's Beach was Harper's Ridge. Along with being a much more populated area further inland, it also held the dubious distinction of being where I had first woken up in that alley. Where Nikki had first befriended me, if you could call it that.

*Fucking Nikki.*

Something tugged at me from deep inside when I thought about her. A part of me wanted to mourn her loss like I'd known her all my life, instead of a few weeks. A piece of me wanted to cry for her, but I shook those thoughts away because she didn't deserve my tears. She'd abandoned me.

The bitch *shot* me.

Preppy gave me a tour as he drove. When we crossed over

a steep bridge, I learned that it was 'The Causeway' referred to by the graffiti on the side of the house.

I found myself sticking my head out the window like a dog. When I opened my mouth, I could taste the salty air on my tongue.

I could be back on the street at any minute, so I decided to enjoy the time I had free of the burden of my immediate survival.

Our first stop was at a tiny well-kept home with white siding. Preppy put the car in park. "Stay here," he ordered, before getting out and slamming the door.

I leaned back in the seat, preparing to wait for him when he startled me by suddenly appearing at my window.

"I want to be your friend, kid," he told me. "I feel real fucking sorry for what you've been through. I know what it's like to go through shit and end up on the other side of it. I'm a nice guy, for the most part. But just because I'm nice doesn't mean you should take advantage. You did that once, and I let that shit go. I just hope you're not fucking stupid enough to do it again. So, this shouldn't need to be said, but I feel like I need to say it anyway. Don't go anywhere, okay? Don't try and run away. 'Cause it doesn't matter that you're my friend. I'll slit your fucking throat and leave you to rot somewhere no one would ever find you, mmmmkay?"

He tapped the tip of my nose and jogged up the driveway. Leaving me stunned in the passenger seat.

The front door partially opened as Preppy stepped up onto the porch, like the person on the other side had been waiting for him. Preppy shuffled sideways and disappeared into the house.

I sat back against the cushy leather seat. Thankfully, he'd

left the car running and the A/C blasting. Although there was a breeze on top of the causeway, here on flat land the air was stagnant, the humidity so thick I could see it rising from the grass.

I rolled my jeans up to above the knee in order to keep cool.

Preppy's warning, although freaky as shit, wasn't necessary. There was nowhere for me to go.

*I'll protect you*, King had said.

And sometime over Preppy's pancakes, I'd resolved to stay. King said he wouldn't force himself on me, so all I had to do was enjoy the free room and board and not give into King.

*You're going to beg for it.*

Yeah, right. He could keep on believing that while I kept on eating pancakes.

It was forty-five minutes before the front door opened. An older woman walked out onto the porch with Preppy and brought him in for an extended hug. She held his face in her hands and spoke to him intimately, her forehead almost touching his. Preppy gave her a kiss on the cheek and waved to her as he got back in the car.

"You okay?" he asked, turning the car back onto the road.

"Yeah. Why? Are you surprised I'm still here?"

"Nah, but there is just no cloud cover today. The sun is fucking BRUTAL even with the A/C on high, and that took a lot longer than usual. Gladys, she's a talker." He gestured to my rolled up jeans. "But it looks like you worked it out."

"I'm fine. Is Gladys your grandmother?" I asked.

"Not exactly," Preppy said with a devious grin on his face. "She's business."

"Business? What kind of business do you have that includes

spending forty-five minutes in an older woman's home?"

Then, it hit me. Preppy must have seen the recognition cross my face.

"What?" he asked.

"Did you have sex with her?"

"Oh my god, you think I'm a hooker!" Preppy pounded his fist against the steering wheel. He pulled over to the side of the road and wiped the tears from his eyes as he laughed himself into an uncontrollable fit.

"It's not *that* funny," I muttered, crossing my arms over my chest.

"Yes, yes it is, kid. What exactly did King tell you about me? Did he somehow mention I got a thing for old ladies? Because if he did, I'm gonna kick his fucking ass, cause it ain't true."

"No, he didn't say that, but you were in there for a while, and she seemed to like you. A lot. If she wasn't your grandmother, then I just thought…"

"Go ahead and say it. You thought I was a hooker, pleasuring her with my man meat and getting paid for it." He turned toward me and leaned back against the driver's side door.

"Well, yeah, but now that you say it that way, it sounds ridiculous."

"That's because it *is* ridiculous," Preppy said, plucking a pack of cigarettes from the center console. He cranked down his window and lit one, turning his head from me to blow the smoke outside the car. He put the car back in drive and pulled onto the road. "I think I'll like being your babysitter after all."

I felt my face redden, "You don't have to make fun of me. I may not have much of a memory, but I do have feelings, so can we please just pretend like this never happened?"

"Yes ma'am, I'll forget all about it," Preppy said, although the amused look on his face said that was never going to happen. Preppy pulled up in front of another house that looked almost identical to the first one, except this one was blue instead of white. "I'll tell you what, kid. Why don't you come inside and see for yourself what it is that I do?"

"No, thank you. I'll just stay here and melt into the seat," I huffed, sounding very much like the brat I was being.

"Nope. My reputation is on the line here. You're coming in," Preppy said, turning the engine off. With that, the A/C let out a hiss as it expressed the last bit of cold air through the vents.

"I thought you were going to forget all about it."

"Oh, I totally lied," he said, rounding the car and opening my door. "After you my dear."

I walked to the front door with Preppy following close behind. He rang the bell, and another woman around the same age as the one before opened it and waved us inside.

"Arlene, this is Doe. She's a friend. Okay if she comes in? Gets awful hot waitin' in the car." Preppy's slight southern accent was suddenly a full out drawl.

"Why, of course my dear. On a day like today, nobody should be made to sit in the car. Shame on you, Samuel, if you've already made her wait for you." She playfully swatted his shoulder as she stepped aside and shuffled us into her living room. "Sit, sit. I have tea all ready. Let me just grab another setting."

Preppy sat on an overstuffed couched draped with lace doilies and motioned for me to sit next to him. A silver tea set that looked as if it had just been recently polished sat on the glass coffee table. Next to it was a three-tiered serving tray filled with cookies and crackers.

"Help yourself, dear," Arlene said, coming back into the room with another saucer and plate set. She handed it to me and filled my cup. I looked over at Preppy who was stuffing cookies into his mouth at an alarming rate.

"Arlene makes the best cookies," he said through a mouthful of food. Crumbs shot out of his mouth.

Arlene put a cookie on my plate, and I took a small bite. It was warm and soft and the chocolate melted on my tongue. Now, I saw why Preppy was shoveling them. I finished the rest in one bite and tried not to lunge for the remaining ones before he could get to them. Instead, I sat back and crossed my legs, sipping my tea while secretly hoping Preppy would choke and die so that I could finish them off.

It was a bit dramatic, but the cookies were that good.

"See, Samuel. This one has manners. You might learn a thing or two from her," Arlene said over the brim of her teacup. "So, is this your new lady?"

"No ma'am, just a friend who's helping out today." I noticed that when Preppy spoke to Arlene he didn't swear.

"That's wonderful, dear. Friends are fantastic. Well, just the other day in bridge club…" Arlene went off on a tangent about friends that began with her bridge club, and lost me somewhere around the time when she abruptly veered off into talking about being a nurse in the war. Which war I wasn't quite sure. I smiled politely and nodded while Preppy inhaled the treats she'd set out for him.

He looked ridiculous in her living room. His tattoos and suspenders stood out amongst the lace and tea cozies.

Okay, so he wasn't a hooker, but maybe Preppy was some sort of granny nanny? Maybe, like a rent-a-friend?

I thought when he'd said I would be helping him on his

errands for the day that we would be going to a bunch of dark alleys and seedy places where he would slyly exchange drugs for money with a carefully choreographed handshake.

I certainly didn't expect to be smack dab in the living room of a house that could belong to anyone's grandma.

"Oh, I don't mean to keep you. I know you have other stops. Janine just phoned before you got here, and I know she is looking forward to your visit as well. She made you a cherry pie," Arlene said.

"You ladies are going to make me fat." Preppy leaned back and patted his flat stomach.

Arlene stood up. "Samuel, you do what you need to do. I'll be out in the garden. Come say good-bye before you leave." Arlene set down her teacup, picked up a wide brimmed hat and a pair of gardening gloves, and disappeared through the front door.

"Let's do the damn thing," Preppy said. He stood and walked down the hall, pausing at a door furthest down the small hallway. "Are you coming or do you think this is where I keep all my old lady bondage gear? Because I'm not wearing the ball-gag again, totally hurts my jaw."

"Ha ha very funny." At this point, there could be a three-ring circus behind that door, and I wouldn't have been surprised. "We've already established that you're not getting paid to be a man-whore."

"Nope. Just a man-whore for fun."

"So enlighten me. Why exactly are we here?"

"We're gardening." Preppy opened the door and stepped aside, allowing me to enter first. What I came face to face with was far more surprising than a three-ring circus. Rows upon rows of leafy green plants filled the small space. High tech machinery lined the walls. A ventilation system hung from the ceiling. A mister chirped out a puff of vapor every few seconds. Preppy pushed his way past me and set his backpack down on the floor. He opened it and took out some tools. Walking through the rows of plants he inspected each one. Occasionally he used magnifying glass to closely inspect the leaves.

"You're growing pot?"

"BINGO."

"In an old lady's house, you're growing pot. Why?"

"If you had to guess what it was I was doing here would this have ever entered your mind as a possibility?"

"No."

"That's why."

"So Gladys, too?"

"And several others around town. We pay their mortgages or other bills, or just give them cash if that's what they want, and in return they let us use a room in their house to grow our plants."

"So, you aren't a granny nanny?"

"Was that your second guess? Well, I suppose that's better than hooker, but no, I'm not a fucking granny nanny. Although I do make it a point to be friendly with all of our greenhouse contributors. Keeps them happy. Keeps them wanting to do business with us. Keeps the law off our backs."

"I think I liked it better when I thought you were a hooker."

Preppy opened his arms wide and looked around the room with pride. "Kid, welcome to my brain-child. Welcome to Granny Growhouse."

"So, that's what you call your operation? Granny Growhouse?" We were back in the car after another three stops, and Preppy just announced that Betty had been our last stop for the day.

"That's what I call it. King hates the name, but he hasn't been back long enough to meet all the ladies and get a feel for it. He'll come around."

"You did this while King was in prison?"

"Yeah, kept getting fucked over by our main supplier who only wanted to deal with King, so I phased them out and started Granny Growhouse. It was how we earned while the big man was away."

"Have you thought of getting a job?"

"What would you call this?" he asked.

"No, like a real job."

"Fuck no. Never had a real job a day in my life. Don't plan on it either. Fuck the man."

"I don't know if you are completely odd or oddly brilliant."

"I can't decide if you are always this blunt or just have a bad case of can't-shut-the-fuck-ups," he countered.

"It's an always kind of thing," I said honestly.

"King sort of has a real job with the tattooing. It's how he stays under the radar. But he loves it, too. You should see some of his art. It's fucking amazing. He's been doing it since we were kids, using me as his human test dummy."

It wasn't until we arrived back at the house, car parked in the garage that I began to dread the reality that awaited me.

All six foot three of him.

Preppy saw me staring up at the house. "I know he's a little rough on the surface, but he's the best guy I've ever met."

"Oh yeah? You must not know a lot of people."

"She's got jokes!" Preppy said as he pulled down the garage door. "But seriously, he's not all bad."

We started to walk toward the house when a large shadow passed over the far window on the second floor, sending shivers down my spine. "You should probably tell him that."

## Doe

PREPPY MADE DINNER, A DELICIOUS PASTA WITH SAUSAGE dish. I think the old ladies were starting to rub off on him because we ate our meals on the living room recliners off of folding TV trays.

After dinner, Preppy disappeared into his room and since I was a glutton for punishment, I went upstairs to look for King. Or maybe, I just wanted to find him before he found me. It wasn't exactly the upper hand, but it was something.

A buzzing sound caught my attention. It was coming from the same room where I'd walked in on King with a girl.

The door was partially open. Inside was a girl with long,

straight red hair straddling a low-backed chair. King sat behind her, but it was nothing like the scene from last time. King was perched on a stool, wearing black gloves. He held a buzzing tattoo gun that every so often, he would dip into a small plastic container before continuing on with his work.

A man with sandy-blonde hair that fell to his chin and bright blue eyes sat in the corner, reading a GUNS AND AMMO magazine. The redhead's eyes were closed, and King lightly tapped his foot to the Lynnyrd Skynnyrd song playing over the speakers.

Not knowing how King would feel about me watching him work, I turned to leave, but he stopped me. "Pup, I need more paper towels."

I turned back around. The blonde's eyes were on me immediately. The red head took out her ear buds, but King hadn't looked up.

"Me?" I asked, unsure if King was talking to me or if he called everyone *Pup*.

"Yes, you. Unless I'm calling Jake *pup* now, and something tells me he wouldn't like it all that much."

The man in the corner stared at me straight-faced with no readable emotion. The girl offered me a knowing look before putting her ear buds back in and closing her eyes.

"On the counter," King added impatiently.

I looked over to the corner of the room and spied the roll of paper towels. I grabbed them and walked over to King, setting them on the small table next to him. I was about to walk back out of the room when he spoke again.

"Stay," he ordered. Unfolding a piece of towel, he sprayed the girl's back with the liquid from a plastic water bottle and then wiped at the tattoo until he seemed satisfied. "I'm done here." He wiped something from a jar onto her back then taped the edges of the plastic with gauze tape. King tapped on the girl's shoulders and she again removed her ear buds. "You can take the plastic off tomorrow. Keep it clean."

"Always do," she said.

I hadn't seen Jake stand up, but suddenly, he was next to the redhead, helping her up off the chair.

"My feet always fall asleep when I'm getting tattooed," she explained to me. She leaned forward onto the blond man for a few moments until she was able to stand up on her own.

I got a brief glimpse of the new ink on her back. It was a tree, a delicate yet bold orange tree at sunset. The leaves spelled out *Georgia* through the middle. The tattoo looked as if it were in motion, like oranges were falling from the branches.

It was heart-breakingly beautiful.

They both wore wedding bands, so I assumed Jake was her husband. When he saw me staring at her new artwork, he reached behind her and released the clip that held up her shirt, rearranging it until she was covered.

"What do I owe you, brother?" he asked King.

"A favor," King said. "Keep your phone on."

"Done." Jake held his wife close as they made their way to the door.

When they passed me, she turned to me. "Hi I'm Ab—"

"We were just leaving," her husband interrupted, looking down at her as if to remind her of something she'd forgotten.

She nodded, and then flashed me a small smile before they left the room. I'd only been around them for ten minutes, but the guy seemed to be two different people. He sent out vibes of being antisocial and an asshole, but he looked at her like she was his most prized possession. But he didn't own her. That much was obvious.

She owned *him*.

"Who was that?" I asked. I watched from the window as the couple climbed onto a shiny black motorcycle. Her husband helped her with her helmet before they rode off down the drive, disappearing under the trees.

"If they wanted you to know, they would've told you."

"They're in love."

"I sure as shit hope so. They're married. Got a kid, too."

King took off his gloves and tossed them into a stainless steel bin beside his worktable. He stood and joined me at the window. I could feel the heat from his body radiating onto my back. He leaned over me, his cheek brushing up against my temple. I closed my eyes and tried not to allow his nearness to affect me.

*I'm stronger than this.*

"There are plenty of married people in the world, but it doesn't mean all of them are in love. Not like that, anyway."

"No," King agreed. "It doesn't." He stepped away, leaving nothing but cold air in his place. I let out a breath I didn't know I was holding.

"Do you want me to leave?" I asked, turning from the window. King was sitting on the couch with his phone in his hands.

"No, I have a lot of people coming tonight. You can help me."

"You're really talented," I offered.

"You don't have to say that," King said, tapping away at the screen.

"I'm not trying to be nice. It's true. Her tattoo was seriously amazing."

"Hhmpf," he grunted, not looking up from his phone.

"You know, it's customary to say thank you when someone compliments you."

"Thanks for the heads up."

A car door slammed below, and two girls about my age giggled as they approached the door. The bell rang.

"Bring them up," he ordered.

My job over the next several hours consisted of shuffling the music when King needed a change of pace, running downstairs to get him Red Bulls, and sitting around doing nothing. At one point, I stood up, told King that I was just taking up space, and that I should get out of his way. He glared at me and nodded back to the couch.

"Why do you do this when you do...other things?" I asked him between clients while I was washing out paint containers in the small sink. "And why don't you have a real shop instead of doing this out of your house?"

"You ask a lot of fucking questions," King pointed out.

"Two."

"What?"

"You said I ask a lot of questions. I only asked two."

King folded his arms over his chest, accentuating his toned biceps. "If you must know, I do this because I've always done it. Art was the only class I liked as a kid. And I do this in my house because the places around here that are any sort of decent are on the other side of the causeway, and the rent wouldn't make the business worth having. Happy?"

"So you do this because art was the only class you were good at in school?"

"More fucking questions," King sighed. "And you don't listen. I did well in school. Very well, actually. I said art was the only class I liked, not the only class I was good at."

"Oh," I said, feeling stupid that I'd jumped to that conclusion. "I'm sorry. I just thought…"

"I'm a bad guy, Pup, not a dumb guy."

"I didn't say you were dumb."

"Look in that drawer over there." He pointed at a tool box. I opened the drawer. In it was a framed degree from the University of South Florida. Under it was a gun.

"Why do you keep this in here? Why don't you hang it up?"

"Because I earned the degree online."

"That's not a big…"

"While in prison," King interrupted. "And I'm glad I did it. I like having it, but putting it on the wall would mean I was proud of it. My feelings are a lot more mixed than that. Besides, Grace says you should always have a drawer that reminds you that who you are and what you do aren't always the same thing."

"Who's Grace?"

"You'll find out."

"Well, why don't you just start your own business?"

King laughed.

"What's so funny?"

"You are, Pup."

"Why is that?"

"Because you just asked me why I didn't start my own business."

"And?"

"And, it's funny, because…" King gestured to the gun. His face went serious. "I did."

A knock at the door interrupted us. I quickly returned the frame to the drawer and shut it just as Preppy let in King's next client.

A woman, older than me, strutted through the door wearing a tight tube top and shorts so short the bottom of her ass cheeks hung out. She set herself up on the table like she owned the place, popping her gum as she explained to King, in detail, the Orchid tattoo she wanted on her left ass cheek.

King told me what he needed set up, and I started gathering his supplies.

"Who's she?" the girl asked, casting me a sideways glare.

"She's none of your business."

"Can't she step out? I'm really shy," she whined, even as she pushed her shorts off in a suggestive manner. Leaving on her heels she crawled onto the table and stuck her thong-clad ass into the air.

"No, she can't," King said. Grabbing a marker, he freehanded the outline of an orchid onto her butt.

The girl made a pouting noise but didn't push the issue. After an hour, she asked if I could go get her something to drink. King nodded to me, and I went downstairs to grab beers from the fridge.

When I came back up, I paused at the door.

"Come on, baby. You don't remember me? You should. Your work is right here." The girl turned around and sat up on her elbows, spreading her legs, she revealed tattooed butterfly wings on both sides of her inner thighs.

"I remember the work. I don't remember you," King said stiffly. "Do you want me to finish this fucking tattoo or not?"

"Yes, but I want your big cock first," she cooed.

"That's not gonna fucking happen."

"Is it because of that ugly skinny bitch? She doesn't even have any fucking tits!"

There was a commotion, and before I could figure out

124

what exactly was going on, King had thrown the girl's shorts out into the hallway and was pushing her out the door by her elbow.

"You can get that shit finished by someone else. We're fucking done here."

She grabbed her shorts off the floor and stomped past me. "Fucking ugly bitch. Fucking asshole," she muttered as she practically tripped in her rush to get to the stairs.

King stood in the doorway. "And if I hear you ever talk shit about her again, I'll find you and take that butterfly tattoo back."

"Oh yeah?" she shouted, stopping on the landing. "How the fuck are you going to do that?"

King was in the doorway one second and an inch from her face the next. "I'll tell you how," he seethed. "I'm going to find you, and then I'm going to take my time carving those fucking butterfly wings from that nasty pussy of yours with my knife. Sleep on that before you decide to open that good for nothing dick-sucker of yours again."

Her eyes went wide with fear. She couldn't move fast enough as she rushed out of the house, slamming the door behind her. The gravel spun under the tires of her car as she sped down the driveway.

"Clean up," King ordered. He grabbed one of the beers from my arms as he passed me in the hallway and went back into his studio. I stood with my mouth open for a full minute before following him.

"What the hell was that?" I asked, putting the rest of the drinks into the cooler by the door.

"It was nothing. Clean up. We aren't done yet." King chugged the beer, crushed the can in his hands and tossed it into the trash bin.

The clock above the door read three am.

The next client was a man named Neil who King had being doing a full sleeve for before he went to prison. Neil had waited three years for King to be released so he could finish it. He said he just didn't trust anyone else to do it right.

I sat on the leather couch and watched King as he scrunched his face up in concentration. How could someone so talented also be so menacing?

*You already know how talented his hands are.*

I bit my lip and remembered the way his fingers felt inside me. My face flushed.

"I can feel you staring at me," King said, snapping me out of my daydream. Neil had a huge set of red headphones on with his eyes closed. He was either engrossed in the music or fast asleep.

"I'm kind of bored," I admitted, embarrassed I'd been caught staring.

King stood and removed a glove. He opened another drawer on the toolbox and removed something, tossing it over to me. A sketchbook landed next to me on the couch, followed by a box of colored pencils.

"Maybe, this will help you stop fucking fidgeting," he said. "It always helped me."

Then, he turned up the volume on the iPod docking station before picking up his tattoo gun and diving back into his work.

I opened the sketchbook, which wasn't blank. The first few sketches were variations of the orange tree tattoo I'd seen King tattoo on the redhead earlier. Each one better than the next until I got to the one he used as a template for her tattoo.

Several pages of stunning artwork later, a beautiful dragon, a skull made completely of flowers, and a pin-up girl dressed as a nurse, and I was finally at a blank page. Doodling, I quickly found, was a much better way to pass the time than wondering about the man who made my head spin, and other parts of me throb.

I drew happy faces and stick figures at first. But then I started shading and one of the stick figures started to look like a person. I wasn't actually drawing. It felt more like I could already see the completed design in my mind and was just filling in what was already on the page.

When I finished, I was staring into the chestnut eyes from my dream. I looked up at King, who was still engrossed in his work. I quietly tore the page from the book and folded it up, shoving it deep between the cushions of the couch. Part of me was hiding it so I could come back to it later and maybe add to it. Another part of me wanted to keep this one thing that I knew was somehow connected to my past to myself.

I then decided to sketch the bird I saw earlier flying over the water. I visualized it just as I had with the eyes I'd just drawn. Before I knew it, my pencil was flying over the page. I wasn't just drawing. I was shading, smudging, and contouring.

When I was done, it wasn't exactly the bird I'd seen earlier, but a more exotic version of it. Dark. Fierce. Its feathers were ruffled wildly, and the snake dangling from his beak had it's mouth open with it's fangs exposed. I created smoke billowing out of the small nostrils on the bird's beak, as if he could breathe fire. But then I decided that he looked too harsh, too intimidating, so I gave the bird a broken wing, and in the reflection of his eye, I drew the snake before he'd killed it, swallowing a mouse. The final product was both brilliant beauty and vulnerability. Tears formed in my eyes, and I wiped them away before they could spill onto my cheek.

*I can draw.*

Not only could I draw, but I could draw well. It came as naturally as breathing.

The second thing connecting me to *her*.

When I put the book down, I looked up, and King's client was gone. King sat on his stool alone, watching me. "You were in the zone," he said. "You looked so fucking cute sitting there concentrating."

I swallowed hard, "I…uuuhhh…got caught up."

His words took me by surprise. I visualized stalking over to him and climbing onto his lap. His big strong hands coming around my back and resting underneath my shirt on my bare skin. I thought about what it would be like to let him do more than what he'd done before.

*What would it be like if he used more than his fingers?*

I shuddered.

"Bring it here," King said, holding out his hand, snapping me out of my own imagination where I was naked and writhing underneath him.

"No, you don't want to see it. I was just messing around. I'll just put it back in the drawer and clean up now." I walked over to the sink with the book under my arm. King reached out and snatched it away from me, flipping the pages in search of my sketch.

"Holy Go-go-Gadget arms," I quipped. I'd clearly underestimated King's reach.

"How do you know that?" he asked.

"What do you mean? How do I know what?" I asked.

"The 'Go-go gadget' thing. That's a reference to a cartoon.

Have you ever even seen it?"

"Um…I think so. It's this guy who wears a trench coat and has a billion little gadgets all over the place that usually don't work the way he wants them to."

"I know who it is. What I want to know is have you watched it since you lost your memory?"

"No, I haven't watched any TV until earlier tonight when Preppy put on something called American Ninja Warrior." I stepped back and leaned against the counter. "What are you trying to get at? I thought you believed me."

"That's not it. I'm just trying to figure it out. Help me understand." King leaned forward and rested his elbows on his knees. "If you haven't watched it, then it's something that carries over from before. How exactly does that work?"

"I'm not really sure. When I was living in the group home, I saw a psychologist or a psychiatrist or one of those. He told me that memory loss works differently for everyone. For me, it wiped out all personal information. Names, faces, memories. But I can still walk and talk, so I retained all my functions. I also know facts. Like, I know who the president is, and I can sing to you the jingle for Harry's House of Falafel's commercial. I just don't know HOW I know those things."

King nodded. I bit my lip.

"You know, you're the only person besides the psychologist guy who's even asked me about it," I added.

King turned a page in the book and found my sketch. He studied it for several minutes. Time seemed to tick by slower and slower. I grew restless wondering what he thought of it. He was probably trying to figure out how to tell me it was complete crap. But then again I didn't take him for someone who would go out of his way in order to avoid offending anyone.

So, what the hell was he staring at for so long?

And why the hell did I need his approval so badly?

"Are you done for the night?" I asked, trying to draw his attention away from the sketch. If he hated it, I'd rather just not talk about it at all. He lifted his eyes from my sketch just long enough to give my body a slow once over, like he was looking at me for the very first time. His gaze ignited my skin as if he'd actually touched me.

"Am I done?" he repeated my question. King ran the underside of his tongue across his bottom lip, leaving a sheen where he'd made it wet. "I'm not sure. I'm thinking I could just be getting started."

*Holy Shit.*

The familiar redness burned its way up my neck and my ears grew hot.

The clock read 4:45am, and although I should have been tired due to the time, I was more alert than ever. The caffeine and sugar from the four Red Bulls I'd drunk felt like it could keep me awake for days, but I needed to get away from King because I felt myself starting to forget all the reasons why letting him strip me down and have his way with me would be a bad idea.

"What does that mean, exactly?"

"It means that I'm done with clients. But it also means that I'm not done with *you*." King grabbed my wrist and dragged me onto his lap, the very place I'd just fantasized about being.

I gasped.

The hard muscles of his thighs rippled under mine. His smell—a light mixture of soap and sweat—was intoxicating. He fisted a handful of my hair and yanked my head sideways, exposing my neck to him. He breathed me in, running his nose along my neck, followed by a long leisurely lick from my collar-bone to the sensitive spot on the back of my ear. I moaned, and he chuckled. I could feel it vibrate through his body and into mine. "Oh, Pup. How much fun this is going to be."

Just like that, he released my hair and pushed me off his lap. My shaky knees almost gave way, and I had to hold onto the counter to avoid falling forward onto the floor.

"We've got one more," King said.

"I thought you just said no more clients tonight," I said, breathlessly.

King proceeded to set up three small containers of black ink. "Here." He handed me a thin-tipped black marker.

"What do you want me to do with this?" I asked.

"I want you to draw your sketch again. The same one. Hold it up for reference."

"Draw it on what?"

"On the back of my hand, it's a much smaller canvas than your sketch so you'll have to downsize a bit, but it's one of the few spaces of blank canvas I have left.

"Why?"

"Why do you always ask so many fucking questions?"

"Don't you have a machine that does this? You can copy this picture and just stick it on there if that's what you really want."

King sighed with frustration. "Yes, I do. But it's not the point. I want you to draw it on me. I want you to put that pen to my skin and recreate your sketch. I don't care if it's crooked. I don't care if it's not perfect, just fucking draw it!" he shouted, standing up. He took a few steps toward me until I was backed up against the counter, clutching the sketch book to my chest. "Please?"

A 'please' from the man who didn't say 'please'.

"Okay," I agreed. "But why?"

"Because I looked over at you while you were drawing this, and you looked all cute, biting your lip, your face flushed, the back of the pencil pressed against those pink lips. Then, when you showed me what you drew, I saw it right away."

"Saw what?"

"Me. The bird. You drew me." I opened my mouth to argue that it was just a bird, but I couldn't. He was right.

Dark and dangerous.

Hard but beautiful, taking what he wanted from the world. It *was* him.

King propped the sketchbook on the table so I could reference my drawing. I did the best I could to create a smaller version of it onto the back of his hand. I worked even harder trying to ignore the electricity humming between us. King never took his eyes off of me.

It took me twice as long to complete than the sketch, but when I was finally done, I put the marker down and sat back.

"Okay?" I asked.

King held his hand up and examined my work. "It will work," he confirmed. "Now, go get me a coffee."

"No Red Bull?" I asked, standing up from the table.

"It's after 5am. After 5am calls for coffee."

"Okay, coffee then," I said, making my way down to the kitchen. By the time I figured out the single cup coffee machine thing they had—the only modern appliance in the kitchen—and got back to the studio, King was hunched over his hand with his tattoo gun buzzing.

"What the hell are you doing?"

Silence.

"So what? You're ignoring me now?"

He lifted the gun from his skin. "Yes, because if I talk to you, I'll be giving this bird a dick in his mouth instead of a snake," King said.

"I will get back to the fact that you sort of made a joke later, something which I didn't think you were capable of doing, but right now, the only thing I can concentrate on is that you are tattooing my sketch onto your hand!" I shouted.

"What did you think I was going to do with it?" King dipped his gun into the ink.

"I don't know, but not that!"

"Pup?" King asked softly.

"Yeah?"

"Enough with the questions. You're distracting me. Go the fuck to bed."

"But—" I started to argue.

"Pup?"

"Yeah?"

"Bed. Now. Or you can choose to stay, but I'm warning you, if that's the decision you make and you are still here when I'm done, I'm bending you over that couch and fucking you into next week."

*Shit.*

I scurried out of the room as fast as I could, not stopping to catch my breath, I could still hear him laughing as I closed the door and sank to the floor.

I was totally and utterly, for lack of a better word, FUCKED.

## KING

YOU LOOKED SO FUCKING CUTE, SITTING THERE *concentrating.* Where the fuck did that come from? I hadn't even realized I'd said it out loud until I saw the redness rise in her cheeks. On the other hand, flirting with her and making her uncomfortable was by far becoming my newest and most favorite source of entertainment.

Since she started eating Preppy's cooking, it only took a couple of days for Pup to pack on some weight. The additional few pounds had done amazing things for her figure. Her sunken cheeks were a little fuller and somehow made her appear even more innocent and cherub-like. Her tits and ass were rounder and begging to be touched even more so than before.

134

She had the body of a woman and the face of an angel and I was constantly walking around like a thirteen year old who had to keep adjusting himself to hide his raging hard-on.

The truth was I didn't bother her while she was sketching because I didn't want her to move, and I was perfectly content to just sit and stare at her all night. But then, she would cross and uncross her legs while biting her lip, and all I could think about was how I wanted to be the one to bite that lip. How wet I could make her between those legs.

I didn't get up from my stool after Neil left because I was afraid she'd look up from her sketch and see my cock standing at attention through my jeans. If she were any other chick, I would draw her attention to it, but I didn't want to send her running into the other room. I already felt her fighting off whatever attraction she had for me. The horrible truth of the matter is that I didn't want to scare her away.

Because I actually liked having her around.

Somewhere, somehow, my anger toward her had turned to some sort of fucked-up affection.

Which I had to put a stop to right a fucking away, because any sort of feelings for her other than contention and lust would only get in the way of the plans I had for her.

She was afraid of me. That much was obvious, but there was a fire there, too, and the more she fought it, the more it turned me on.

The way her body reacted to me told me that there was only so long she could resist the inevitable. The inevitable being me fucking her until she couldn't remember her own name.

It's not like she knew it anyway.

But I did.

An unfamiliar nagging feeling tugged at my gut.

Guilt maybe?

I brushed it off. There wasn't time to entertain any feelings of guilt. A better opportunity to get Max back was not going to just fall into my lap like this again. And in the meantime, I was going to spend my time with her as I pleased. In her case, that meant doing everything I had to make her warm, wet, and willing.

"Boss-man!" Preppy shouted, bounding into my studio with his pupils dilated, forgetting to blink like he'd just snorted blow by the fucking truck full.

"What's up, Prep?" I asked, putting the finishing touches on the tattoo Pup had sketched for me. After I saw it, I needed it on my skin, immediately and permanently and for the life of me I didn't know why. But after it was done, I felt like a weight was lifted.

"What the fuck is that?" Preppy asked, pointing to the back of my hand. I wiped off the excess ink and blood and held it up so he could see.

"It's a tattoo, dumb-ass. Or did you forget what it is I do in this room?"

"I know it's a tattoo, fucker. I just wanted to know why you were tattooing yourself right now."

"You've seen me do it a hundred times so what's the fucking big deal?" I barked, not liking Preppy's third degree.

"What exactly is it?" he asked, leaning over my shoulder as I put a layer of plastic wrap over the top.

"It's nothing. Pup drew it. What exactly is it you wanted?" I hated being short with him, but I wasn't about to answer questions I myself didn't exactly know the answers to.

"I came to tell you two things actually. One is that Bear called, and he overheard his dad talking. Isaac's coming to town.

He's not sure when, just knows he's coming. Got eyes on him though. He hasn't left Dallas yet." The MC had a long-standing relationship with our former primary source of weed.

"And?"

"AND I'm pretty sure he's probably a little pissed the fuck off that we cut him out as our supplier."

"I was locked up, and he didn't want to deal with anyone but me. If he expected us to just do nothing until I got out, that was his mistake. We saw opportunity. We seized it. End of story."

"Yeah man, that's the way you and I see it. But Bear over-heard his dad saying that Isaac sees it more like a kick to his balls that he wants to pay back to us a thousand times over."

"I'm not hiding from Isaac, or anyone else. If he wants to talk to me, he knows where the fuck I live. Now, what's the oth-er thing you wanted to tell me?" I snapped.

"Dude, you're so fucking moody since you got out. You're like a bitch on the rag twenty-four hours a day. The second thing I wanted to tell you is that I'm going to take Doe out on a date Saturday night."

"You're going to fucking WHAT?" I suddenly wished my tattoo gun was a real one because with that one sentence, Preppy was walking into dangerous fucking territory.

"She's cool as shit, so I'm going to take her out. Maybe, a movie or something. The drive-in is playing some scary para-normal thing, and chicks fucking love that shit. Makes 'em all cuddly," Preppy said, hugging himself with his arms.

"Like fuck you are." Not only was he not taking her out, I got the impression that scary wasn't exactly Doe's favorite genre. The girl's been scared enough in real life.

"Dude, I'm not going to fuck her. Unless that's cool with

you. In which case, I will most *definitely* fuck her."

I stood from my stool. It rolled back and crashed against the wall. "Not. A Fucking. Chance." The thought of his hands on her made my stomach twist.

"You don't even like her," he barked. "Besides, you don't know anything about her. And that's your fault because she may not know a lot about herself, but the little she does know you haven't even bothered to ask her about."

He had a point, but Preppy didn't know that there was a reason for that, and I planned to keep that reason to myself for the time being.

"What exactly would you like for me to talk to her about? Because the *where do you come from, what's your name,* thing doesn't exactly apply in her case."

Preppy huffed and linked his fingers together behind his neck. "I don't know. You could ask her something simple, like maybe, how she likes her sandwiches or something."

"Sandwiches. You want me to ask her about sandwiches?"

"Why the fuck not? Everyone likes a delicious sandwich, and talking about them is better than talking about the heavy shit you seem to be carrying around these days."

This is why Preppy was my best friend. He saw right through me.

"I know Max is important. I know we need to get her back, but until then, you still have a life to live, man. And talking to the girl, who for all intents and purposes is living in our house, isn't going to get in the way of that."

*That's what you think.*

"Have you even fucked her yet? I mean, the chick sleeps in your bed and shit. What the fuck is that all about?"

"That's none of your fucking business," I warned. He was

crossing a line.

He rolled his eyes. "I'll take that as a no. Maybe, that's why you've been so fucking grumpy since you got out. Maybe you just need to get some ass. Get laid. Get all up in there before your dick shrivels up and falls the fuck off."

"I've gotten laid since I've gotten out, so shut the fuck up about it. This isn't about liking her or about fucking her. This is about me saying NO and you listening to me for once!"

"King, you've been my best friend since the dinosaurs roamed the earth, so listen to me when I tell you that you look at her like you want to fuck her brains out, but you treat her like she's garbage under your shoe. It's not cool, man. You're the one who decided to keep her here, which wasn't the brightest idea to begin with, so let me have a little fun with her for fuck's sake."

"This is about a debt that needs to be paid," I said, unconvincingly.

"Oh come on! We both know she didn't take anything. And since when is it up to you to dole out life lessons on who needs to pay for what? You some kind of life coach now? Besides, she's not your property. She's a person, not a fucking car."

"That's rich coming from you." I've witnessed Preppy doing things that made even my skin crawl, but if he was going to throw my shit in my face, then I was going to throw his shit in his.

"Seriously, she isn't yours. You can't just take her."

"Yes, she *is* mine, and I *did* just take her. She sleeps in my bed, doesn't she? Next to me. I may not have fucked her, but it was me she turned to when she wanted to get off the other night, and me who gave her what she needed. So no, I haven't fucked her, *yet*. But the answer is still no, you can't fucking take her out," I said through gritted teeth, I could feel my veins tighten as my blood pressure sky-rocketed.

Preppy cocked his head to the side and smiled. A recognition of some sort settled over his face. "Well, she's not my property. She's my friend. So, if I can't take her out, then you have to take her. I'm not doing this for me. I'm doing it for her. She's been through some shit, and we both know what that's like. The kid deserves a break. A little fucking fun."

"Fuck no. I'm not going to fucking date her. And this isn't up for debate. No date. No nothing. Just fucking drop it." For the first time in my life, I felt like punching Preppy. He's never coaxed that kind of anger from me before.

"Man, get your fucking head out of your ass. She's just a confused kid. Either you take her, or you let me take her. I may call you Boss-Man, but we're friends, and that doesn't mean you can make all my decisions for me. You may call the shots, but I'm still my own person. I'm not asking you here. I'm telling you."

"Fine!" I shouted. Throwing my arms up in the air. "Take her out on a fucking date. What the fuck do I care anyway? Go! Have a fucking blast!"

I sat back down on my stool and pretended to fiddle with my equipment. Why the fuck I was getting so riled up to begin with was beyond me.

Maybe, I'd just forgotten how to interact with people who weren't wearing orange jumpsuits or correctional officer uniforms.

"Awesome!" Preppy hopped from one foot to the other. "I'm going to go iron my good bow tie."

"Prep?"

"Yeah, Boss-Man?"

"It's six in the fucking morning."

"And?"

"You want to take her out on Saturday right?"

"Yeah."

"It's Monday."

"Ah."

"So how about you go wipe the fucking blow from under your nose and get some fucking sleep. Iron your good bow tie tomorrow." Preppy may not have to listen to me, but the need to tell him what to do would never go away.

I'd forgotten while I was away that Preppy was one hell of a partier.

We both were.

Or, I used to be.

Before Max.

Before prison.

Before *her.*

Preppy wiped the powder from under his nostrils and rubbed it onto his gums.

"Yes, sir," Preppy said with a mock salute. He turned to leave.

"And Prep?" I called out.

"Yeah, Boss?" he asked, stopping mid-stride.

"You're taking her out as her friend only. You've got that?"

"I've got that."

"Good. Because if you so much as touch her, I'll fucking kill you."

Doe

"WHAT IS ALL THIS?" I ASKED, STARING DOWN AT the plate upon plate of sliced meats and cheese.

"Sandwich stuff." King said, tossing me a roll.

"Yes, I can see that. But why are we making sandwiches on the dock?"

I wandered what his ulterior motive was. King didn't seem like the type to picnic on the dock, no matter what the situation. Plus, in the entire time I'd been staying with King, he'd never once made a meal for me.

Or even eaten a meal with me.

"Because it's a nice day to be outside, and because who the fuck doesn't like sandwiches?" King sat on one of the plastic chairs surrounding wooden table that was screwed to the dock so it wouldn't fly away during a storm. "And Preppy said…I don't fucking know, just go with it." King loaded his roll with salami and cheese and dug out a huge scoop of mayo from the jar with a spatula.

"That's enough mayo to choke a horse," I said, carefully selecting turkey and bacon for my own sandwich.

"Have you actually seen a horse choke from ingesting too much mayo?" he asked.

"I very well could have. I just don't remember." I grabbed a handful of Cheetos from the bag and smashed them into the top slice of bread with both hands. King pulled the other chair up along side his until the arms were touching and motioned for me to sit down.

And then OUR arms were touching.

"So what's it like?" King asked, popping the top off a beer and handing it to me.

"What's what like?" I asked, setting my paper plate in my lap.

"Not remembering anything. I keep thinking about what that would be like and I can't imagine it."

"It's…" I searched my brain for the words but only one popped into my mind over and over, "…empty."

"You're a lot of things, Pup, but empty isn't one of them." King tucked an unruly strand of hair behind my ear.

"Oh yeah? Then, you tell me what I am, because I can't think of anything that doesn't have to do with me losing my memory." I took a bite of my lunch that was so big I could barely close my mouth around it.

King laughed. "Well, for starters…you're kind of quirky."

"Quirky?"

"Pup, did you or did you not just put Cheetos on your sandwich?"

"Duly noted. Okay, quirky. I can handle that. Keep going. What else do you think you know about me?"

"Well, you're bold. Brave. I would even go as far as to say that you're irritatingly feisty. You speak about three hours before you think. You ask way too many goddamn questions. You have this dimple on your left cheek that comes out when you're smiling, but it also shows up, along with the one on the right cheek, when you're pissed off." Embarrassment burned my neck as if I was standing too close to a fire. "Your neck and your face get red when you're embarrassed. It starts at your neck. Right here." King lightly wrapped the palm of his hand around my throat. "Then, it jumps up to your cheeks." He brushed his thumb over my cheekbone. "Then, it travels all the way up to these ears."

He leaned in and sucked my earlobe into his mouth, trailing his tongue along the delicate flesh of my ears sending sparks of pleasure down my body. My nipples hardened and pressed up against my shirt.

King chuckled and pulled back. "So don't say that you're empty, Pup, because you are anything but." There was a mischievous glimmer in his eyes. Something I hadn't seen before. "I think you are, by far, the most interesting person I've ever met."

"Thank you," I said. "But stop trying to imagine what it would be like without your memory. You're lucky you know who you are and where you belong."

King pulled at the label on his beer and sighed. "Sometimes,

I wish I didn't."

"What do you mean?"

"If I could choose to wake up tomorrow and not remember who I am, the shit I've done, the people I would be leaving behind, I would do it. I could just start over. Be someone else."

"I don't want you to be anyone else," I blurted, interrupting his confession.

"You should hate me," King said, taking my plate from my lap and setting it on the table. "If I were you, I would hate me."

"I thought I did."

"And now? What do you think of me now?" King asked, leaning in closer.

"I think you are the most stubborn, overbearing, anger inducing, obnoxious, complicated, and beautiful man that has ever lived."

"I think you are beautiful, too," King breathed. In one graceful movement, he had me out of my chair and onto his lap.

His hands had just slid into my hair when a loud crash sounded from the other side of the mangroves.

"Stay the fuck here," King ordered. He stood and tossed me off his lap. I crouched behind the cement retaining wall that separated the dock from the yard. King leapt over it effortlessly and ran in the direction of the garage, toward where the sound had come from.

It seemed like I was there for hours, waiting for King to come back or for something to happen.

Nothing.

My stomach growled, and I was reminded that I had barely started my lunch. I scooted down to my ass and stretched out my leg in an effort to drag the chair that held my plate toward me. I hooked my foot around the leg of the chair and slowly pulled. It made a horrible scraping noise against the wood planks of the dock. I paused and waited.

Nothing.

So, I continued. Slowly, inch my inch, I dragged my lunch closer to me until my Cheetos smashed sandwich was within my reach. I pulled my plate off the seat and picked up my sandwich. I opened my mouth and was about to chomp down on victory when someone cleared their throat.

With my sandwich still in launch-into-my-mouth position, I looked up from behind the bread to see both King and Bear standing on the top of the seawall, peering down at me.

Bear looked just a good as he did the night I met him, but now, he looked even better. Because he was shirtless. His ab muscles glistened with sweat. I thought King had a lot of tattoos, but Bear didn't have a single inch of available real estate left on his skin.

King spoke first. "Oh no, don't worry about me. I'm fine. Just went to check out what that bomb like noise was, but you go ahead and finish your sandwich. We'll wait." He was smiling out of the corner of his mouth.

Bear crouched down. "Oh shit. Check you out. Didn't think you'd still be alive."

I put my plate down and stood up. "If you two are done mocking me, can one of you tell me what the fuck that noise was?"

"Oh shit. Sorry, that was all me. This girl came over, and she's got this old Volkswagen Bug. One thing led to another..."

"I don't want to know," I interrupted.

Bear continued, "All I was going to say is that while her lips were wrapped around my cock, I vaguely remembered promising to fix her bug for her. What you heard was that very car backfiring. For what I'm thinking was the very last time, because it's dead. Like super dead. Like there is no coming back from that dead. Which totally blows cause the girl could suck the—"

King held up a hand. "Okay, Bear, cut the bullshit, you can tell her what really happened."

Bear nodded and his phone rang. He pulled it out of his back pocket and clicked a button on the screen. "Yeah." He scratched his beard. "Fuck. Okay. Yeah. Yeah, I'll tell him." He clicked the phone again and put in back in his pocket.

"Isaac is on the move. Jimmy and BJ spotted him and his boys in Coral Pines this morning. Looks like they've got business there. BJ spoke to a guy in Isaac's crew. They'll be riding into our corner of the world in a week or so."

"Shit," King cursed.

"I told you to fucking get out of town, dude. You knew he was coming."

"Yeah, and when you told me that, I didn't care if he came right up to my front door, guns-a-fucking-blazing."

"But now?" Bear asked.

King nodded to me.

"Ah. I see. What do you want to do, man? Your call. You know I'm behind you no matter what." Bear lit a cigarette.

"I think we go on the offense," King said.

"Wait, what does all this mean? Who is Isaac?"

King ignored me. "I'll get her to Grace's before then," he told Bear.

"King, who the fuck is Isaac? Who the fuck is Grace?" I shouted, jumping up and down to make my presence in the conversation known.

"Pup, when Preppy took you out with him, did he tell you that when he and I started the granny operation, we cut out our main supplier?"

"Yeah. He did."

"Well, Isaac, was that supplier."

"Shit," I said.

Bear took a long drag of his cigarette and blew out the smoke through his nose, looking very much like the bird recently tattooed on King's hand. "Yeah, that about sums it up."

"What you heard was a warning," King said.

"What kind of warning?" I asked.

Bear stubbed out his cigarette into the concrete of the retaining wall. "The kind that goes boom."

"What was blown up?"

Preppy's wail broke through the air like another explosion.

"WHAT THE FUCK HAPPENED TO MY MOTHERFUCKING CAR?"

## Doe

ANY SIGN OF THE PLAYFUL VERSION OF KING FROM lunch were gone. He gave me ten minutes to get ready and *get my ass in the fucking truck.*

I didn't know where we were going, and something about the way he'd barked it at me made it clear he didn't exactly want me to ask.

We traveled together in a silence so heavy it had its own presence in the truck. Like an uninvited guest, it awkwardly sat between us on the bench seat. We turned down a narrow, dirt road. My curiosity piqued when King pulled over to the side of the road next to the gate of a yellow ranch style home with a short, white picket fence lining the front yard.

"Let's go," King said.

Getting out of the truck, he unlatched the gate and started up the cement walkway. I followed behind him, jogging to catch up to him and match his long strides. Several pinwheel lawn ornaments spun as we passed them, our motion creating the only breeze in the stagnant heat of the day. I thought that maybe King was making a pickup for Preppy, and that this was another one of their Granny Growhouses that I had not yet seen.

When we reached the door, King didn't knock, just shoved it open and walked inside. For a split second, my heart skipped a beat because I thought that maybe he was robbing the place, but I quickly squashed that idea when I heard him call out, "Grace?"

*Grace.* I recognized the name from earlier.

I followed him into the house and closed the door behind me. When I turned back around, I came face to face with a thousand tiny eyes staring back at me. The small living room was covered with them. From the plant shelves to the buffet style table in the entryway to the coffee table and on top of the old TV, ceramic rabbits of all shapes and sizes were everywhere.

King didn't pay them any attention as he strode through the living room to the sliding glass doors on the back of the eat-in kitchen where large stuffed rabbits occupied all six chairs of the table like they were about to enjoy a meal together.

*I guess Grace likes rabbits.*

"Out here!" shouted a high-pitched, yet scratchy voice.

King held the sliding glass doors open so I could pass, but he didn't step aside. I had to brush against his chest to get through. In my attempt to touch him as little as possible,

I stumbled outside onto a wooden deck where a little woman with pixie-style, gray hair sat in a plush navy blue deck chair. Her feet were resting on top of the table, crossed at the ankles. She drank out of a tall glass with light green liquid. A leaf floated on the top of the ice.

Instead of asking me who I was, she stood up and brought me in for a hug. She was easily in her seventies, and wore a denim-colored sweater, matching pants, and white orthopedic shoes.

"I'm Grace," she said, pushing me far enough away that she could study my face, but keeping her hands on my elbows.

"Hi." I wasn't sure what the protocol was about introducing myself to her, but King solved that problem for me.

"This is Doe."

"What an unusual name. What does it mean?"

I looked to King, and he nodded. "Doe as in Jane Doe," I told her.

"Are your parents into true crime novels, or are they hippies who fried their brains on too much acid? Lots of them peculiar types around here. Although I've never met you before, so I don't believe you're from Logan's Beach."

"I'm not sure what my parents are into, ma'am."

Grace looked at me quizzically and then over to King, who was still standing in the doorway. He shrugged.

"You're letting all the bought air out over there," Grace scolded King. "Come out here. Sit. Have a drink."

Grace waved King over and tugged me to a chair. She poured us both a glass of the green liquid from the glass pitcher on the table.

"I hope you like mojitos!" she exclaimed, finishing her drink and pouring herself another.

I took a sip. The ice clinked against my front teeth. The drink was both sweet and bitter, but under the heat of the noon sun, it tasted heavenly.

Thankfully, my sunburn was fully healed, and I no longer needed to hide in the shade. Nor did I resemble a ripe tomato.

King took the seat next to me and across from Grace.

"What you got for me?" Grace asked King.

He laughed and shifted in his seat. He removed a small black plastic bag from his pocket and slid it across the table.

"Thank you, sweet boy," Grace said, hugging the bag to her chest. She set it down on the table and turned to me. "So, how did you two kids meet? Tell me everything."

"Um…" I had no idea how to answer her, so I started with the truth. As I spoke, it became like word vomit of epic proportions, and I couldn't stop it from barreling out of my mouth. "Well Grace, we met on the night I decided to sell myself for a hot meal and a place to sleep. I was about to suck this guy's dick when he realized I was being skittish about the whole thing and threw me out. Then, my friend, who was a hooker, stole some money from him. Then, she shot me, or grazed me, or whatever. Then, he found my only friend dead in a hotel room with a needle in her arm, but that was before I escaped. Then, he killed my would-be rapist and brought me back to his house for a bath and a conversation about how I was now his possession and didn't have a choice about it."

I stopped and looked up at Grace whose glass was paused mid-air.

King cleared his throat. "She came to my coming home party." It was the truth, but he was leaving out all the cringe-worthy details I'd just laid out for her. Grace set her glass down and threw her head back in laughter.

"I don't think you two could be any cuter together," she said, ignoring everything I'd just told her. "I'm so glad you found someone, dear boy. I'd missed you so much while you were gone, and I prayed every single day that you would find someone who made you as happy as my Edmund made me." Grace turned a small silver band on her ring finger.

"We're not—" I started, but King put his arm over my chair and tugged me into him.

"I wanted you to meet her," he said, running his thumb against the side of my neck in an unexpected sign of affection.

Show or not, my skin came alive under his seemingly innocent touch, and I'm pretty sure I gasped out loud because King's shoulders shook with silent laughter. Grace stood and rounded the table. Pausing above King, she kissed him on the top of the head.

"You've made this old woman very happy," Grace said, wiping a tear from under her eye. She sniffled and clasped her hands together. "I'm going to start dinner. Doe, darling, would you like to help me?"

"Sure," I said, standing up from the table.

I still wasn't entirely sure why we were there, but I liked Grace, and having someone else besides the three tattooed amigos around was a nice change. She had a grandmotherly thing going on that set you at ease the moment she opened her mouth. I was going to enjoy it while I could until I had to go back to the house with Mr. Mood Swings.

"I've got stuff in the truck," King said, hopping down off the deck and disappearing around the side of the house. Grace led me into the kitchen and took out ingredients for pasta with meatballs. She moved one of the stuffed rabbits so I could sit at the table and chop vegetables while she used her hands to mix together all the ingredients for the meatballs.

"How you do know King?" I asked, chopping green peppers onto a cutting board. I used the knife to wipe them into a bowl and started on the onions.

"He didn't tell you?"

"He doesn't say much," I admitted.

"Man of few words, that one," Grace said warmly. "I've known Brantley since he was a snot-nosed middle schooler. He tried to steal from my garden one day. He wasn't a day over twelve."

"Brantley?"

"He really doesn't tell you anything, does he?" Grace cast me a sideways glance.

"What did you do when you caught him?" I was curious about how King forged a relationship with a lady three times his own age.

"I got a switch off the tree, just like my mama would have done, ripped his jeans down past his little, white butt, and whipped some sense into him," Grace said, casually as she rinsed a tomato under the tap and dried it with a paper towel.

"No, you didn't!" I said, half in disbelief and half because I couldn't imagine this little sprig of woman giving King a spanking.

"Yes, I sure did. Then, Edmund called Brantley's mom while I made dinner, but she didn't answer. Edmund left a message, but his mom never came. So, he stayed for dinner. Then, he stayed the night. He's come over every Sunday since. Well, every Sunday he hasn't been mixed up in something or sitting in prison. In that case, we went to him."

"You knew he was in prison?"

"Of course. Visited him every week. And when my

Edmund died, that little boy came to his funeral wearing a green tuxedo he bought from the thrift shop that was three sizes too big. I've offered to let him live here a thousand times, but that boy was never one who could be contained. He chose to stay out there, do what he does, and he comes to take care of me and the house in between."

"So, you know…everything?"

Grace nodded. "Not the nitty gritty details but I'm no dim-witted woman. I know my boy isn't exactly walking on the right side of the law. But I know that I love him like a son, and he loves me like his mama so that's all that matters to me." Grace didn't pause when she continued. "Love is what you would do for the other person, not what you do in general. There is no doubt in my mind that he would throw his life down for me. I would do the same without hesitation." She opened the refrigerator and pulled out a bowl of green peppers. "I also know that everything you said out there, about how you two met, is true."

"Why didn't you say something?" I asked.

Grace sighed and looked away, deep in thought. "There was this movie I watched as a little girl. This black and white picture about a cowboy who robbed trains. I'll never forget the ending. You see, the cowboy turns to the woman he loves, after she just found out that he was the train robber, and he tells her that although he did horrible things, he stole from people, killed people, it didn't mean he loved her any less or that he wasn't capable of love."

Grace motioned for me to pick up the salad bowl and follow her out onto the deck. I set the bowl on the table, and Grace arranged the plates and forks. When she was done, she guided me to the railing and nodded over to where King stood on a ladder, replacing a light bulb on a small shed in the corner of the yard.

"What I'm trying to say, dear, and what I think the cowboy was trying to say to his love in that movie, is that there is a difference between being bad and being evil. Just because he was a very bad boy, that doesn't mean he couldn't be a truly great man." I was rolling her words around in my brain when she added, "And God help me, little one, you break his heart, and I will cut you where you stand. If I'm long gone when that happens, be assured that death will not stop me from bringing you down." Grace smiled like she hadn't just threatened my life and brought me in for another hug. "Now, let's go get the meatballs."

Grace may have been a little thing, and she definitely had the wrong idea about what was going on between myself and King, but I had no doubt that if I crossed her, she would carry through on her threat without blinking an eye.

King ducked inside the bathroom to wash his hands and then joined us out on the deck. The sun had just started to set when I noticed the strands of lights crisscrossing over our heads. As the sun sank lower, the lights got brighter until they looked like thousands of tiny stars shining over our meal.

We ate, and Grace did most of the talking. She frequently refilled my mojito, and at one point rushed inside to make another pitcher. She was curious about me and asked a lot of questions. In between shoveling meatballs into my mouth, I filled her in on my story.

"It's a good thing you have each other." She pointed out.

"She's not my girlfriend, Grace," King said, his lips compressed in a thin, straight line.

Grace shrugged and took another sip of her drink.

"Edmund and I had an arranged marriage, you know. His mother and mine conspired together since we were still on the tit. The first few years we were together, I couldn't stand the man, but after a while, I learned to love him. Then, I fell in love with him and felt that way up until the day he died. Things don't always start out the way we want them to. It's how they end that's important. I may not have loved Ed in the beginning, but he grew to be the love of my life."

Grace had the most optimistic, if not bordering on warped, perception of relationships. But what did I expect? The woman was a walking, talking contradiction. A tiny little thing that drank like a fish and swore like a sailor. Not to mention that her house looked like an episode of HOARDERS: RABBIT EDITION.

"It didn't hurt that the sex was off the charts fantastic," Grace said, staring up into the lights.

I spit out a mouthful of mojito. Half of it splattered against King's shirt. I braced myself for his anger, slowly lifting my eyes to his, but there was none. His shoulders shook as he chuckled. Grace was downright howling.

I helped Grace clean up while King disappeared down the hall. I heard the bathtub running and thought maybe he was ringing the mojito out of his shirt.

"Grace, what's with the rabbits?" I asked her, needing to know. She smiled and closed the dishwasher. She turned the dial, and it sounded like Preppy's car exploding all over again.

"Ed used to bring me home a ceramic rabbit after every business trip." She looked around at the table. "I know it's odd, and I know they've taken over the house. But each one was a moment my husband wasn't with me, but was still thinking about me." Grace looked as if she was getting tired. My heart seized. I wasn't expecting the reason to be so sentimental, and I hated that I ever thought that she might have been just a crazy rabbit lady.

"I'll finish this up, Grace. Why don't you go lie down?"

She nodded and wiped her hands on the dishcloth hanging off her shoulder. Setting it around the faucet, she brought me in for another hug. "Thank you. Take care of my boy, will you? He's been having a hard time since he got out. I worry about him."

I didn't know how to respond, so I took the coward's way out and went with what I knew she wanted to hear. "Of course."

Grace made her way down the hall where I heard a door open and then shut. I finished the dishes and sat at the kitchen table for a good hour. It was getting late. Grace obviously needed to go to bed.

Where was King?

I padded down the hall and paused outside a door when I heard voices speaking in hushed tones. The door wasn't latched, so I pushed it open a little, hoping it wouldn't creak. Peering through the crack, I caught a glimpse of King and Grace in the mirror of a large ornate walnut dresser that took up most of the small room. Grace sat on the side of the bed in bright orange button-up pajamas with matching slippers. Her feet didn't touch the floor. King crouched in front of her and held up what looked like some sort of glass pipe.

"Like this," he said, lighting the pipe he took a hit and held it in his lungs before blowing out the smoke. Then, he passed the pipe over to Grace who did the same, looking to King for reassurance. When she exhaled, she started having a coughing fit. King held her arm while she laughed and coughed at the same time.

"Will I do that every time?" she asked when she was finally able to manage a sentence.

"No, just the first few times." King assured her with a small smile.

"Good. I hate coughing," Grace said.

"Are you sure there isn't anything else you need?" He asked.

"I'm an old lady, and a dying one at that, and you still come over to fix my house and take care of me like I'm still going to be around in six months. You do too much already."

"Don't talk like that," King scolded, pinching the bridge of his nose. Grace reached out, took King's hands in her own, and held them on her lap.

"You are the closest thing to a son I ever had," she confessed.

King looked to the floor. "You've always been more of a mother to me than...*her*."

Grace's face grew serious. "I'm only sorry I didn't kill that bitch myself."

It was on those words that I lost my footing and came tumbling forward into the room, landing on my hands and knees in front of the bed.

"Is she always this graceful?" Grace asked.

King kissed Grace on the top of her head and turned off the lights. I gave her a sad little wave as he ushered me from the room, closing the door behind us. He turned off all the lights in the house and locked the back sliding door. Just as we reached the front of the house, King stopped and reached into his pocket, then placed something on the edge of the table on the hall. I fell a few steps behind so I could inspect what it was he'd left for Grace. When I saw it, my breath caught in my throat.

It was a tiny white ceramic rabbit.

Doe

"WE HAVE ANOTHER STOP TO MAKE," KING declared, punching out a text on his phone with his thumb as we got back into the truck. I looked at him, really looked at him as if I were seeing him for the first time. What I saw was a man who when you stripped away the intimidation and constant mood swings was someone who was taking care of a woman he loved in her final days. The man who I'd started out believing was a monster was capable of love.

"Why were you showing Grace how to smoke pot?" I asked.

"She puts up a good front, but Grace is in a lot of pain." King winced. "All the medications they give her are a bunch of bullshit. It's all supposed to make her comfortable, but she gets really sick from most of it."

"What does she have?"

"Some fucking bullshit aggressive cancer." King's hands tightened around the wheel until his knuckles turned white.

"Does she really only have six months?"

King looked uncomfortable, but, I felt like after meeting Grace and bonding with her I needed to know more about her condition.

He propped his elbow up on the ledge of the open drivers side window, thoughtfully resting his jaw on the back of his hand. "They say six months, but I've been told to take that and divide it in half because they usually exaggerate when they tell you how much time you have left."

"Who told you that?"

"Her doctor."

"Oh."

We spent nearly twenty minutes in silence as we rode to our next stop, which was another residential neighborhood, This time when King parked and I grabbed the door handle, he stopped me with his forearm across my chest.

"What?" I asked.

"We aren't getting out."

Killing the engine, he leaned back in his seat. I opened my mouth to ask why, but the dark look in his eyes said that he wasn't up for conversation. I folded my arms over my chest, waiting for the reason why we were there to produce itself.

After a few minutes, there it was. A light. Not from the house we were parked in front of but the one behind it. From where we sat, we had a perfect view of the back of the house and the illuminated sunroom. A tall woman with short black hair was sorting through some toys on the ground, when a small blonde girl came bounding into the sunroom.

King sat up straight.

We may have been a hundred feet or so away from the house, but I instantly recognized the girl prancing around in her PJ's.

"That's the girl from your picture, right? Is she your sister? Do you want to go say hi? I'll wait here if you want me to."

King remained silent, staring intently at the little girl until the woman found what she was looking for and ushered her back into the house, switching off the light. King looked into the darkness long after they were out of sight.

"I can't go see her. I have no rights. I'm her only family. She needs me, but to the courts, I'm just another felon. I don't even have visitation. I did everything I could in prison, hired every lawyer I could, but there's nothing they could do to help. I had to bribe a clerk to give me the address of her foster home. It's the only way I know where she is.

"I'm sorry." I said, and I meant it. King knew who and where his family was and they still couldn't be together. "She really is beautiful."

"She is," he agreed. He turned the key and started up the truck. "Max."

"What?" I asked.

"Max. Her name is Max."

"Short for Maxine?"

King smiled and shook his head, turning back onto the main road. "Like Maximillian."

"For a girl?" I wrinkled my nose.

"Yeah, and shut the fuck up. It's the best fucking name ever," King said, still smiling. There was a hint of pride in his tone that I didn't want to step on. "A strong name for a strong girl."

"It's a great name," I said softly.

"Yeah, it is."

"Why did you bring me here? And to see Grace?" I asked, using the small moment of vulnerability to my advantage.

"Because I don't know what the fuck I'm doing with you, Pup," King confessed. "You make me fucking crazy and I feel shit that I can't—" He paused. "Prison fucked me up, made me rethink things, but you've managed to fuck me up more than prison ever did. For some reason, I want you around. And since I'm shit with words, I figured the best way for you to get to know me, the real me, was for you to meet the two most important girls in my life."

"Oh." I bit my lip. I don't know what kind of answer I expected from him, if any answer at all, but what he said took me by complete surprise.

*He WANTS me around?*

"I've been in a maximum security prison. I've been around the worst of the worst. I've had to sleep with one eye open, thinking my next breath could be my last."

"Why are you telling me all this?"

He turned toward me and our eyes locked. He reached out and ran the back of his pointer finger along my cheek. "Because I want you to know that none of those motherfuckers ever scared me as much as you do."

King's phone buzzed from the cup holder in the console, and he answered it, leaving me with my mouth open in shock.

"Yeah," King said, holding the phone up to his ear.

"Motherfucker! No, I've got it. You stay where you are, and I'll come get you in a bit. Yes, I know. I'm sure. I got this."

King tossed the phone into my lap and turned the wheel of the truck so hard I swear we were up on two wheels.

"What's going on?"

"One last stop," King said through gritted teeth. Whoever it was on the other end had told him something he obviously didn't want to hear.

After a few minutes, we pulled up in front of a small dive bar with a neon green sign that flashed the name HANSEN'S with a symbol of a ship below it. There were only a few scattered cars in the gravel parking lot. King threw the truck in park and jumped out.

"Stay here," he ordered. He leaned into the bed of the truck and grabbed something out of it before making his way into the bar. King had to duck to pass through the low doorway.

I'd seen three sides of him in one day. The dark crazy scary shit. The sexy as hell shit that made my knees quake with the smallest look. And the side that I didn't think he had, the side that genuinely cared for someone other than himself. It was nice to know he wasn't a misogynist after all.

There was a commotion inside. The door to the bar swung open. A woman's screams followed King as his massive shadow emerged from the bar.

Less than an hour ago, he was pining for life where he could have his sister in it. Shortly before that, he was helping his elderly friend find relief during her last days.

Now, he walked back to the truck in long strides, an explosively angry look in his dark and dangerous eyes. It wasn't until he was within ten feet of me, standing under the buzzing street light, that I was able to take a good look at him.

King clutched a wooden baseball bat tightly in his grip. Dark spots were splattered across both him and the bat, droplets splattered across his chest and face. When he turned to put the bat back into the bed of the truck, he stepped fully into the light, and my breath hitched.

Both King and the baseball bat were covered in blood.

King tore out of the parking lot. When we hit the highway, he pulled off on the first exit and parked the truck under an overpass that was under construction. My heart was beating in my chest, quick and heavy.

Thud. Thud.

Thud. Thud.

The light of the moon shone through the front window, making the dried blood on his forehead look like it was shimmering.

"What the fuck just happened?" I shrieked, unbuckling my seat belt.

"Business," King said with no discernable emotion.

"You're covered in blood! Did you kill…whoever it was?"

"No, I didn't, but he'll think twice about fucking with my shit again."

"Who was that?"

"Someone who used to roll with Isaac. Preppy found out he was the narc who told Isaac about our granny operation. He needed to learn a lesson. He doesn't need to be running his mouth when he doesn't know shit about shit." King ran his hand over his head. "About starting wars that don't need to be started."

"Is that what's going to happen? A war?" I asked. "What are we going to do?"

"There won't be a war if I can help it. I've reached out to Isaac's people, asked for a meet. I want to get in front of this thing before it gets any worse." King turned to me. "You're not going to do anything. I've got this handled. And you should not be worried about any of this. I promise that nothing will happen to you. I told you I'd protect you, and I meant it."

"You think I'm worried about myself? Preppy's car got literally blown up. Bear lives in the garage ten feet away. You've got a guy, a dangerous guy by the sound of it, after you, and you think it's ME I'm worried about!?" I huffed. "How fucking selfish do you think I am?"

"You're worried about me, Pup?" King teased, cocking an eyebrow.

"No! I mean yes. Why are you so fucking irritating?" I yelled. King cut the engine. "And why are we parked under a—"

King interrupted my tirade by grabbing my hips and roughly sliding me down until the back of my head landed on the bench seat.

"I love that you worry about me," he said, covering my body with his, his mouth crashing down against mine. His were lips soft and full, but hard and needy at the same time. "Your lips are so fucking sexy. I've imagined them wrapped around my cock a thousand times." He slid a hand underneath my shirt, cupping my breast, kneading it with his palm. "I love your perfect fucking tits." His knee parted my legs, and he settled between them. His hard cock rested against an area that was already hot and wet with need. "I can't wait to be inside you." He trailed his lips to my neck where he licked and sucked and teased while he rolled my nipple between his fingers and rocked against me.

I arched my back off the seat. His every touch sent shock waves of need rippling through me, crippling every thought of resistance that ever floated around in my head.

"Tell me you want this, Pup. Tell me you want this as much as I do," he panted against my neck. With one flick of his fingers, he opened the button on my jeans and pushed his hand down the front until he found what he was looking for. I moaned when he reached the spot already humming from the friction of his erection. "You're so fucking wet. You want this. I can feel it." He used my own wetness to rub circles against my clit. "You're so ready for me. Tell me you want me to fuck you. Let me hear you say it."

I threw my head back, unable to form the words. He was right. He was so fucking right. I wanted him. I wanted this.

Maybe, Grace was right when she said that he could be both a bad boy and a good man. That one didn't necessarily dictate the other.

My brain may not have been on board with the idea, but my body reacted to his every touch like it was made to be pleasured by him, like it couldn't get enough. Like I was going to wither away and die without him inside me. I liked him on top of me. Touching me. Wanting me.

No. I didn't like it. I *loved* it.

I loved sleeping with his big body next to me. I loved the way he made me feel so small. I loved the way his nostrils flared when he was about to kiss me, and then when he did, I loved that he kissed me like he was mad at me. Like it was my fault I was so desirable that he just had to put his lips to mine, his hands on me.

King sat up, and I had to hold my thighs together to stave

off the ache that started building the second he'd touched me. King reached behind him, pulling his shirt up and over his head. He tossed it on the floor.

My hands went to his chest because there was no way they couldn't go there. It was glistening with his sweat, heaving with his labored breaths, and covered in the most fantastic art. I leaned up and licked his nipple.

He groaned and fisted my hair, forcing my head back roughly. His lips came back to mine. His tongue slid in and out of my mouth, moving in sync with my own. He rocked against me, and I no longer felt like my body was my own.

"I need to hear you say it, Pup. Say you want this, and it's yours. Tell me you want me," King panted.

He pushed my jeans and panties down over my ass. He'd only gotten them to my knees when he leaned down and dove in, flattening his tongue against my clit. I almost leapt out of the truck at the sensation, but finally settled when he held me down by my thighs. Over and over again, he licked me and sucked on my folds. His tongue pushed inside me. If it wasn't for him holding me down, I would've crushed his head with my legs.

He wasn't just licking me to make me come.

He was kissing me down there just like he was kissing my lips, my mouth. He was making out with my pussy.

A pressure started to build in my lower stomach, and I writhed under him, seeking the release I needed.

King mumbled something that I couldn't quite make out as I neared the edge. I was about to jump off into the most amazing life-changing orgasm when suddenly he was gone, and the cool night air brushed against all the parts of me that he'd made sopping wet.

Suddenly all too aware that I was lying there with my legs spread, my nakedness fully exposed to him. My cheeks flushed.

"What's wrong?" I asked, breathless like I'd just run a marathon.

King leaned back in his seat. Other than his raging hard-on straining against the front of his jeans, he looked completely unaffected by what we'd almost done.

"I'm not going to take you unless you tell me you want me. If you can't say the words while I've got my tongue in your pussy, then it's not something you really want. I told you before, when I fuck you, it's going to be because you want it so bad you'll be begging for it."

"When you touched me," I said slowly, "did it not seem like I wanted it? Did it not seem like I wanted you?"

King shook his head.

"Your body wants me. Just like my body wants you. But if you can't say the words, there's an underlying problem. What's got you so wrapped up that you can't tell me you want me when you're obviously about to come apart around me?" King leaned in, tucking a strand of hair behind my ears. "Are you still afraid of me?"

My eyes shot up to his. Is that what he thought? Sure, he was scary as shit, and at one point, I'd feared what he might do to me. But, he hasn't hurt me. He hasn't done anything but give me a place to stay and food to eat.

Because of him, I found a friend in Preppy.

Because of him, I was living in a state of the female equivalent of blue balls.

"No," I answered honestly. "I was. I mean, you can be a lot to take in."

"Yes, that I am." He glanced down at his erection.

I licked my lips wondering what he would taste like in my mouth.

"No," he groaned. "Don't you go looking at me like that. We need to have this conversation. If you keep looking at me like that, any resolve I have to stop is going to disappear, and I will bend you over the hood of this truck and pound you into oblivion." His words sent a spasm to the area still throbbing with want. I almost came right there in the truck without him even touching me. "So what is it? What is holding you back if it isn't me?"

I squeezed my eyes shut. "It's not you. It's me."

"Said in every cheesy break-up movie ever."

"No, you don't understand. I'm not just making decisions for myself. I have to think about her, too."

"Pup, I like a good threesome as much as the next guy, but I don't see anyone else in the truck with us. Who, exactly, are you referring to?"

"You know I don't remember anything before the summer, before I woke up, feeling like I'd just been put through a meat grinder."

King nodded, dragging me closer so that our thighs touched. I closed my eyes and focused on what I was trying to tell him instead of the rock hard thigh making my spine tingle.

"Go on," he urged, softly kissing my jaw, trailing his lips behind my ear.

"I'm not going to be able to talk if you keep doing that."

"Yes, you are. Keep going. I'm listening."

My insides clenched, and I spat out the rest of my story while being pummeled with the sensation of King's lips on me.

"Well, I refer to the person I was before, when I had a memory, as HER. Someone else entirely, because that's who I was. A different person."

"Get to the fucking point. Because if you don't have one in the next minute, I'm putting my cock in you. Before I do that, though, I'm going to let you take me in your mouth and give you a taste because I know that's what you were thinking about just now."

Again, I closed my eyes and attempted to concentrate as King lifted me by the hips and sat me on his lap so that I was straddling him with my back to the steering wheel. In this intimate position, there was nowhere for me to hide. Although his hard cock was rocking against me, I had to push aside thoughts of him sinking into me in order to finish my story.

"The point is that I can't do anything that could potentially be life-changing because it isn't just my life I have to think about. I have to consider that one day all my memories, everything I am and everything I was, will come back to me. It may never happen, but I can't take the risk. Because the possibility that it might happen is out there. That day, when and if I become HER again, I will have to deal with all the things I did when I didn't know who I was. That's why even though I think your artwork is beyond amazing and I've imagined you creating something for me since I saw you tattoo for the very first time, I just can't do that to her. What if she hates it? What if she is morally against tattoos and I've left her with something she can't get rid of? That's why although my body wants you, and I want you, it doesn't matter. Because the person you see in front of you is just temporary." King pulled back and was now staring into my eyes as I spoke. "I can't help but melt into you when you touch me, but I can't do this to her. What if she has a boyfriend, a fiancé? What if being with you means ruining her?"

I sniffled. Tears welled up and were about to spill from my

eyes. King forced me toward him with a hand on the back of my neck, and just as I thought he was going to kiss me again, he turned my face and licked my cheek, wiping my tears away with his tongue.

"What if she's a virgin?" I whispered.

King slowly shifted me off his lap and set me back on the passenger seat.

"I hadn't thought of that," he said softly. "And while I am both appalled and incredibly turned on by the idea of being the first one inside that pretty pussy of yours, I feel it necessary to point out the holes in your little theory about the person you were, before you came stumbling into my life."

"What would those holes be?" I asked.

"First, your virginity theory. Who the fuck cares? If your memory comes back and you go back to a life where I'm not around, at least you'll have enough amazing memories to last you through faking the orgasms with whatever schmuck you're with."

"Why is he a schmuck?"

"Trust me. A guy who let you wander far away and hasn't found you by now, if he's even looking for you at all, is a fucking schmuck. I didn't even like you at first. In fact, I downright fucking hated you, and I still didn't want you more than ten feet from me. Neither did my cock."

I shuddered. "And the next hole in my theory?" My voice was strained.

"Tattoos. Anyone who doesn't like my art can kick rocks."

"It's that simple?"

"Yes, it's that simple," he stated flatly. Then, his face grew serious. "It's that simple, but not because of some guy who may or may not be out there pining for you or the fear that you will regret letting me fuck you or tattoo you." King traced a line from the back of my hand to the top of my shoulder like he was creating an imaginary tattoo. "It's that simple because you can't live your life for someone you *might* be. So what if your memories come back and the person you were before comes with them? She will just have to fucking deal with the fact that you were here when she wasn't. Make your mark while you still can, Pup."

"You make it sound so easy."

"It is."

"It's not. I just...I can't," I breathed. I wouldn't be able to live with myself knowing that I wasn't protecting her.

"You made a promise that you would protect me. Well, I made a promise that I would protect her," I said, my voice barely a whisper.

"Have you even thought that who you are now is exactly the person you're supposed to be? That maybe with the slate wiped clean of bullshit outside influences that you are now more yourself than ever before?" he asked, with each point he was trying to make he grew louder.

"No." I hadn't thought of that. King had a point. "But living life thinking that was the truth was a gamble I'm not willing to take." I looked down to the floor and wished it would open up and suck me down into it.

"So, let me get this straight. You were willing to fuck random bikers, but you can't be with me?" There was a hint of cruelty in his voice. If his intentions were to sting, they worked.

"That's a low blow."

But King continued on as if I hadn't just interrupted. "So I'm just like them to you? Just like a biker you don't want to fuck and end up regretting?

King turned the key and started the truck, pulling back onto the highway.

"No, you're not like them at all," I whispered, unsure if he heard me.

"How is it that you can see me as worse than them when I know you want me? I can feel it. Don't fucking deny it. Because it's bullshit, and you know it." King looked straight ahead at the road. He turned up the radio until Johnny Cash was singing so loud it rattled my eardrums. The tears in my eyes spilled over onto my cheeks.

I leaned against the window and hugged my arms to my chest. The lights from businesses and signs blurred together as we passed into streams of colored lights.

"You're right. You're much worse than them," I whispered, knowing full well that King couldn't hear me over the music. "Because with them, it wouldn't hurt this much."

## Doe

KING HADN'T COME TO BED IN DAYS. I STILL HELPED him at night in his studio but our conversation never escalated to anything more than him barking orders at me.

On Saturday morning I'd found a box on the kitchen counter with a note addressed to me. The card read:

FOR OUR DATE. BE ON THE PORCH AT EIGHT-PREPPY

Our date? Why would we go out on a date? Inside the box was a short black strapless dress and a pair of matching heels.

Preppy had made sure I had a bunch of jeans and tank

175

tops to wear on a daily basis. He even stopped at a store and let me pick out some underwear and bath stuff one day, but I didn't have anything like this.

The clock on the stove read only ten am. I was disappointed I'd have to wait so long to put it on.

At eight o'clock sharp, I stood by the steps and fidgeted with the hem of my new dress. I'd spent hours showering, shaving, and blow-drying my hair. I was beyond ready, thrilled to be doing something new and grateful for the distraction.

I had no clue what Preppy had up his tattooed sleeves.

"You ready, Doe?" he asked, bounding out from the door under the stairs.

He draped an arm over my shoulder and ushered me toward King's truck, which was already parked in front. "I wish I could take you in my car. But you know, it fucking blew up and shit," he said bitterly.

His usual short-sleeved dress shirt had been swapped out for a dark blue long-sleeved button down that he wore untucked over a pair of dark boot cut jeans. His usual bow tie carefully in place. He smelled like he'd just gotten out of the shower. Like soap and shaving cream.

"Did you shave?" I asked. His beard looked just as long as it had that morning.

"Huh?" he asked, looking down at me.

"You smell like shaving cream, but you still have your beard."

"It's a date, baby girl. I manscaped in case I get lucky."

I laughed. "You're not getting lucky."

"I know. King would kill me, and I rather like my life. So, I think we'll leave that off the table. For now." He winked. "Besides, you may not let me get my cock wet, but maybe someone else will take pity on me when the night's over and let me get it in."

I laughed at Preppy, his smile taking the edge of his crude words.

"You look nice," I said. If I didn't know any better, I would say that Preppy actually blushed.

"Thanks. But tonight, I'm not Preppy."

"You're not?" I asked. "Then, who are you exactly?"

"Nope, this is a date. So tonight, you can call me Samuel. I would say that you look nice, too, but you look way more than nice. I would say…"

Preppy took a step back and slid his hand down my arm, to lock his fingers around my wrist. He, then, lifted my arm and twirled me around slowly to appraise me. My face flushed with embarrassment when I noticed he was staring at my ass.

"Hot. You look HOT, baby girl. Pancakes do a body good. Real fucking good."

"Thanks." I felt my cheeks redden. "I wish you could call me by my real name, too, but I don't know—"

The roar of a motorcycle drowned out my words. We both turned toward the noise. King pulled up the gravel drive and parked a shiny black bike next to one of the house pilings. It was the first time I'd seen him drive anything other than his beat-up old truck. He swung off his bike and ripped his helmet off his head, tossing it to the ground as he stomped toward us with furious steps. His brows furrowed, and his fists clenched at his sides. His eyes firmly locked on me as he approached, looking me up and down and then to where Preppy was still holding my hand.

My heart beat in a quick, uneven rhythm as he approached. My palms began to sweat. I plastered a fake smile on my face.

"Where the fuck did you get THAT thing?" King roared, pointing to my dress. His gaze darted back and forth from me to Preppy.

Preppy smiled and released my hand. Once again draping his arm over my shoulders, he tugged me into his side.

King's eyes widened at the gesture, and I thought for sure he was going to punch one or both of us. Preppy, however, seemed unaffected by King's mood.

"We're gonna paint the town red, Boss-Man," Preppy answered coolly. "How do we look?"

Something in the way he asked made me think he was goading King.

"He bought me the dress," I added, slightly embarrassed that King obviously didn't like it. It was strapless and form-fitting. Showing off the curves I'd developed in the days I'd been stuffing my face.

"Fuck no, you're not. I've changed my mind," King said, staring Preppy dead in the eyes. "You're gonna get your fucking ass back in the house before I put a fucking bullet in your skull. That's what you're going to fucking do."

"Why not?" I heard myself ask before I had time to register the fact that I had also shook off Preppy and stepped to King. He came forward, too. Our feet touched at the toes. Since I was much shorter than him, I had to look up to meet his disapproving gaze.

"Cause I fucking said so, Pup," King growled, his nostrils flaring.

His usual green eyes were now shining black pools of anger. There was a hardness to his features that suggested this was a fight I'd never be able to win.

That didn't mean I wasn't going to try.

"I'm here because I don't have any other options! I get that you're fucking mad at me, or that you fucking hate me. I do. But I just wanted to pretend for one fucking night that I'm a normal girl on a normal date in a normal place!"

Just as I turned to head back into the house, King grabbed my elbow and spun me around, he tipped my chin up.

"Stay. Here," he ordered, his face still hard and angry. "You." King pointed to Preppy. "A fucking word. *Now.*"

He gestured with his chin to the house, releasing me as he stormed up the steps and slammed the front door behind him. Preppy looked amused, although I'm not sure how he could've been with King steaming in such close proximity.

"Sorry, babe," Preppy said with a knowing smile. "Maybe, another time?" He bounded up the steps, taking them two at a time. I thought about following them in, but I didn't want to provoke King further.

I spent the next ten minutes stewing on the porch, wondering if they'd killed each other because I hadn't heard anything inside. The sun had long since set over the trees, so I stayed under the safety of the light of the porch. I soon got tired of standing. My ass had barely touched the bottom step when the front door swung open, and King came bounding out. I jumped up and held onto the railing to keep from falling onto the walkway.

"Let's go," King said, holding out a hand to me. Anger still lingered on his face, along with a bit of confusion.

"Go? Go where?" I asked.

"On a date thing." His brows furrowed again like my question confused him.

"With you?"

King nodded. Since his hand was still extended out to me

and I'd made no move to take it, he reached over and grabbed my hand. That's when I looked at him, I mean *really* looked at him.

He was freshly showered and smelled like he'd just put on cologne. He wore his usual dark jeans and a tight black t-shirt. His stubble was still there but neatly trimmed. It's amazing what he'd done in the ten minutes he'd left me outside.

"With me," he confirmed, slowly raking his eyes over my body. His gaze burned into me.

"What happened to Preppy?" King stiffened.

"He's no longer available," King spat, obviously put off by the question.

"Oh," I said, looking down at my feet.

"Fuck. Just forget it. It was a fucking stupid idea anyway."

"What? No, I just… this was all Preppy's idea anyway."

"Shut up," he said, silencing my rant. King tugged on my hand and led me over to his bike. He handed me a helmet and straddled the seat. He turned the key and it came roaring to life. He turned and gestured to the space behind him.

I shouted over the engine, "I'm wearing a dress!"

King grabbed my hand and tugged me toward him. "I think we know by now that you know how to straddle, so get the fuck on." I pressed my thighs together, willing the memory of the night in his truck away.

"Why can't we just take the truck, or we can walk," I suggested.

King stared me down. "Pup?"

"Yeah?"

"Get on the fucking bike."

"You really are a fucking asshole, you know that?." I punctuated my words by digging my pointer finger into his chest.

King smiled obnoxiously. I didn't want a smile I wanted a fight. I was beginning to think it was long overdue.

"Took you long enough," he said, grabbing hold of my finger.

"Long enough for what?"

"To figure out I'm an asshole. Now, get on the fucking bike."

"Fuck you," I spat.

King got off the bike and stalked toward me. He snatched the helmet out of my hands and roughly shoved it onto my head. My hair was trapped over my eyes and I was momentarily disoriented. King took advantage of that, by picking me up and setting me on the bike.

I shrieked into my helmet, and before I could protest and jump off, we were in motion. My options were then limited to holding onto King or flying off the back of his bike.

Reluctantly, I wrapped my arms around his waist.

What I really wanted was to wrap my hands around his throat.

We drove for what seemed like only a few minutes but in reality it was more like a half of an hour. The normally stagnant and wet Florida night air blew cool all around us as the bike pressed forward into the night.

My jaw dropped, and my heart sped when the neon lights came into view.

A carnival.

King had brought me to a carnival.

The Ferris wheel overhead appeared so close I thought that if I reached my hands up into the air I might be able to touch one of the swaying carts.

When King brought the bike to a stop in the grass parking

lot, my body was still humming from the vibrations of the engine. In my excitement at being at a real live carnival, I jumped off the bike quickly, grazing my calf on one of the hot pipes.

"Shit, shit, *shit!*" I shouted, bouncing around on one leg.

King set his helmet down and came around to where I was hopping around and wincing in pain. "Come here," he said.

I was still angry, the twenty minute ride doing nothing to take the edge off wanting to do him physical harm. I ignored his request and bent down to inspect the damage on my leg.

King shook his head and walked over to me, picking me up under my shoulders and setting me on top of a nearby picnic table. "You need to learn to do what you're told," he said, lifting my leg to inspect the burn.

I huffed. "Picking me up and tossing me around is unnecessary, you know."

King leaned down and gently blew across the burn, sending hot chills up my spine. I was all too aware that the dress I wore had ridden up my thighs when he'd picked me up. I caught him glancing at the exposed white fabric between my legs.

"Then, do what you're fucking told the first time." He then proceeded to inspect me thoroughly. "It's not a bad burn," he said, but I could barely hear him over the memory of his breath against my skin.

"I thought you didn't do gentle," I teased.

King helped me set my foot back on the ground and reached for my hand.

"I don't." He turned to the gate, roughly yanking me behind him as to prove his point.

King paid for our tickets, and we entered through a turnstile. Once inside, my inner child sprang to life, and my anger was temporarily forgotten. Neon lights, carnival music, corn dog and cotton candy stands.

It was everything I ever wanted in a first date. Well, except maybe for a date who actually wanted to be there. I yanked my hand out of King's grip, but he grabbed me again and held my hand tighter, pulling me closer into his side.

"What do you want to do first, Pup?"

"Everything. I want to do absolutely everything!" I craned my neck to get a better look at the giant Ferris wheel.

"The Ferris wheel is last," King said, pushing me toward the row of games.

As we moved deeper and deeper into the crowd, the noise level around us increased tenfold. A group of kids whizzed by us, leaving bursts of laughter in their wake.

The carnival workers shouted the names of their games and advertised how easy it was to win one of the big stuffed animal prizes they held up.

King stopped at a game where the goal was to shoot water from a gun into a hippo's mouth in order to move the baby hippo up the ladder. Whoever shot their gun the steadiest and moved their baby hippo to the top the fastest was the winner.

"You in?"

"I'm so in," I answered, barely able to contain my excitement. I bounced up on the balls of my feet.

"Two," King said He removed a money clip from his pocket and plucked out a few bills, handing it to the man controlling the game. King took a seat on one of the ripped leather stools, and I took a seat a few stools down.

"Afraid to sit next to me?" King asked.

"No, but you're huge and these stools are small. I don't want to bump into your arm and lose just because you haven't missed a workout in three years." I closed one eye and readied my water gun.

King shook his head, "That mouth of yours," he said. There are several ways I could have taken that statement, but I didn't have time to think about it because I had a game to win.

"I'm warning you. I'm really good at this game," King said to me.

Was he being playful?

"Competitive, are we?" I asked, keeping my focus straight ahead at the bulls-eye.

"Oh, Pup. You have no idea."

The bell rang, and the carnie shouted, "GO!"

I squeezed the trigger. Water sprayed out of my gun and directly onto the target. My little hippo shot up the ladder, and just as quickly as it had started, the game was over. I looked over to King who was sitting back smiling. What was he smiling over? I was the one who won.

"Winner! Winner!" the Carni shouted He unclipped a huge stuffed deer from the top of the tent and handed it to King, who received the prize and then started to walk away.

*He'd won? How was that possible?*

"Hey!" I shouted, chasing after him. "Why did you get the prize? I won. My hippo was so far ahead of yours that I didn't even see yours move." King stopped.

"Pup, you didn't see my hippo move because I was done before you even began." He was smiling. A genuine, real–life, swoon-worthy smile that reached his eyes. It was a good look on him.

No, it was a GREAT look on him.

"You've got to be kidding me!" I shouted.

"Competitive, are we?" King asked, mocking me. "I told

you I was good at that game."

King seemed like any other young man who was taking a girl out on a date. Well, any other six-foot-something tattooed wall of muscle who looked like he could be an underwear model.

I liked playful King.

I liked him a lot.

"You must have played that game before," I pouted. "Unfair advantage."

"Yeah, I'll give you that. This carnival has come here every year since I was a kid. Preppy and I used to sneak in the back. Over there." King pointed toward a gate in a chain-link fence with a huge padlock keeping it shut. "We'd steal corn dogs from the food stands, right out of the fryer. Although the padlock happened only after they found out how we were getting in."

I knew Preppy and King were best friends, but this was the first time I'd ever heard any stories from their childhood together.

"I tell you what," King started. "Since this is a date and all, and guys usually give their dates their prizes, I will let you have my deer." He held out the stuffed animal.

I didn't know if he was toying with me. If I didn't know how to handle ornery King, I certainly didn't know how to handle nice and playful King.

I snatched it out of his hands like he was going to reconsider his offer, and I tucked it tightly under my arm. King laughed.

"What's so funny now?" I asked.

"Doe…holding a doe." Okay, he'd got me on that one. I held my hand over my mouth to contain my laughter.

For the next few hours, we played every single game the place had to offer.

I won none of them.

King made a point of handing me each of his prizes. Soon, I ran out of arm space to carry them all.

"I don't think we can play anymore," I told him, gesturing to the huge stack of cheap toys up to my chin.

The bell sounded for one of the games, and I was just about to walk away when King stopped me. "No, wait a sec."

We watched as a tiny boy tried three times to win a prize against two much older teenagers. After a minute the boy's dad pulled him aside. "That's enough, Sam. We can try again another time."

"But I wanted the stuffed alligator," the boy complained.

"You'll get it. Maybe, next year when you're a little bit bigger." The dad smiled.

King plucked a stuffed penguin from my arms and approached the boy and his father who were walking away from the game, the boy's bottom lip set in a pout. Tears welling up in his eyes.

"Excuse me," King said, getting their attention. The father looked alarmed and pulled his son into his leg.

King ignored the dad's reaction and bent down to the boy, holding out the penguin. "I know it's not an alligator, but penguins are just as cool. As a matter of fact, they're cooler. They live in the snow, and they're the only bird that doesn't fly. Did you know that?"

"No, I didn't know that," the boy said, with a thumb in his mouth.

"They also slide around on their bellies on the ice."

"Cooool," the boy said, staring at the penguin.

"Now, you take good care of him, okay?" The boy nodded and took the penguin.

"Thank you." The boy's dad mouthed to King.

He nodded, and they disappeared into the crowd.

King made his way back to me. "You're up next," he said as he approached.

We stood behind the games and gave out my prizes to kids who lost their games one by one until all I had left was the deer King had given me first.

We ate cotton candy. We ate corn dogs. We ate fried Oreos. We laughed like kids. We rode a gravity ride that locked you to the sides as it spun, and for ten minutes afterwards, I thought all the food was going to come back up.

"Here," King said, pushing a cup in front of me. "Grace says that a ginger ale is the best cure for an upset stomach."

I slowly sipped the bubbly drink, and I started to feel better almost instantly. King grabbed my cup and walked a few steps to toss it in the trash when I noticed a nearby woman ogling him.

I looked around, and it seemed like every woman at the fair, whether she was with a man or not, was undressing King with her eyes.

"Do they all have to do that?" I muttered under my breath.

"Does all who have to do what?" King asked.

"Do all the women have to look at you like they want to jump your bones?" I scoffed.

King put an arm around me. His lips brushed my ear when he whispered, "Unlike some people, they aren't hiding what they want." I opened my mouth to say something, but I couldn't find the words. "It's cute that you're jealous though."

"I'm not—"

"Time for the Ferris wheel," King announced. It was getting late, and the crowd had thinned.

"Why did we save it for last?" I asked.

"Because it's the best part," King said. "You always save the best for last."

King helped me into the squeaky cart while the carnival worker closed the little door to the bucket. There was barely enough room on the seat for the two of us. When I shoved my deer between us, King picked it up and handed it to the carnie, along with a bill from his pocket. "Take care of this for me until we get down will ya?"

"Sure thing, man!" He set the deer on the chair next to the ride's control panel.

King rested his arm on the back of the seat over my shoulder.

Then, we were lifting up into the air. Higher and higher we rose, stopping every so often to allow for other riders to board. Once we were almost at the top, we started to move more fluidly. Round and round we went, watching the city lights beneath us flicker and glow.

"Wow," I said, watching the people scurry around below. "They all look like ants from up here." I glanced over at King but he wasn't looking at the lights of the city or at the crowd.

He was looking at me.

The depth of his stare pinned me to the seat. "Pup, what I learned from being in prison is that we're all just a bunch of ants."

"How do you mean?"

"I mean we're all scurrying around, doing insignificant bullshit. We get this one life. ONE. And we spend too much time doing shit we don't want to do. I don't want to do that anymore."

"What do you mean?"

"I don't want to be remembered as the notorious Brantley King."

"Then, how do you want to be remembered?"

"I don't. I want to be forgotten."

"You can't mean that."

"I do. I used to want to go out in a blaze of glory. Now, I just want to live in my house, fish on a weekday, and tattoo when the mood strikes. And when it's my time to go, I want to fade out like the ending of a movie and be quickly forgotten."

"That sounds lonely."

"Not if you're with me, it won't be."

"Please, you already told me that I'm gone the second you get tired of me." I laughed.

King wasn't laughing. "I'm serious. What if I said I changed my mind? What if I wanted you to stay for real?"

I shook my head. "I wouldn't know what to say to that. I don't even know if you mean that or not." I sighed. "It's just not that simple. You know that I have to look out for her."

"Fuck that. Fuck HER," King said, raising his voice. "As I said, we get this one life. One. As of right this fucking second, I'm no longer going to spend it doing anything other than what I want to do. I don't want to grow old and look back and realize that I may have had a life, but I forgot to live it." King brushed his lips against mine. "Are you with me, Pup?"

"What are you doing?" I asked, my breath shallow and quick. King leaned into me and kissed the spot behind my ear, his lips igniting my skin. I felt the kiss to my very core, and I trembled.

"After everything, you still have no idea. Do you?"

"No idea of what?" I panted.

No sooner were the words out of my mouth than his lips

crashed onto mine. His kiss was harsh and demanding. His tongue parted my lips, gaining entrance into my mouth, licking and dancing with my own. I moaned into him.

I was on fire. King's hand slipped up under my dress and found the place where I was already wet and ready for him. He groaned and pressed a finger into me, his thick cock nudged my thigh. He ran a hand up my neck and fisted a handful of my hair, turning me up to him so he could gain better access to my mouth while his fingers pushed in and out of me. I clenched around him, my orgasm building, when he suddenly pulled away.

"Why did you stop?" I asked, flustered, my legs still parted for him.

"Because, Pup, the ride's over."

I hadn't even noticed that we were at the bottom. The carnival worker came over and let us out of the bucket. I adjusted my dress and stood on shaky legs while King retrieved my deer.

We walked to the parking lot in complete silence.

We passed some sort of tool shed on our way to the bike. King suddenly grabbed me and dragged me into the shadows, pinning me hard against the wall of the shed.

"This is the last time I'm going to ask you this, Pup. Do you want me?" King asked, his lips finding mine again, asking the same question with his demanding kiss. My skin came alive and danced with anticipation. "I can't stay away from you anymore. I tried, and I can't do it. I want you. I need you to tell me all that hesitation bullshit is over and that I can have you. Stop being alive, and start living." He pulled a hair's breadth away and sought the answer in my face.

"Yes," I answered breathlessly. Because it was true. Every part of me wanted him. I'd been fighting it for too long for reasons that the longer I was around him seemed less and less important. "I want to be alive."

"I want you so fucking bad," King said, pinning me to the wall with his hips pressed against mine. His erection hard and ready against my core. My dress was up around my waist. Only his jeans and my panties separated us.

"Why do you call me *pup*?" I asked breathlessly while he lifted the sides of my dress so his hands could dip into the back of my panties. He dug his fingers into my ass cheeks and I gasped.

"Because when I first saw these wide, innocent eyes, you looked like a lost puppy dog."

I was disappointed with the comparison to a puppy, especially after Preppy had called me a stray.

"And," he continued, "I knew at that very moment when you stood in my doorway, that I wanted to keep you."

He emphasized his statement with a thrust of his hips. I let out a guttural moan, and he laughed softly into my ear, his tongue licking and sucking along my jawline and back to my mouth.

"Not here" he said, pulling away from me and adjusting my dress back down to cover my ass.

He led me back to his bike, making quick work of putting on my helmet. When I hopped on behind him and wrapped my arms around him, I felt him shudder under my touch. I let my hands slip just under his belt onto the bare flesh of his abs, and I heard him groan over the roar of the engine.

He wanted *me*.

Whoever that was.

And I wanted *him*.

As crazy as that was.

At least for the night, I wasn't going to think about what the girl with the memories would do, the girl who I tried to please on a daily basis. I was going to be selfish, and I was only going to think about what I wanted.

*Who* I wanted.

I'd made the decision to *live.*

## Doe

WHEN WE PULLED UP TO THE HOUSE, I DIDN'T expect to see a party in full swing. Bikes lined the street, blocking our entrance to the property. King drove past them and turned onto another small dirt path I hadn't noticed before that led us right up to the garage.

King parked the bike and cut the engine. I took my helmet off and passed it to him so he could set it on the seat.

"What's going on?" I asked.

"It seems my hospitality is being taken advantage of," he muttered. King dragged me into the house by my hand and up the stairs to the main floor. In the living room, we passed a bunch of bikers standing around, watching an older, dark-skinned woman bounce up and down naked on the lap of a boy who looked younger than me, his pants around his feet. The patch on his vest read PROSPECT. His face was turned up to the ceiling, his eyes hooded in ecstasy, his mouth partially open.

"King!" Bear shouted, motioning to him. "Come over here, and watch this. Billy's just popped his cherry."

"What the fuck, Bear! What is all this?" King growled. His fist was clenched at his side, and the hand that held mine grew tighter and tighter. I could feel his pulse racing in his wrist.

Bear smiled and held out his arms. "Dude, it's a party. It's Saturday. We used to throw ten of these in a seven day week. Didn't think you'd mind."

"Don't go anywhere. I'm coming back down. You and I need to talk." King pointed at Bear then dragged me upstairs to his room.

"I need you to stay in here while I talk to Bear. I'll be right back." For once, he wasn't barking orders at me. It sounded more like a plea. "Close the door. Keep it locked."

"Okay," I said, stepping into the room and shutting the door. It was the first time he'd told me to do something that I didn't feel the overwhelming need to argue with him.

Three hours later, there was still no sign of King, and the music seemed to be getting louder and louder. I'd read for a bit, clicked through some channels, and done my best to distract myself, but my curiosity was getting the best of me.

I didn't want to disobey him, but maybe, I could at least change locations. I figured going into the tattoo studio in the next room wouldn't be disobeying his orders too much. Besides, King's sketchbook was in there, and it could help occupy me until he came back.

I crept out of the room. The party downstairs still raged although none of the party-goers had made their way upstairs like last time. I pushed open the door and stepped inside.

I wasn't prepared for what I found.

My jaw fell to the floor along with my heart and any faith I had in King and his promises. My heart disintegrated in my chest.

It was dark in the room except for the neon lights beating in time with the bass of the Nine Inch Nails song playing on the iPod dock. King was perched on his chair with his eyes closed, a joint at his lips. His jeans were down around his ankles. A topless brunette was down on her knees in front of him, reaching for the waistband of his boxers.

"What the fuck," I gasped. I was going to be sick. The asshole was just toying with me the entire time. He hadn't meant a word. Maybe, that was the revenge he'd been wanting since Nikki stole from him. Maybe, that was his game the entire time and now that I was humiliated my debt had officially been paid.

King's eyes opened suddenly, and I half-expected an apology for walking in and catching him in the act. At least, I expected an attempt at pulling up his pants. But it was my fault for thinking that way. Somewhere between the tattoos, the sandwiches on the dock, Grace's house, and the carnival, I'd forgotten who I was dealing with.

This was the man who held me against my will. Handcuffed me to his bed. Threatened my life.

*Killed his own mother.*

He was the fucking devil himself. And all it took was a slutty brunette on her knees to remind me of that.

"Get out," he barked. He took a long drag from the joint,

then tugged on the brunette's hair, tipping her head back. He leaned over until his lips were almost touching hers and made a show of blowing the smoke directly into her mouth.

I slammed the door and ran down the hall. I grabbed a bottle of something off of the kitchen table and headed outside to the dock, ignoring catcalls from some of the bikers I left in my wake.

I walked past the raging bonfire and toward the water.

I sat down on the end of the small pier and dangled my legs over the edge. I tore the cap off the bottle and tossed it into the water. I held up the bottom of the bottle and chugged a few mouthfuls of the amber liquid. It tasted like pure gasoline mixed with pine-cleaner, burning my throat and stomach on its way down. I took a breath and kept on drinking, swallowing one horrible tasting mouthful after another. I didn't stop until I felt the hazy warmth begin to spread through me.

I wiped my mouth with my wrist and looked out onto the water.

I may not have known who I was in the past, but I knew who I didn't want to be, and who I didn't want to be was someone weak.

I'd fallen for it. His words. His body.

I'd fallen for him.

I may have set out to be a whore, but I sure as shit wasn't going to allow myself to be treated like one.

He may have been the notorious Brantley King to everyone back in that house and everyone in that town, but to me, he just became the asshole. The asshole who just minutes before had broken my fucking heart.

*Things were so much easier when I hated him.*

"This seat taken?" A deep voice asked. I shrugged. Bear sat

down next to me and lit a cigarette. "Something bothering you, pretty girl?"

"Nope," I lied.

"I may not know shit about shit, but I can tell you that when a girl goes running from a party with only a bottle of whiskey for company, something is most definitely bothering her. In my experience, that something usually has a cock attached to it." Bear exhaled the smoke.

"Well, you're not completely wrong," I admitted. Turning up the bottle again, the liquid no longer burned when I swallowed.

"Easy, girl," Bear said, grabbing the bottle from me. He took a swig. "What's going on between you and King, anyway? You his now? Cause he sure looks at you like you are. And seeing as he didn't kill you and all, I'm thinking what he feels for you might be pretty fucking serious."

I shook my head. "Right now, he's in his studio, belonging to a brunette with fake tits." My eyes welled up with tears, but I refused to cry at my own stupidity.

"Ah, I see," Bear said, passing me back the bottle. "The kid doesn't appreciate what's right in front of him."

"He's not exactly a kid, Bear. Actually, I'm pretty sure he's older than you, and it's not that he doesn't see what's in front of him. It's that he just doesn't give a shit." I was more than tipsy, working my way to more than drunk. My words grew bolder in my mouth before I spat them out. Any filter I ever had was completely gone. "What do you see when you look at me?"

Bear looked out on the water and scratched his beard. "I see a very, very fucking beautiful girl who shouldn't be hanging out with the likes of anyone up in that house. Or anyone sitting next to her, for that matter. We're bad seeds, little girl. You're a good seed. I can tell. Shit, anyone within a hundred miles of here can tell. You don't belong here. That much is obvious."

"I don't belong anywhere," I admitted. A fog started to settle over the water, emerging from the trees on the other side of the bay, traveling toward, and brushing my ankles as it spread under the pier.

"Sure you do. First, you have to figure out where that someplace is. Then, you just have to want to belong there."

I'm not sure if Bear knew my entire story, but what he said was way too simplified of an answer, especially in my case.

I laughed. "Oh yeah? Well, I'm leaving here tonight, and I have nowhere to go. I don't want to live on the streets again, but that's where I'm going to be. It takes a lot more than wanting to belong somewhere, or not belong, or whatever," I said, my words slurring together.

"I remember talking to you that first night. Do you remember what I told you about coming back to the clubhouse with me?" Bear asked.

"Yes."

"I should've never sent you up to King. I should have dragged you away right then and there and made you mine that night before King had his way with you."

"King has never had his way with me," I slurred. "His way or the highway, maybe."

"No shit? Well that changes everything, baby," Bear said. His smile reached all the way to his eyes which were shockingly bright and beautiful. I was pretty sure his beard hid even more of his good looks, and a very drunk part of me wanted to pull on it to see if it would come off.

"It changes nothing, Bear. I'm still leaving. He's still with the brunette girl with the…" I cupped my hands in front of my chest. Bear laughed out loud, revealing a perfectly straight line of pearly white teeth.

"It changes everything, actually. Our bro code only goes so far. Seeing as how he's not claimed you as his, as stupid as that is, my offer is still good. What's fair is fair," Bear said, again taking the bottle from my hands.

I looked over at him and half-expected to find him laughing at his own joke, but his lips were in a straight line.

He was dead serious.

He also wasn't bad to look at. That night was the first time I'd seen his blonde hair pulled into a high bun on the back of his head.

"Listen," Bear said. "King's been my friend almost my entire life, but he knows the rules I live by. In my world, you're fair game, and I would love to put you on your back in my bed."

"You're just saying that. The truth is that you're not gonna want me when you find out that I don't know what I'm doing when it comes to—" I darted my eyes to the bulge in his jeans. "—that."

"Fuck," Bear swore, biting his bottom lip. "Darlin', I believe I want you even more now."

"You've got freckles under your eyes," I said, leaning toward him. He grabbed onto my shoulders before I fell forward.

"Yeah, kid. So I've been told." He laughed. He also had a dimple on his left cheek, which was on it's own a ridiculous contradiction when it came to the big biker man sitting next to me.

"Why did you send me to him?" I asked. "I would've gone with you. You're nice. I needed a place to stay, and you've got freckles under your eyes, and I would've been a good biker whore for you."

Bear's eyebrows shot up. "Oh yeah?" he asked, a crooked smirk on his face. "I don't really see you as the biker whore type. But I can definitely see you on the back of my bike."

"But you said I don't belong here. That I shouldn't hang out with you. Or any of those—" I waved the bottle around behind me, missing Bear's jaw by only an inch or two. "—people up there in the stupid house. Stupid people in the stupid house on stupid stilts." My shoulders slumped. "Bear, my heart was just getting warm. Now, it's all cold again."

Bear grabbed the bottle from my hand and set it down on the dock.

"I said you didn't belong here. I said you were too good to hang out with me. I didn't say that I wouldn't hang out with you. You may be too good for me, but I'm the kind of guy who can live with that." Bear placed a hand against my cheek. I could see why they called him Bear. He was strong and warm and his hands were so big they reminded me of giant paws. I closed my eyes and swayed into him. He leaned in close, his lips only a breath away from mine.

"Will you come with me, baby girl? I don't know if I can warm your heart, but I sure as shit can warm your body. I know for a fact that you can warm my bed. Then, maybe, we'll work on that cold heart of yours. We'll take it one day at a time." He assured me.

Bear sounded sincere, and what he was offering was exactly what I was looking for weeks earlier.

It seemed like a lifetime ago.

A lifetime ago when King wasn't in my life.

"I don't know," I answered honestly.

I couldn't stay with King anymore; that much I was certain of. And all the liquid courage in the world wouldn't be enough for me to convince myself that I could survive out on the streets again, scrounging for food and shelter.

Bear's offer was all I had, but I couldn't bring myself to say yes. Saying yes meant closing the door on King altogether. Was that something I was ready to do? I looked back up at the house. The light was now off in King's studio.

I may not have been ready to close that door, but just as I'd thought he'd opened it, he'd slammed it in my face.

It was time for me to do the same.

"I guess I'm going to have to do a little more to convince you." Bear wrapped his arms around me and pulled me into his big warm body. Right before his lips touched mine, I felt it.

Or rather, I felt *him*.

"Get the fuck away from her, Bear," King seethed. A clicking sound grabbed my attention, and I whipped my head around to where King stood behind us on the dock, his gun cocked and aimed at Bear.

"Done already?" I asked, all too aware of Bear's arms still wrapped around my waist. I made no move to push him away. "She must be disappointed that the almighty Brantley King, The King of the stupid Causeway, couldn't last longer."

Bear chuckled.

I've spent so much time trying not to make King angry, and it's never worked. I was tired of walking on eggshells around him. I wanted to make him angry. I wanted to fight with him more than I wanted anything. I wanted to scream.

I wanted to claw his fucking eyes out.

I wanted to hurt him the way he hurt me.

"Get the fuck away from her, Bear," King repeated.

"We're just talking man," Bear said, no sign of fear in his voice. If anything, he was amused.

"Looks like you're doing more than that. Get your fucking hands off her, and go fucking talk to someone else," King warned. "She's. Mine."

"Oh yeah? Well, you may want to tell her that because you ain't got her thinking the same thing."

"The only reason you don't have a bullet in your fucking skull is because we've got history. But in two fucking seconds, if you don't get your dirty fucking hands off my girl, I will say fuck-all to our history and blow your mother fucking head off," King said angrily through gritted teeth.

"Ain't gotta get your pretty panties all up in a twist, brother." Bear got up and brushed off his jeans. "Sorry darlin'. Maybe, some other time." He winked at me and whispered, "Offer still stands. You need me, you come find me."

I could feel the anger radiating off King when Bear walked past him, nudging his shoulder. "You might want to put your claim on that before the boys get wind that you haven't," Bear told him. "She's fair game to the bikers in these parts, including me, so you best do it and do it soon. That is, if she still wants your dumb ass."

Bear was one brave soul to talk to King while the look on his face screamed nothing but murderous rage. I half-expected King to go ape shit and make good on his promise to shoot Bear but the second he'd disappeared into the shadows, King stepped onto the dock.

"I hate the way you make me feel. Well, most of the time," I spat. I was tired of dancing around the truth. "I hate the confusion you bring into my already confused life. I need this back and forth shit to end." I took a deep breath. "I can't take it anymore. You like me. You hate me. You like me. You want to kill me. You want to fuck me. You want me to stay. You want me to *live*. My head is fucking spinning over here."

My buzz faded faster than the setting sun.

"You should leave. I don't want you here," I added.

"I know. I don't care," King said.

"Oh, I'm fully aware that you don't care. That I know."

"You don't know shit, Pup," King barked.

"Oh yeah? So you didn't just spend the entire night at the carnival all over me, saying sweet shit to me, making me feel like this stupid thing between us is something more than just a stupid thing, only to whip out your dick with someone else the very first chance you got? Go back to the fucking house, King. Go back to that girl. I hope she's everything you wanted."

"I can't," King said evenly.

"Why not? Seemed easy for you before."

"Because, Pup, I don't want to. No matter how hard I try to fight this, I'm drawn to you. You think I like this back and forth shit? You think you're the only one who's fucking confused here?" He shook his head like he couldn't believe the words that were coming out of his mouth. "I'm drawn to you," he repeated turning my chin up to him.

"What do you expect? Am I supposed to fall at your feet and thank you for being 'drawn to me'?" Not only was he confusing, he was fucking infuriating. "Drawn to me? You're drawn to me! Well, let me just take off my fucking panties then, and let's do this shit. Yeah, you were really drawn to me. Tell me something, *KING*. Do most first dates end with the guy getting sucked off by another girl? I mean, I've never been on one, so you tell me. I could be wrong here. Because if the answer is yes, then this date has gone fucking swimmingly!"

"I'm...FUCK! You think you know everything, but you don't. All you do is run those pretty lips of yours and expect me to be able to just give into you!" King threw his hands up in the air. "You make me fucking crazy, you know that!" he shouted.

"I make YOU crazy? How the fuck do you think I feel? Most of the time I don't know if you want to kill me or fuck me!" I screamed, every single word he spoke ignited my anger until it wasn't something I could even begin to hold back.

King had the audacity to actually smile. He leaned forward and whispered seductively against my cheek, "Can't I want both, Pup?"

I pulled back and stood up.

"NO! You can't! And stop calling me, Pup. It's a stupid fucking name. I'm not your fucking pet!"

I paced the dock. My rage was at a boiling point I couldn't turn off. This was his fault. He'd made me into this lunatic.

King stood and grabbed my face with both hands, forcing me to look at him. "Yes, you are," he said, as he lowered his lips and brushed them softly against mine in a move so gentle, so unlike him, it took me a few seconds before I registered what was happening.

Then, my anger returned, in full force. Using both my hands, I pushed against his chest until he had no choice but to release me.

"Fuck you! You don't want to keep me!" I shouted over my shoulder as I made my way to the front of the house and started down the gravel driveway. "Do you think I'm stupid? You wouldn't be getting your jollies while I'm in the next room if it was me you wanted."

A large hand grabbed my shoulder and spun me around.

"Let go of me!" I shouted.

"Listen, Pup. I've tried it your way. I tried gentle just now, but you didn't listen. Now, we're going to do it my way, and you're going to fucking listen. Don't make me have to cuff you again," he warned.

King's tone was all anger and confidence. I didn't doubt for a moment that he would make good on his threat. He wrapped his arms around my waist and held my hands together behind my back, locking my struggling body against his.

"I did that to push you away," he admitted. "I wanted you to see it."

"Congratulations, it worked," I spat. "You should be fucking happy."

"You and that tongue of yours." King shook his head. "No, I'm not happy. I'm far from fucking happy. I've been far from fucking happy since I got out of prison. If I think back, I wasn't exactly happy before prison either, and it's your fucking fault!"

"How the fuck is that my fault?" Now, he'd gone too far, blaming me for his life years before I was even in it.

"Because you are the one who made me realize I was fucking unhappy. Because with you, I think I can actually BE happy!" He shook me when he spoke, like he wanted to shake the words into my brain to make me understand what it was he was saying.

I needed it all to be over. It was too much. The mind fuck was more torture than I could take. I wanted him. I wanted to believe him. But words were just words, and coming from King, they were probably just another method to keep torturing me.

I just wanted to be left alone. It was time for me to go. "I'm leaving. Just let me go," I begged, softly.

King shook his head. "No. You're not going anywhere."

"You can't keep me here," I stated.

"See, that's where you're wrong. I think I've proven that I

can," King argued. "Besides, where would you go? Back out on streets?"

"Maybe. What do you care, anyway?" I bit back.

"You seem to forget what it's like out there on your own. Or maybe we can dig up Ed, and he can tell you how he planned to dispose of your body when he was done raping you," King spat.

"I'd rather take chances with my life out there—" My chest constricted. "—than take chances with my heart here."

"No," King argued.

"What the hell do you want from me?" I asked. My anger battled against the heartbreaking thought of leaving and never seeing King again. "Why don't you just gut me, and get it over with? Do whatever it is you want to do to me. Hit me. Fuck me. Fucking *KILL* me. Just. Stop. *HURTING*. Me."

Sobs emerged from my throat, and I fell limp into his arms.

"Baby," King said, holding me tighter so that I wouldn't drop to the ground. It was the first time he'd ever called me that, and when I tried to register the endearment, it fell flat. "I'm so sorry. I didn't fuck that girl. I couldn't do it. She didn't touch me. I stopped the second you shut the door. I swear. I'm so sorry. You're the last person I want to hurt. I just don't know how to fucking do this."

"Do what?" I asked him. A tear fell from my cheek and onto his arm. As much as I didn't want to, I buried my face into his shirt and clenched the fabric in my fists.

His voice cracked when he whispered, "I don't know. Any of it. I don't even fucking know what this is."

"That's not good enough," I said, not really sure what part I was talking about. Maybe, his apology. Maybe his actions. Maybe, his uncertainty. Maybe, all of it.

"I think that's the problem," King said. "You deserve so

much more than an ex-con who has nothing to offer you. You deserve so much more than me. It was easy to keep you when you were just my mine, my property. It's hard to keep you as my girl. I don't know when it all shifted, but it did. And that's what I want, but it's something I've never wanted before. I'd never even taken a girl out on a date before tonight. I want you in my life more than anything, but it's so much more complicated than just wanting it. So much more than you know."

"If you're going to let me go, let me go. If you're going to let me in, let me in. But, you have to pick one. You can't hold me close at night and push me away every morning when the sun comes out." I pushed off of his chest again and turned to walk away, but he pulled me back.

King kissed the top of my head. "I know, baby. I know."

"You don't know shit!"

Breaking free, I headed to the front of the house, away from the party, and away from King. I needed to be alone. I needed to think. King caught up with me easily, each one of his strides accounting for at least three of my own.

"I'm done with nice, Pup," King shouted from close behind me. I continued marching away, trying to put some space between us.

"You're done being nice?" I called back over my shoulder. "You've never been nice. You've lied to me and toyed with me, and that is not *nice*."

King caught me from behind just as I approached the first pillar under the house. He pushed me up against it and pressed himself to my back, his erection prodding the seam of my ass.

"Bear is nice," I said with my cheek pressed sideways against the pillar. "Bear offered to take me in. He wanted me to stay with him at the clubhouse. He wants me to keep his bed warm, fuck his brains out. Told me he wanted me on the back of his bike."

"What the fuck did you just say to me?" King hissed into my neck, his teeth against my skin. I didn't let that stop me from raining down my wrath on him. He deserved every last bit of it. I spun myself around in his arms, but he was too fast. Before I could bolt, he had me pegged against the pillar, my back to his front. His eyes darkened. A vein pulsed in his neck. His jaw was set on a hard line.

"You heard me," I said. "I was going to say yes, too. I was going to go with him and let him put his hands on me. You saw us. He was about to kiss me. I was going to let him." I was wild with power, crazed with lust, and completely reckless of the consequences of my actions.

I was free.

I gave zero fucks.

It was fucking amazing.

"What the fuck have I been telling you?" King roared pushing his knee between my legs, spreading them apart until I was straddling his thigh.

"Nothing. You've been telling me nothing but some fucking bullshit about being yours for weeks now."

"Newsflash, little girl. You were mine from the first moment you walked in on me fucking that girl on my table. You were mine then, and you're mine now." King looked as if any control he had was gone. He'd snapped.

I didn't care.

"You're a fucking liar," I spat.

"I've never lied about that. You. Are. Mine."

"Fuck you. I don't belong to you or anyone else!" I yelled. King pressed his forehead against mine.

"I'm only going to say this once more. You." He thrust up against me, his erection against my core, and I gasped. "Are." He did it again. This time, I had to put my arms on his shoulders to prevent myself from falling. "Mine," he said, hammering in his point with another trust of his hips.

I pulled back and looked him dead in the eye. "Fucking prove it," I challenged.

King growled and pushed his hands up my dress, forcefully ripping my panties down my legs. We were in the shadows, but anyone walking by the side of the house could see us. The instant he touched me, I was too lost in sensation to care.

Zero fucks.

King kissed me. An all encompassing kiss. A possession. He wasn't kissing my mouth. He was claiming me as his, and I was going to leave my mark on him in every way I could.

My entire body ignited into the flame he'd been stoking inside of me for weeks. He kneaded my breasts through my dress and attacked my neck with his lips. He lifted me up and wrapped my thighs around his waist. I grunted in frustration, gyrating against his erection. I couldn't get close enough. I couldn't find the friction I needed.

"You a virgin, Pup?" King asked wickedly.

"You know I don't know that," I panted.

"Cause I'm letting you know right now that there won't be a question if you are after tonight. I'm going to be buried so deep inside your sweet pussy you won't ever again forget who owns it."

He pushed down my dress, exposing my breasts, then yanked up the bottom until I was naked except for a scrap of fabric lingering around my midsection.

"Fuck yes," he hissed through his teeth.

After that, we were all hands and mouths. Touching, exploring, needing, biting. Teeth clacking together in an effort to get closer to one another. It was sloppy and wet and wonderful, and it wasn't enough. King reached down between us, released his belt, and pushed down the front of his jeans. His erection sprang free. Smooth, soft, and hard as stone prodded up against warm and wet, seeking entrance.

"Yes," I breathed. I was ready. I needed him inside me more than I needed to breathe.

King lined up his cock with his hand, and in one long thrust, he was inside of me. He groaned as he pushed his way into my tightness, stretching and filling me until I thought I was going to fall apart from the inside out. It hurt, but it was a pleasurable kind of pain, caused by the unfamiliar feeling of being so full.

The pain he caused was a pleasure all its own.

"Fuck yes," King moaned, now fully seated inside me.

I groaned loudly, not caring who heard me. King thrust up inside me, and my insides clenched around him. Every time he pulled out, he rubbed against that spot inside that made me see stars before thrusting angrily back in.

Again and again.

"I told you," he said. "I told you you're mine. This pussy. This pussy is mine. Don't fucking forget that shit again."

He thrust hard and angry. I took him. All of him. His cock. His anger. His possession. I let him claim me with his kiss, his cock, his words.

We were fighting with our sex.

A back and forth.

A give and take.

With our sex, we told each other *I hate you* and *I want you* and *I don't want you to leave.*

"Fuck, Pup. Fuck. I knew it. I knew it would be like this," King said breathlessly.

A pressure was building inside of me that was ten times more powerful then when King had made me come on his fingers. Growing with each stroke. Faster and faster he plunged into my depths until he didn't just give me an orgasm; he ripped it from my body.

I shouted out my release as I came and held onto King for dear life, tightening my thighs around him, digging the heels of my feet into his ass as he furiously pumped into me. I saw stars, bright and vivid, dancing in front of my eyes until I thought that I might pass out and die right there in his arms. Maybe, I did choose King being inside of me over breathing, because I couldn't seem to catch my breath.

"Look at me," King ordered, his voice deep and raspy like he was trying to hold onto his control. I was too lost in coming down from my orgasm high to pay any attention to what he was saying. "Look at me!"

This time he emphasized his words with a thrust of his hips. I moaned and opened my eyes.

"Don't look away," he ordered, holding my gaze as his cock hardened and twitched. He groaned as he came inside of me, spilling his wet warmth into my depths.

We'd said all the things with our bodies that our mouths had failed to communicate over and over again. He'd told me that I was his before, that I belonged to him. But before that night, I hadn't believed him.

It was what his body told me that took me by surprise and shook me to my very core.

He was mine.

# Doe

"COME WITH ME," KING SAID. RIGHTING MY clothes, he took my hand and led me back to the pier. When we passed the bonfire, we were greeted with a lot of whistling and applause.

They'd obviously heard us.

I didn't care.

We sat on the dock with our legs dangling over the side. The fog had lifted off the water. The full moon cast our shadows over the glass-like bay, making it appear like black ice.

King held my hand in his, and when I tried to pry it away, he tightened his grip.

"King," I started.

"Brantley," he corrected. "Call me by my first name."

"Brantley," I said, testing his name out.

"I hated it growing up, but for good or for worse, it's the only thing my mama ever gave me. Grace is the only other person who uses it." He paused, then added, "I like the way it sounds when you say it." His serious tone and soft eyes made me question where he was going with this, but then, it hit me.

He was letting me in.

"Okay, Brantley, what else you got?" I nudged his shoulder. He took a deep breath.

"You know about Max?"

I nodded. The girl we went to see, the one from the picture. "Your sister."

"Pup, Max isn't my sister," King admitted.

"Then, who is she to you?" I asked. If she wasn't family, then why did he have so much interest in her?

"She's my daughter."

*Holy. Shit.*

"Your daughter?" I asked, my throat tightening.

"Yeah, Max is my daughter. She's the real reason why I went to prison, and only Preppy and Bear know the truth about her." He squeezed my hand tighter. Looking out over the water, he seemed pained to be recalling memories associated with Max. "Do you want to know the story? Because you asked me if I wanted to let you go or keep you, and I want to let you in. I want to keep you, but it's a hard story for me to tell. I've never told it to anyone. The only people who know were there in some way."

"I want to know."

"Do you know why I was in prison?"

"Because of your mom."

"Yeah," he agreed. "I don't make apologies for the things I've needed to do for the sake of business. Preppy and I had shit lives growing up. We did everything we could to turn it around for ourselves, most of those things were far outside the law, but we did it. Shit was amazing for a while. But my anger would get the best of me, and I would almost always be the one who ended up in jail here and there, usually just overnight. Sometimes, for thirty or sixty day stretches, depending on the charges. The other players in the game we play know the rules. They also know that when you step out of line, things happen. Things that make you dead. But this wasn't one of those times. I didn't pull a trigger, or use a knife, or send someone after her."

"Your mom?" I asked.

He nodded, then told me his story.

*By the time I was fifteen, Me, Prep, and Bear were our own little crew. Just three young shitheads who just wanted to have a good time, get laid, and make some fucking money. Surprisingly, we did make money. Enough for me to buy the house.*

*The three of us were on top of the world for a while. I'm not gonna lie. It was the best fucking time of my entire life.*

*But then, I got pinched. It wasn't the first time, and it wasn't for anything I should've actually gotten pinched for. A stupid bar fight in an upscale place Preppy wanted to check out across the river in Coral Pines. Some shitty tourist spot.*

*I was talking to a girl when some pink sweater-tied-around-his-shoulders douche-bag stepped to me for talking to her. We got into it, broke some shit in the bar, chairs, glasses, tables.*

*I'm covered in tattoos, and I have a record. He's got a pink fucking sweater tied around his shoulders. It was easy to figure out which one of us was going to jail when the sheriff showed up.*

*I got ninety days because of my priors. When I was in county, this girl I used to screw around with showed up for visitation. She was as big as a fucking house. I thought that she was going to give birth right there in the visitors' room. She told me the baby was mine, said that she wanted to raise it with me when I got out.*

*I didn't think much of the girl, but she was nice enough, and after I got over the initial shock of it all, I was really excited to be a dad. I made a plan, made promises to myself that I was going to be a good dad, especially since I could only narrow down who my father was to every man in town except Mr. Wong who ran the corner store, for obvious reasons.*

*I wrote the baby letters from prison, though Tricia didn't know then if it was a boy or a girl. She'd said they tried to find out on the ultrasound but he or she was moving around too much. It was exactly what I needed. And then it was what I wanted.*

*Sure I had money, but the baby gave me a reason to want more out of life.*

Purpose.

*The morning I got out of county, Tricia was supposed to pick me up but never showed. I walked to a payphone to call her, and when she answered, she told me she'd had the baby the week before.*

*A girl.*

*She'd named her Max, the girl name we picked out when she was still pregnant.*

*I asked her where the baby was, and she mumbled something about it being too hard and that she couldn't handle it. That the whole motherhood thing wasn't for her. She said she wasn't coming back. There was a lot of noise in the background, glasses clinking, music. It sounded like she was at a bar. She was shouting into the phone.*

Where the fuck is she? *I kept asking her over and over again. For a second, I thought she was going to say she gave her up or something, and I was already thinking about who the fuck I was going to have to kill to get her back when Tricia said something that surprised me and turned my stomach.*

I LEFT HER WITH YOUR MOTHER

*Before that day, I hadn't seen my mom but a handful of times in years, and none of those times were on purpose. Most of the time, when I ran into her, she didn't know who I was. The very last time I'd seen her, she called me Travis and asked me how Bermuda was.*

*As soon as Tricia told her where the baby was, I hung up and called my mom, but the phone line was dead, and I didn't know if she had a cell.*

*I took a cab to Mom's and called Preppy to meet me there.*

*I got there before he did.*

*I knew walking up to the door that something was wrong. I could feel it in my gut.*

*I banged on the door of her apartment until my knuckles bled, but there wasn't any answer. I could hear the static from a TV inside. I screamed out for my mom, but there was no response. I was about to turn around and walk away, check with some of the neighbors to see if she even still lived there, but then I heard it.*

*I heard her.*

My Baby.

Crying.

*My baby was crying.*

*Not just a little cry or a cranky cry, but a strangled cry straight from the gut, the kind that says that shit ain't right.*

*It's like she knew I was there, and she was calling out to me.*

216

*I kicked in the front door. The living room was dark except for the TV. When I took a step, trash got stuck on my shoes, fast food wrappers, cigarette butts. The counter was littered with garbage. The trash can was overflowing. Flies circled the kitchen sink which was piled high with dirty dishes.*

*I heard her cry again. It was coming from the back of the apartment.*

*I ran into one of the spare rooms and turned on the switch, but nothing came on. It took a second for my eyes to adjust to the dark, but when they did, I saw this little baby, this beautiful, scared, skinny, little baby, no bigger than half my forearm, covered in shit from head to fucking toe. Her eyes were red and crusted over from crying. She wasn't in a crib. She was lying on a dirty sheet on the floor. No bottle. No blanket. No lights. No nothing.*

*I gently scooped her up in my arms, and she weighed practically nothing. Even though she was visibly hurting and I was hurting for her, I remember that first feeling of holding her. Before she was even born, she became the most important thing in the world to me, but holding her sealed the deal. There was nothing I wouldn't do for her. Nothing.*

*I would hurt anyone and everyone who ever made my baby cry like that again. I would burn down cities for her.*

*I fell to the ground with my back against the wall and rocked her until she calmed. I told her about all the things I was going to buy for her. I told her that daddy was here, that she was safe. I got up and found the cleanest towel I could and wrapped her up in it. She settled against my chest and fell asleep.*

*I was fighting mad. Deeply disturbed. And completely in love. All at the same time.*

*I was leaving with Max in my arms when the light from the*

*TV flashed, and I saw a shadow in the Lazyboy. Sure enough, it was my Mom. Next to her was an empty bottle of some cheap fucking whiskey and an ashtray full of little bags of leftover crystal.*

*She didn't take care of my newborn baby because she was too fucking busy getting drunk and high.*

*Max would've died if I hadn't gotten to her in time.*

*It was that thought that set me off. It still pisses me off to this day, and it makes remembering what happened next a whole lot easier to digest when I recall the memory.*

*Rage consumed me. The kind that makes you want to rip out someone's throat with your bare fucking hands.*

*A lit cigarette hung from her bottom lip, an open newspaper on her lap. Her face was covered in pock marks and her skin was draping off of it like it was melting. As much as I wanted to hurt her, it was like the fucking karma cosmos or whatever aligned, because the lit cigarette fell from her mouth, and the newspaper ignited.*

*I stood there and watched it happen.*

*I was happy. It couldn't have gone better if I lit the fire myself. It was a horrible way to die, but knowing what could have happened to Max, I really didn't give a shit if it was the most horrible death imaginable. To me, in that moment, she deserved it.*

*I still feel that way.*

*Mom's chest rose and fell, so I knew she was alive, but she was so far gone into whatever high she'd been chasing that not even a fire on her lap disturbed her.*

*When the paper fell to the ground, the carpet caught fire. The light from the flames allowed me to get a good look at the place. There wasn't a section of the floor that wasn't covered in filth and rusty syringes poked out of the couch like it was a pin-cushion.*

*When the flames got higher, I made the decision.*

*I turned around and left.*

*I felt the heat behind me as I walked away. I was halfway across the street when the windows exploded and the glass shattered.*

*I bought diapers, bottles, and formula from the nearby convenient store and hosed Max off in the restroom the best I could. It took me ten minutes to figure out how to put on the diaper.*

*Preppy saw the flames from my mom's trailer and pulled up behind the gas station.*

*He took us home.*

*He sang to her made up, profanity laced, lullabies.*

*Max gulped down a bottle so quick she would pause to choke, and my heart skipped out of my chest every time she did it, but then she would keep going.*

*I was so nervous. I was a single guy in my early twenties who'd never so much as been in the same room as a newborn before. I'd never even spent more than a couple of hours with the same woman.*

*And suddenly, I had this baby girl to raise. It was the first time in my life that I can say I was truly terrified.*

*I talked to her again and hummed some Zeppelin to her until she fell asleep on my chest.*

*I covered us both up with a blanket and watched the fan spin around until I saw lights flashing through my front windows.*

*Blue and red.*

"It turns out the convenient store had some pretty decent surveillance. Since I walked away without seeking help and I made no attempt to douse the fire or save my mom, they arrested me. Charged me with manslaughter and put me away.

Max got sent to foster care right away since they couldn't

find Tricia. They wouldn't release the baby to Preppy because he was a felon himself, not to mention he didn't have a legit job on record, anyway. Grace was in Georgia, getting treatment for her first fight with her cancer at the time.

"Do you know what ever happened to Tricia?"

"No, but if she's smart, she'll never show her fucking face in this town again." King sighed. "They took her from me. I was her dad for only three hours, and they were the three best hours of my fucking life. And they fucking took her from me."

"You're still her dad," I offered.

"Yeah, I've been trying to be," King said. "While I was away, I did everything I could. Filed papers. Hired lawyers. But it got me nowhere."

"Is there anything else you can do?" I asked. "There has to be. This can't be it."

"There are two options left, at least two that I know of. The first one is a long shot." King flashed a sad smile. "But there's this guy, a big shot judge. A dirty fucking politician. Bear has ties to him through the MC. The senator thinks he can make him see things my way and rule for custody in my favor."

"So what are you waiting for? Do that!" I shouted excitedly.

"It will cost me about a mil," King said flatly, killing my growing enthusiasm.

"Shit," I cursed. "A mil? As in a million dollars?"

King laughed. "Yes, Pup, as in one million green-backed American fucking dollars."

"Do you have that kind of money?" I asked.

"I did," King said. "I don't anymore. We sunk everything into getting the granny operation going. Even if I sold the house, it needs work, and that costs even more money. And the market sucks right now, so even if I sold it I wouldn't be able to come up with even half that."

"And if you do get custody, you need a home to bring her to," I added.

"Yeah, I've imagined building her a tree house in the big oak by the garage and turning my studio into her room, move my tattoo shit into the garage apartment."

"Then, where would Bear go?" I asked.

"Home! Bear has a room at his pop's place and a room at the clubhouse. He just likes to take up all the rent-free space he can." King laughed.

"I am so, so sorry, about all of it," I said, tears spilling out onto my cheeks. He wiped them away with the pad of his thumb.

"Don't be sorry, Pup. I'll never be the good guy in the story. I let my mom burn to death. I lost my daughter because of who I am and the things I've done. That shit's on me. That's my cross to carry."

The deep need to help reunite King with his daughter dictated my decision-making. I took a deep breath and grabbed his hands, folding them onto my lap.

"What do we need to do next?"

"We?"

"Yeah." I let the word sink in. "We."

"WE don't need to do anything. I'll figure something out."

"But wait. You said there was a second option."

King shook his head. "It's a worst case scenario, and honestly, it's going to be bad whether I decide to do it or not. I can't win either way."

"Tell me what exactly is it you'd have to do."

"It's a dark road to travel down, and I'm not sure it's one I could ever come back from." It was the lingering sadness in his voice that made my heart break for him and made me not want to press him further. "But it's a worst case scenario, so I'll cross that bridge when and if it comes down to it." King looked at me thoughtfully. "For now, I'm going to kick the granny thing in high gear and see what we can come up with."

"Let me know if you need my help. I'll do anything."

"I'll remember you said that," King said, pulling me onto his lap.

"I mean it."

"So did I," King replied, squeezing me tighter. He buried his nose in my neck. "I might need you to stay with Grace a while."

"Why, is she okay? I mean…you know." I stammered.

"Grace is fine for now, but we might have some shit going down here soon, and I need you far away from it."

"The Isaac thing?" I asked.

"Yeah, the Isaac thing. But don't worry about it. Just know that when I say you need to go to Grace's that's where you need to be. No questions asked. No arguing bullshit. You got me?"

"I got you."

"Can we talk more later, Pup? I feel like a fucking chick right now, spilling my guts to you." King laughed.

"Yeah, we can talk more later," I said.

I wrapped my arms around King's neck and looked over the water. The bird that was the inspiration for my sketch sat on top of a crab trap buoy in the middle of the bay. His beak was down, searching in the water for his next meal.

"So what now?" I asked, turning back to King.

"Now? Now, we need to go upstairs, and I need to get you in my bed because I'm not even fucking close to being done with you tonight."

## Doe

"GET UP," KING SAID.

He took me by the hand and lifted me off the mattress. I was still half asleep. Knocked into a sex coma after King proved that when he said he wasn't nearly done with me, he wasn't lying.

Heat coursed from his hand into mine and shot directly into my erratically beating heart, causing my breath to hitch in my throat.

"Where are we going?" I managed to squeak out as I pulled on a tank top and my underwear.

Looking down into my eyes, King slowly tucked an unruly

strand of hair behind my ear, allowing the very tips of his fingers to brush against my skin.

"Pup," he said, his voice almost hoarse, "it's time for you to stop living for who you might've been and start living for who you are now."

"I thought that's what I was doing," I said with a yawn. King's grip tightened around my palm. He dragged me down the hall into his tattoo studio and switched on the light.

"Sit," he commanded, releasing my hand and gesturing to the chair in the middle of the room.

"Why?" I asked becoming more aware as I slowly woke up.

My palms started to sweat. "You want me in THAT chair?" I asked.

King walked over to the iPod docking station, and with his back to me, he flipped through the songs. After a few minutes, the sounds of Florida Georgia Line's STAY filled the room.

When King turned back around and noticed I was still standing by the door, he narrowed his gaze and again pointed to the chair. "Sit, or I will come over there, pick you up, and toss you onto it."

His tone did not imply that I had another option. I reluctantly moved over to the chair and tentatively perched myself on the edge.

"Take off your shirt." His voice so suddenly strained, he had to clear his throat. King sat down on his rolling stool and opened the bottom drawer of his tool box. He started sorting out materials just as if he were getting ready to tattoo a client, just like I'd seen him do many times over the past few weeks.

"What? Why? What are you doing?" I asked, unable to hide the panic in my voice.

"Because, Pup, it will be very hard to do this fucking tattoo with your shirt on. So, take the goddamn thing off, yeah?" King was demanding, but his tone hinted at a softness that wasn't there when I'd first met him.

"I already told you. I can't," I said. "You just don't get it. I may want one, but I just can't. I've told you this." Then, another thought crossed my mind.

He wouldn't tattoo me against my will, would he?

King stood from his stool and slowly approached. A menacing look in his eyes. He pushed my knees apart and settled his large frame between my thighs. He rested his forehead against mine in a gesture that was both intimate and new.

"How many times do I need to tell you? You need to learn to do what you are told, Pup," he growled, his cool breath floating across the skin on my cheek and neck.

In one fluid movement, he yanked my tank top over my head and tossed it onto his toolbox. "You're mine now. In every way. And I need you to know that if you regain your memory and remember who you are, you're still going to be mine. If you have a boyfriend out there waiting for you? You're still mine." He paused. "And if you *ever* leave me to go back to your old life, just know that no matter who you are with, every inch of this beautiful body of yours will always belong to me."

Braless and feeling very exposed in every way, I made a move to cover my breasts with my hand. I looked down to the floor to avoid eye contact. I could feel his gaze on my body. The hair on my arms stood on end. My nipples hardened.

King's lips curled upward in a wicked smile. He leaned back into me and placed his hands over mine, removing them from my breasts, fully exposing me to his hungry gaze. He blew out a long-held breath. His tongue darted out, licking his bottom lip before sucking it into his mouth. After what seemed like a lifetime, he shook his head and lightly chuckled.

"This isn't about me right now," he said. I got the feeling he was talking to himself rather than to me. "Lay on your stomach." He snapped on a pair of black latex gloves.

"You can't. I can't," I argued.

He sat down on his stool and rolled it toward me with his feet. "You said you wanted a tattoo, right?"

"Yes, I did, and I do. But I can't. I can't because what if—"

"No. Let me guess, you can't because it may be what you want, but it may not be what SHE wants?" He didn't wait for me to answer. Probably because he knew that was exactly what I was going to say. "But what you aren't understanding is that you are her!" King roared, standing up so abruptly his stool slid back and hit wall behind him. "Don't you see? You can't second guess everything you want because you are afraid of remembering another life!"

He paced the room and wrung out his hands, cracking his knuckles.

"Fuck who you were!" King screamed, the veins in his neck pulsing with each of his ragged breaths. "Be you, this fantastic, amazing, fucking beautiful…" His tone softened, and he stopped pacing, lifting his eyes to meet mine. "We're not just going to have a life, remember? We're going to live."

He slowly approached me. Again, he moved my hands away from my breasts. He pressed his chest into mine. His hands circled around my lower back, his hardness to my softness.

"I fucking love who you are, Pup, and it's about damn time you learned to love her, too," he said, placing a soft kiss on the edge of my mouth, igniting a sensation deep within that caused my entire body to shake.

LOVE?

I started to protest again, but the fog of desire wouldn't lift, and instead, I just sat there with my mouth open, waiting for King to make the next move.

Much to my disappointment, he sat back onto his stool and opened another drawer of his toolbox. He took out a sheet of paper that was almost see-through with colorful lines already drawn onto the page.

"Here." He passed me the paper, averting his gaze to the floor. "I made this for you."

I reached for the paper. It took me a minute to figure out what it was. The lines were all colorful, deep purples, pinks, and blues. The design was ornate, and at first, it just looked like beautiful vine work, but when you looked closely, hidden in the design was...me.

Concealed in the design was a book opened to the middle with wings protruding out the sides as it perched upon a pink pair of brass knuckles. Further down and off to the side was a quote woven into vines, '*I don't want to repeat my innocence. I want the pleasure of losing it all over again.*'

My breath hitched in my throat, and I couldn't form the words. It was completely me.

I had to have it.

Suddenly, nothing mattered anymore because this man knew exactly who I was. Not who I used to be, not some girl I was waiting for to return while putting my current life on hold in the process.

I was tired of standing still. I wanted to move forward. All that mattered was what I wanted now, and what I wanted was right in front of me.

"Where?" I asked, unable to tear my eyes away from it.

"Do you trust me?" King asked.

"Yes," I said without hesitation. Because it was true.

"Good. Then, lay down." King took the paper from me, and with one hand on my shoulder, he pressed me down onto the table, placing his knee on the outside of my thigh. His face hovered just inches above mine. "Now, be a good girl," he whispered on my neck, "and roll the fuck over." A crooked smile on his lips.

"Yes, sir," I said, no longer able to contain my own smile, my belly doing flips as I thought back to where those beautiful lips had been not long before.

"Good girl. Now, you're learning," King praised me, sealing his compliment with a smack on my ass as I did what I was told and rolled over.

He shuffled around, preparing his tools. The tattoo needle started to hum, and shortly after he applied the template, I felt the first sharp sting on my skin, followed by a scratching sensation.

It didn't hurt as bad as I thought it would. In an odd way, I welcomed the pain. I closed my eyes and lost myself in the sensation of the needle across my skin.

The sensation of taking over my life and making it my own.

The needle stung and scraped its way across my back and shoulders. At the same time, I said a silent goodbye to the girl I'd been protecting for months.

I wasn't going to miss her.

As King branded my skin, I embraced the girl whose life was just beginning. I embraced life.

*My* life.

King filled me so completely. Not just my body. My heart. My soul. My life. I didn't give a shit if I ever got my memory back.

Because with King, I knew exactly who I was.

I was his.

## KING

TATTOOING DOE WAS THE SINGLE MOST EROTIC moment of my life. Marking her perfect, pale skin with a tattoo I'd designed for her made me so fucking hard I had to adjust myself every thirty seconds in order to concentrate on my work.

When I was done, I handed her the hand mirror, and she walked over to the full-sized mirror that hung on the back of the door, like she'd seen dozens of my other clients do before. When she held up the hand mirror, she gasped.

"What?" I asked in a panic, hoping she didn't already see what I'd hidden in the tattoo. I was an asshole for putting it there. I was an asshole for tattooing her in the first place.

I was just an asshole.

But I couldn't help myself. My name needed to be on her. It wasn't enough just to call her mine. I needed to mark her as well. So hidden in the vine work under the quote I found that I thought was perfect for her, was my name.

KING was woven into the design. In order to see it you had to tilt your head or otherwise you wouldn't notice it. But it was there.

I would tell her eventually, of course, but I wanted it to be my secret for a while. She'd stopped being my possession a while ago, a lot longer before I cared to admit it, but I still felt the need to mark her as mine.

I still liked the idea of owning her.

Only now, she owned me, too.

She didn't notice the name. Tears filled her eyes. She stood there staring at the hand mirror in just her panties. Little cheeky ones where her ass hung out of the bottoms. Her tits were only inches from my face. Her tears of happiness made my dick twitch. Although her sad tears evoked the same response.

My dick wasn't partial to which kind of tears he liked.

I took the mirror from her hand and lifted her up onto the counter. "You like it?" I asked, pushing her panties down her legs.

"I love it," she panted, wrapping her legs around me, drawing me close. Her wetness soaking my boxers. I pushed them down with one hand. I'd been hard for three hours, the entire time I'd been working on her, and couldn't wait any longer. I pushed inside her tight, wet heat.

We both moaned at the contact.

"You love it?" I asked, needing to hear her say it again.

231

"Yes, I love it!" she said as I thrust up into her, hard. "I love it. So much. I love you."

I froze when I heard the words, and when I did, her eyes flung open.

"I didn't mean—"

"Shut the fuck up."

"Oh my god, I have that word vomit thing. I'm sorry. Shit, I just meant that—"

"Shut the fuck up!" I demanded, thrusting hard to get her attention. She closed her eyes, and her head fell back. "That's fucking better. Now, keep that pretty mouth of yours shut while I fuck you."

"Okay," she whispered, breathless.

"Shut up," I said again, and she closed her mouth. "Shut up so I can fuck you…and show you how much I love you."

She nodded and although her eyes stayed shut, a tear rolled down her cheek. I sucked it off her chin before it could fall to the floor.

Then, I fucked her.

Hard.

I showed her how much I loved her until I couldn't tell where I started and she began. Until all that was in that room was me and her and the thing between us that kept pulling us together like magnets. Until we were lost in sensations and orgasms.

And in each other.

I fucked her until we were one person, and in a way we were, because I'd lost myself along the way, and I found myself again in the most unlikely place.

I'd found myself again in the haunted eyes of a girl who was just as lost as I was.

Or maybe, we didn't find each other at all.
Maybe, we just decided to be lost together.

## KING

D OE AND I WERE LYING IN BED ON A SATURDAY
afternoon, watching Demolition Man. Her idea. Not
mine. Out of all the DVDs in my collection, that
was the one she's watched the most in the past few days. She
also liked Disney movies, but every time she watched them,
I thought about Max and a pain formed in my chest thinking
that she might never be around to watch them with us.

Or Max might be around, and Doe might be gone.

I was going to do everything I could to get them both under one roof with me. Although as the days went by, the reality
of putting together the money for the payoff seemed less and
less likely.

Disney princess movies may have just been a bunch of fairy tales, but the idea of the three of us together—four if you count Preppy—was my idea of happily ever after.

"All restaurants are now Taco Bell," Doe said in sync with Sandra Bullock's character. She knew every line. It was downright adorable. Besides, we were naked, and I had one hand on her tit and the other was cupping her pussy, so I had no complaints. "Why is the house half-painted?" She turned to me abruptly, propping her head on my chest.

"Cause when Preppy and I first moved in, it was already an old house, but we kind of trashed it with all the parties and didn't think much of fixing it up. Then, I asked Preppy to fix it up a bit because I expected to bring Tricia and Max here.

"But why did he stop?"

"Because I went to prison, and the house being painted didn't seem to matter to either of us anymore. There wasn't a chance in hell they'd let me have her at that point. Besides, Preppy may be able to cook, and he's a killer mechanic, but he's a shit handyman. So, the place kind of went to hell while I was gone."

"Well," she said, stretching her arms over her head. Her perky tits bounced as she yawned and hooked her leg over my thigh. "You better get to painting again because we're going to get the money, and she's going to come home."

"Yeah, baby. We're going to get her back." I was unsure if I was speaking to her or trying to convince myself. The truth was that each and every day that passed by, Max was slipping further and further away.

Preppy opened the door, and Doe sat up quickly, pulling the sheet over her bare chest.

"Dude, fucking knock much?" I asked.

235

Preppy ignored me and hopped up onto the bed, settling himself between me and Doe. He slung an arm around each of us.

"I just love you guys," he said, squeezing the three of us together like we were one big, fat, odd-as-fuck family.

"Is there a purpose to this love fest?" Doe asked, giggling as Preppy leaned in to tickle her.

It should've pissed me off that he was even touching her, but there was nothing sexual about their connection. Although I often found myself jealous of their easy friendship. I had to work my ass off to get Pup to like me, and even then, I was shit at it.

But, Preppy wore both his crazy and his heart on his sleeve, and I was always a little envious of how easy it was to be around him.

All of us together just made sense. Doe could read bedtime stories to Max as she fell asleep at night. Uncle Preppy could teach her how to make pancakes. Those were the kind of images that made it all come together for me. It was clear. I had to do whatever it was going to take to make this shit work.

Max had to come home.

Pup had to stay.

I'd told her I was a selfish prick, and I'd meant it. I just didn't think she realized how true that statement really was. I guarantee that she had no clue that I was hiding the truth about her past from her.

I didn't plan to fall for her, but I did. Now, she wasn't just a pawn I was going to use to get Max back. Now, she was a part of my life.

A part I wasn't willing to give back.

Even if that means keeping the truth about who she really

is a secret until I'm rotting in the ground.

"As a matter of fact, there is a point. So glad you asked!" Preppy turned to me, and his face went serious. "Bear wants us to come to the compound tonight. They're having a party since daddy over here got pissed when he threw the last one and grounded him for a month."

"Cut the sarcasm, Prep," I said, I had no patience for Preppy's humor because all I wanted was for him to leave so I could be alone again with my girl.

"Yes, a par-tay with the bikers and the four B's."

"Four B's?" Doe asked.

"Yep. Beer. Booze. Blow. Babes." Preppy looked between us. "Well, maybe not the babes since you two seem to be an exclusive thing. Are you an exclusive thing? Should I be getting out the fine china and calling the preacher?" Preppy turned to Doe. "Are you with child?"

"What?" she asked. "No! I'm not." She laughed while Preppy pretended to pass out on the mattress.

"But we are exclusive," I chimed in. I'm not sure why I felt the need to say it, but I did. I needed Preppy to get the message loud and clear. It may be an innocent friendship between them, but the warning to your fellow horn-ball friends about your woman could never be too obvious or too loud.

"Ahhhhh, so what do you say, my friends? Par-tay with Preppy tonight?" He rubbed his hands together like an evil warlock casting a spell.

"Do you want to go?" I asked Doe who was all smiles.

"Really?" She asked.

"Really." I replied. If going to a party was all it took to coax that kind of smile from her, I'd take her to one every fucking night if she wanted.

"Yipeeeee motherfuckers! Get dressed, lovers. We're going to the clubhouse." Preppy stood up on the bed, jumping up and down until his head hit a spinning blade of the ceiling fan. He dropped back down to his ass, clutching his forehead. "That's gonna leave a mark."

Doe leaned over Preppy and pushed his hand off his head to inspect his injury. She'd let the sheet fall from her chest, her bare breasts swayed in front of Preppy's face.

Preppy was no longer concerned about his wound. He openly stared at her nipples and licked his lips.

I might not have been mad that they were friends, but my best friend was about to take a fist to the face for ogling my girl like that.

I grabbed her waist and dragged her back to me, covering her chest with the sheet. She blushed.

If she thought my homecoming party was wild, she would be shocked to see what went on over at the Beach Bastards' compound. "Shit, I forgot about those fucking bikers," I said.

"Oh stop it," Preppy said. "Bear's people are harmless now. You've staked your claim, flagged your territory, put your sausage in the onion ring. That's all they care about. That's bible to them. She won't be fucked with. Besides, I'll be there, and so will Bear, and so will you."

"I'm not all that trusting of Bear these days," I said. "It wasn't a week ago that he was asking my girl to be his old lady."

"But as I said, you gots it in. It's all good, play playyyyyyy."

"Preppy, how much coffee have you had this morning?" Doe asked.

"Not much, six, seven cups. Why?" He twitched his fingers like he was playing an imaginary piano.

"We can go, but you're not to leave my fucking sight," I told

Doe. "I mean it. Either me or Preppy are with you at all times, got it? Worst case scenario, go to Bear, but I swear to god if he lays a hand on you, I will chop it the fuck off."

It came out harsher than I intended, but I wasn't fucking around. The reality of what could happen to her if she wandered off on her own was what was really harsh.

Not a motherfucker in that place would survive if they touched her. Just remembering what Ed had almost done made me want to kill that piece of shit all over again.

"Got it," Doe said, recognizing the seriousness in my tone. She placed a hand on my shoulder. "I won't go anywhere unless you or Preppy are with me."

"Good." I let out a breath I didn't know I was holding.

"So, what are we watching?" Preppy asked, leaning back on his elbows and crossing his feet at the ankles. "Ooh, Demolition Man. This is my jayum."

"Get the fuck out," I said, shoving him off the bed.

"You guys are no fucking fun," Preppy pouted, picking himself up off the carpet. "You are all in lovers' land and forgot all about ole Preppy over here." He stuck out his lower lip and drooped his shoulders.

"Have the car ready in twenty," I barked, throwing a pillow at his head.

"You mean the truck. My classic caddy is in a million little pieces, and 'death by bomb' isn't covered by insurance," Preppy said, dodging the pillow.

"You don't fucking have insurance," I said. Preppy didn't believe in anything that kept him on the grid, no matter how illegal it was.

"But if I did, it wouldn't cover it," he said, waving us off and leaving the room.

"Remind me to get a deadbolt for that door," I said.

"Oh, stop. Preppy's great, just highly caffeinated," Doe said in his defense.

"You can back out now if you've changed your mind. We can stay here and stay naked and watch whatever stupid movie you want, as long as we are naked while watching it. We don't have to go to Bear's party if you don't think you will feel comfortable."

"I want to get to know your friends better. I want to get out of the house for a while. I want it all." Doe smiled. "And I want it with you."

I wanted to puff out my chest and beat on it like a gorilla. Her words were empowering. She wanted it all.

With me.

I felt so good about where we were and where we were heading that I almost felt okay about living the rest of my life lying to her.

Almost.

## KING

B EAR'S CLUBHOUSE WAS AN OLD TWO-STORY APARTMENT complex with a courtyard in the center and a small, kidney-shaped pool that had been graffitied a million times over.

Plastic patio chairs with gaping holes in the seats and backs, some missing legs, were scattered everywhere. A few were floating upside down in the deep end the pool in a foot of green sludgy water. There was no sophisticated speaker system. An ancient boom box sat on top of a small round table blaring Johnny Cash. Its cord ran into the shallow water of the pool and across the courtyard where it was plugged into a wall out-let inside one of the rooms.

Scantily clad women were everywhere, and bikers of all ages, shapes, and sizes lingered about in various states of drunkenness. Two muscle heads wearing their cuts with nothing but their bare chests underneath, arm-wrestled in the corner on top of an overturned laundry basket.

Two women with matching bleach blonde hair, both topless, were making out on the second floor balcony against the railing, while a skinny prospect stood close by looking on with heavily lidded lust filled eyes, with a hard-on he wasn't even trying to hide, straining against his jeans.

Bear was the first person to greet us. "King, you motherfucker!" he shouted, standing in the open doorway of one of the motel rooms, his arm draped around the neck of a girl with innocent chubby looking cheeks, but a very weary look in her eyes. "In here!" He waved us over and practically shoved the girl out of the room. She would have landed face-first on the concrete if Preppy hadn't caught her and set her back on her feet.

"Thanks," she said, looking up at Preppy. Preppy scrunched his nose as if he was confused by her thanks, then stepped around her. She looked back at him as she walked away.

"What the fuck was that?" I asked.

"No fucking clue," Preppy said seriously, his usual humor nowhere in sight. "Let's get this party started."

"Doe, baby! You're here!" Bear exclaimed, pulling Doe into a hug that lasted a beat too long. I clenched my fists. Bear didn't seem to notice, and if he did, he didn't seem to care. "Bump, get my friends a drink!"

A freckle-faced redheaded prospect I'd seen a few times before, filled three red cups from the keg and handed them to us.

"Got anything in a bottle for the lady?" I asked, emptying my cup in just a few swallows.

I needed something to take the edge off, but I wouldn't put it past one of these little prospect fuckers to try and slip Doe something. We were friends of the club, but some of these newbies may not know the extent of which we weren't to be fucked with. I was about to explode out of my skin. Why did we come here again? Oh yeah, because Doe wanted to.

I was turning into such a fucking pussy over this girl.

"You heard the man. A bottle for the lady," Bear ordered, taking the cup from Doe's hands before she had a chance to lift it to her lips.

Bear chugged the contents of her cup while Bump handed her an unopened bottle of beer. I discarded my cup and used the buckle on one of the belts around my forearms to pop off the cap for her. "Overreacting much, buddy? Wouldn't let anything happen to her. Not on my watch. Not at my place. You should know that."

I shrugged, and Preppy chimed in before I could say anything. "Don't get all fucking butt hurt about it, Bear. King doesn't even trust me around her, and I only wanted to take her out on a date, and maybe put the tip in a little, but noooooo."

It was a lie. I hope Preppy knew that. I trusted him with my life, and I knew he wouldn't do anything with Doe that meant upsetting me. But that didn't mean I didn't want to slit his throat every time he smiled at her. Especially when every single day since the day I decided I needed her in my life, I'd felt like my every move had to be thought out around her so I wouldn't send her running scared.

Or worse, accidentally tell her the truth.

"You wanna get this shit started?" Bear asked, holding out

his hand he pointed to an old nightstand where several lines of white powder were already cut. I shook my head. I hadn't touched anything but alcohol and weed since I got out, but Preppy stepped up and did two lines. He knew me better than anyone, and he knew that a bump was the last thing I needed with all the adrenaline already coursing through my veins. But he also knew that doing coke with the bikers, especially Bear, was like their version of bringing a nice bottle of wine to a dinner party. A show of respect. Biker etiquette, if that makes any sense. I lit a cigarette and glanced over at Doe, who was looking around the place like she was discovering the lost city of Atlantis.

Another one of Bear's crew popped his head into the room. I recognized him right away as a guy named Harris, who'd been voted in just before I went away. "Bear, your old man's here. He wants to see you and said to bring King and his crew so he can say hi. He's back in the office."

Bear chugged his beer and let out a long belch. He threw his now empty cup at Bump. It bounced off his head and landed on the ground.

"Clean that shit up," Bear ordered, leading us from the room. "Come on, kids. Let's say hi to my old man and get it over with."

Bear's dad was the president of the Beach Bastards. One day, he would take the gavel from him and become the man in charge.

When we walked into the office, the door closed behind us and a clicking noise echoed in the room. Preppy turned back to the door and turned the handle, but it was already locked.

Shit. Bear swore.

Behind the desk, on the far side of the room, a chair sat,

facing away from us. It slowly turned, and where I'd expected to see Bear's dad, was Isaac.

"Motherfucker," Preppy swore.

Isaac's feet were propped up on the top of the desk. He was caressing his long braided beard. A toothpick hung haphazardly from his bottom lip. His eyes immediately narrowed in on Doe.

*Fuck.*

His eyes darted from me to Doe as he spoke. "And who is this?"

I felt my face getting hot with rage. If I ever saw that cocksucker Harris again I was going to tear him limb from chubby limb.

It was at that moment I realized how stupid bringing Doe to the party really was. Isaac was a dangerous man, and although I thought I had time before he rolled into town, I'd known him being around was a possibility. I'd planned to send Doe to Grace's house in a couple of days, at least until this all blew over.

Obviously, it wasn't soon enough.

It was a complete lapse in judgment on my part. My brain had been put on hold because all the blood had been in my cock, which for the better part of a week had been deeply lodged inside Doe's tight as fuck pussy.

"She's with me," I answered, keeping my voice as casual as possible. Trying not to let my words scream SHE'S WITH ME, IN A FOREVER KIND OF WAY SO BACK THE FUCK OFF OF HER, ASSHOLE. Instead, I kept my face hard and unemotional. "They with you?"

I gestured to the two blondes with sketchy looking matching pink BITCH tattoos on their biceps. They were making a show of touching each other's huge fake tits.

"I guess they are," Isaac said with a laugh. He clasped his hands together and gestured to the chair in front of him. "Have a seat, Mr. King."

I sat and pulled Doe down onto my lap where I kept a hand possessively around the back of her neck. It was a gesture that said she was with me, but it was disrespectful enough to Doe to tell Isaac that she wasn't all that important. She let out a surprised little yelp, and I rubbed the back of her neck with the pad of my thumb to comfort her. Her pulse raced in her neck.

Isaac's gaze roamed up her calves and settled between her legs where I was sure he'd caught a glimpse of her panties. I wanted to cross her legs or throw her off of my lap so that he'd stop looking at my girl like he wanted to eat her, but that would show him that she was my weakness. Instead, I slightly parted her knees with my hands to show Isaac more of her. He licked his bottom lip, and his gaze met mine.

"It's been a long time, KING," he said, his eyes glimmered with amusement. I pushed Doe's legs back together.

The way Isaac said my name sent chills up my spine. Doe went along with what I was doing. She trusted me and thank god for that, but the way her body tensed, I knew she was horrified over what I'd just done.

So was I.

"It has. I hear you recently lost your nephew in a tragic construction accident. My condolences," I offered.

Isaac smirked. "It was tragic, Mr. King, but it was no fucking accident. Wolfert was stealing from me. Simple as that. So, I had his throat slit and buried under three feet of concrete. The only real tragedy of it was that I was stupid enough to give him a chance at all, and that his mother calls me weeping three fucking times a day." Isaac lit a cigarette and scratched his head. "I've learned my lesson, Mr. King, and I won't be that stupid again. The number one rule in this business is to make sure that the people who fuck you over get fucked right back, or get dead real quick."

Doe stiffened.

Isaac waved to the blondes who brought over a bottle of expensive whiskey. One of them poured while the other passed around shot glasses. When she got to me, she made a show of brushing her fake tits up against my hand. I was about to tell her to get the fuck away from me when out of the corner of my eye I noticed Isaac watching my every move.

I grabbed the shot glass from the blonde and set it in the other blonde's cleavage. I made a show of licking the salt off her breast before dipping my head between her tits to bite the glass with my teeth. I threw back the shot all while holding Doe tightly to my side. I waved my hand dismissively when I was done, tossing her my empty glass and then redirecting my attention toward Isaac, who for the meantime, seemed satisfied.

Preppy and Bear stood in the back of the room. I had an uneasy feeling about the situation, and obviously so did they because they were in position to where if the shit hit they fan, they would be able to shoot their way out.

"Let's not sit in here and hash this shit out right now," Preppy said. "Let's party tonight and schedule a formal meet for tomorrow, when we've all had a chance to get drunk and get some pussy."

I could sense Preppy's wariness. I was able to read him better than anyone, and what he was really saying was *let's get the fuck out of here.*

Bear chimed in as well, "Yeah man, let's go out to the

courtyard. Strippers should be here by now. Bump and the boys are setting up mud wrestling out back. Let's get loaded, and get our dicks wet before all the serious talk goes down."

"Sounds good." I stood and started toward the door, dragging Doe with me.

Right when we reached the door, two of Isaac's men stepped into the room and closed it, blocking our exit, raising their guns.

When we turned around, three more of Isaac's men emerged from the room right behind the desk. Their pistols drawn and aimed.

"That's it? You fuck me over and expect that I would just party with you and forget all about it?" Isaac asked. He stood and walked in front of the desk. "You can't just shit all over a business I'd spent decades running. I'm not your whore. You can't choose to get in bed with me when it best suits you then leave me hanging after you have thoroughly fucked me."

"I was locked up," I argued, knowing that wouldn't be a good enough reason for Isaac. "You wouldn't deal with Prep. We needed to earn. We didn't cut you out. We made a business decision. A *temporary* one. I've been trying to reach you since my release, but you've had your balls in a knot. I'm not your girlfriend, Isaac. I didn't mean to hurt your feelings. Now, let's move the fuck on, and if you want to talk, we'll talk. But let them get back to the party." I waved my hands at my friends and Doe. "That way, they, at least, can enjoy themselves tonight."

"You think it's that fucking easy do you? This county may belong to you, but this is my coast. Anytime one of you little trailer trash bastards wants to so much as take a shit, you need my fucking permission!" Isaac spat, pounding a fist onto the desk. His face reddened. He turned his head to the side and passed the heel of his hand against his face, cracking his jaw from side to side.

Bear went for his pistol but he wasn't fast enough. One of the men who blocked the door pressed his gun to the back of Bear's neck.

"Don't even fucking think about it," he warned.

Preppy spoke up, "What the fuck do you want, Isaac? You want us to make it up to you? You want money? Fine, we'll up your cut. Make you richer than you already are. I honestly didn't think you'd care. We're small-time compared to your other operations. King was locked up. The idea was all mine. This entire thing is on me." His voice grew louder as he got bolder. "You want someone to blame? Blame me." He wasn't cursing, and his tone was serious. That worried me more than the guns to our heads.

Preppy was being reckless.

And he was doing it for us. So he could take all the blame and all the punishment.

I couldn't allow him to take all the blame, and I couldn't' allow this motherfucker to shit all over us like he ran the world. I wasn't a fucking drug lord, but I wasn't someone you could point a gun at and not pay for it with your life. I held Doe's hand and gave it a squeeze, trying my best to reassure her that I would protect her.

I very well intended to.

"But once I knew about it, I didn't stop it," I chimed in. "The Money was good, man. But we're ready to go big time. Need your help to take us there." I tried appealing to Isaac's sense of business. But there was a reason Isaac was successful. He cut down everyone who'd ever stood in his way like an angry lumberjack.

Even his family.

Isaac bent over and cackled like a possessed witch. The girls on the sofa scooted to the far edge in an effort to escape. "Stay right the fuck there, ladies!" Isaac warned. His laughter vanished instantly. Deep lines etched themselves into his forehead. His lips pursed. "This won't take very long."

"This ain't on them," Bear said, nodding to the girls and then to Doe. "Let all three of the bitches leave, and we'll handle this in any way it needs to be handled. Don't forget this is my house, my people. I don't know what you think is gonna go down, but it ain't going down without a fight. I got a few dozen of my brothers out there that don't sit idle when they hear gun shots."

Isaac strutted toward us. I instinctively shoved Doe behind me. Bad idea, because with that move, I showed Isaac she was more important to me than myself. It was instinct to protect her, but in that situation, instinct wasn't doing me any favors.

He smiled as he approached.

"King of the Causeway," Isaac said, quoting the air with his fingers around the label that had been given to me when I'd started to make a name for myself in Logan's Beach. "You ain't King of shit! The only King around here is me, and if you fuck with what's mine, the only way I see it is that I need to fuck with what's yours." He turned toward Doe. "Or fuck what's yours."

"You're not going to fucking touch her!" I roared, stopping just short of taking Isaac down when I felt the barrel of a gun at my back and Issac's knife at my throat. My gun was still lodged behind my belt buckle in the waistband of my jeans.

There was no way of getting to it without getting us all killed.

Isaac waved to his one of his men. "Bring her to the back

room."

The man stepped up and grabbed Doe, pushing her forward. She stumbled in her heels and fell onto her knees. The shoes fell off her feet and clattered against the floor.

With just a little fall, all my baser instincts screamed at me to go help her, protect her. But I was surrounded, and I couldn't do shit.

I'd never felt so weak in my entire life.

Isaac's man yanked Doe up by her arm and threw her forward. She landed with a smack, her cheek against the door. I growled. He opened the door and pushed her inside. Isaac followed her in and turned back to where I stood surrounded by guns aimed at my fucking head.

"Fuck," Preppy swore. We were utterly helpless.

"Like I said, KING. You fuck me. I fuck you. And since I'm not into cock, your girl here is going to have to do."

He shut the door.

# Doe

A man came up behind me and grabbed me by the arm, shoving me forward into a dark room, slamming the door shut behind me.

A small cot sat in the middle of high walls lined with empty shelving. I peered around Isaac, who entered the room after me and spotted King who mouthed IM SORRY as the door slammed shut.

Then, we were alone.

Dark and alone was my worst fear.

This was worse.

My only family in the world stood in the other room with guns pointed at them.

How fucking ironic was that? Because on the way to the party both Preppy and King were so concerned with my safety, they made me recite their rules to them several times over.

#1 Don't go off on my own.

#2 Make sure one of them was with me at all times.

#3 Don't take drinks from anyone but them.

We hadn't even been there an hour, and what they thought was the worst thing that could happen to me was in no way as bad as what was really happening.

They were worried about me being drugged and date raped.

What happened was so much worse.

Isaac wanted revenge on King, and it was obvious he'd planned it all out before we'd showed up at the party with the help of someone in Bear's MC.

King and Preppy could be killed.

They could've already been dead.

I couldn't feel my limbs, but I could hear the blood rushing to my head.

Maybe, it was all for show. I silently hoped that Isaac just wanted to prove a point and that his intentions weren't as bad as he'd let on.

No. They weren't as bad. They were worse.

Much worse.

Because the second the door closed behind me, the reality set in. I looked around for a weapon, something I could use to ward him off, but it was too late. I was on my back on the cot with Isaac's hand wrapped around my neck, silencing the guttural scream I didn't even know was coming from deep within my throat.

With one hand trapping my wrists, he straddled me, his thighs caging me in. He released my throat to roughly tug down my dress, exposing my breasts. I let out another scream, which was rewarded with his fist cocking back then landing square on my jaw. My brain rattled around in my head. I saw stars and my vision blurred. My insides were in full defense mode.

Every bit of adrenaline I had was being used to fight him off. But being dazed from the blow to the face, my efforts weren't enough because he released one hand from my wrists and fumbled with his pants, his fat, little limp cock rested on my thigh as I tried to buck him off with all I had.

He wasn't as big as King, but he was big enough to do whatever it was he had planned for me without much trouble. Fighting back with all my strength was nothing more to him than a slight amusement and minor annoyance.

I wasn't about to give up. There was no way King would be able to rescue me, this time. I was on my own and was going to survive this, even if that meant I had to rip his dick off with my fucking teeth.

In the meantime, I bit at any body part of his that came near me, my mouth landing on his wrist bone, rattling my teeth and barely piercing his tanned and tough skin. Immediately, I felt something cold against my forehead.

"I will fucking blow your brains all over this room if you don't stop biting me, bitch. Then, I'm going to have my men shoot your boys out there in the head and dump them in the fucking swamp. Is that what you fucking want?" he breathed, pushing the gun harder against my head.

"No," I gasped.

"That's what I thought. King needs to learn his place. He needs to know that when he gets in bed with me I'm the one who calls the fucking shots, and what's his is mine. These are my streets, my product. This is my fucking clubhouse. These are my fucking tits." He snaked his cold, wet tongue around one of my nipples, and I had to swallow down the bile rising in my throat. "That's why I'm going to fuck you right now. I'm going to fuck you without a rubber and send you back out there with my cum dripping down your leg so he can learn that he is the King of *nothing.*"

He slid his hand up my leg and grabbed a hold of my panties. When I screamed, he again he covered my mouth and straddled me with a knee on each side of my rib cage, squeezing his legs together so tightly I heard my rib crack at the same time I felt the explosion of pain in my chest. With his free hand, Isaac reached into his boot and produced a long hunting knife. He raised it into the air, and then brought it down into my thigh until I felt it hit bone.

Twice.

When he pulled the serrated blade out, he took chunks of my flesh with it. "I told you not to fucking scream, you fucking cunt."

Pain coursed through my leg and spread to every nerve ending in my body until it felt like my entire leg had been stabbed, not just my thigh. Tears poured out of my eyes as I struggled to see past the pain-induced blurry vision.

Isaac's hands were back up my dress, yanking my panties down, the cool air blew over my newly exposed parts, letting me know that Isaac had successfully removed them.

He settled himself between my legs and reached down to

position his cock at my entrance. "You fight me, and they're fucking dead," he said, looking me in the eyes.

There was nothing about his demeanor that would make me believe that he wasn't the kind of guy who didn't follow through with his threats. He meant every word. If I screamed, if I fought him off, the only people in the world who I loved would be dead.

King would be dead.

"That a girl," he hissed as I dropped my knees to the sides. With a whole lot of effort, Isaac managed to push himself inside of me. He was struggling. My body was so dry it was like it was fighting its own fight to keep him out. He spit on his hand and reached between us.

I closed my eyes tight. Maybe, if I didn't see it, it wasn't really happening.

But it was. Because although I couldn't see it, I could feel it.

He entered me, fully violating the body I'd finally taken possession over as my own. It wasn't just a violation of my body. It was an invasion of my soul.

*Pop Pop Pop Pop.*

The sound cracked through the air from the other room.

"What the fuck?" Isaac roared, lifting off of me just in time to turn his head toward whoever had just opened the door.

Pop.

Isaac's head exploded above me like a sledge hammer to a watermelon. My face became coated in thick, warm, red. The full weight of his limp body fell onto me, knocking the wind from my chest. Shrapnel of flesh and bone that used to be Isaac's head, landed in my open mouth, and I immediately turned my head and heaved into the floor.

King suddenly appeared beside me, gun in hand. He rolled Isaac off of me pushing his lifeless body to the floor, finally freeing me from his penetration.

King had lost his shirt and was only wearing a black wife-beater. Every inch of available skin on his arms and neck was covered with blood as if he just slaughtered a cow.

Or people.

King's eyes went wide when he looked down to my state of undress. Then even wider when he noticed the blood pumping from my leg.

"Fuck!" King aimed his gun at Isaac and fired twice, his lifeless body jumping when each bullet made contact. "Motherfucker," King muttered. "I am so sorry, baby. I am so fucking sorry."

"What the fuck is going on?" I asked. I was losing blood fast and getting more lightheaded by the second. King lifted me up into his arms. "Where's Preppy? Where's Bear?"

"Cover your eyes, Pup," King ordered.

"Why?"

"Because you may think differently of me if you keep them open," he whispered, carrying me into the other room. "It's not a pretty sight out here."

I knew I should have listened to him, but a part of me, a very stupid part of me, needed to see. But no matter how much I warned myself what was on the other side of the door, it wasn't nearly enough to fully prepare for the reality of what was in front of me.

Bodies.

Bodies. Everywhere.

Slumped over one another on couches, chairs, the floor. The white linoleum was covered in sludgy, dark red footprints.

Preppy sat in the doorway looking pale, clutching his side with one hand, blood saturating the area of his shirt his hand was trying to cover. Bear stood over him with his hands on his knees trying to catch his breath. Preppy looked up as we approached and scratched his head with the barrel of his gun. He flashed us a pained smile. That was so Preppy. Smiling while seriously injured in a room full of dead bodies.

"So…you guys ready to party now?" he asked, his usual loud and chipper voice was raspy, his breathing shallow.

He turned ghost white in a matter of seconds. The blood draining from his face at al alarming rate. His smiled faded as his eyes rolled back in his head until his pupils were replaced with only the whites of his eyes. Bear lunged to catch him as he fell face forward onto the cement.

Preppy exhaled on a strangled moan.

I would have given anything in the world for that smile and that breath, to have not been his very last.

## KING

*Fifteen years old*

"Fuck no! I ain't gonna be nobody's bitch," Preppy slurred at Bear. He took another giant swig from the bottle of cheap tequila we were passing around. The three of us sat on overturned milk crates on the floor of the living room of the shitty apartment Preppy and I had just moved into. The crates were the only furniture we had. "That cut is cool as fucking shit, but you ain't gonna see me announcing to the world that I'm a criminal. I keep my shit on the DL."

The place was a complete shit hole. Two bedrooms, one bathroom, and a kitchen that consisted of a hot plate and a sink

258

that sat on top of two cabinets in the corner of the square living room. One strip of black and white linoleum squares marked off the 'kitchen' area.

It was dirty. There was an ant mound growing under one of the baseboards, flies stuck to traps hanging from the ceiling. A fan with two broken blades that didn't turn on hung uselessly from the living room ceiling. The only window in the main living area was nailed shut so it couldn't be opened.

It was the greatest fucking place ever.

"Nah man, it's totally cool. Cops don't fuck with us cause they're scared of us. Besides, the MC parties all the fucking time. Pussy and blow everywhere, as far as the eye can fucking see, man." Bear swayed to one side and kept himself from falling off his milk crate by straightening one of his legs and anchoring the heel of his boot to the floor. "It's totally tits, man. You gotta join up. Prospect it out like me. Once I'm in, I'll vouch for you guys. Then after a year, it's fucking smooth sailing on the SS Tits and Ass. Besides, you'll love the clubhouse. It has a pool table *and* a fucking bar."

Bear had first told us he was going to turn Prospect for his dad's MC, The Beach Bastards, when he started buying weed from us in the eighth grade. He'd known what his future held for him since the day he was born. Since he spent most of his time with either the MC or us, he'd been trying to get us to Prospect with him since the day he decided that we were all going to be friends.

"Not for us, man. We're like our own MC of two. We're like the non MC, MC," I said. I'd moved on from the tequila and was lighting the two-foot tall purple glass bong that sat in the middle of the living room on yet another overturned milk crate, this one acting as our coffee table.

"You gotta kill people and shit?" Preppy asked in a lowered voice, like someone was listening in and he didn't want them to hear. He reached over to take the bottle back from Bear, stretching out his too-long-for-his-body arm.

Where I was fifteen and taller and more built than most adults, looking several years older than I was, Preppy was smack dab in the middle of an awkward phase that made his arms and legs look like a stretched out Gumby and his face looked as if he'd had a chronic case of the chicken pox.

"Only people that need killing," Bear answered like he was reciting something he'd heard a million times before, and no doubt he had. "No women or kids, nothing like that. Just people who know the score and understand the consequences, or people who fuck with the MC and us earning." Bear looked up at Preppy through his messy white hair and brushed it out of his eyes. "Why? You got someone who needs killing?"

He sounded very much like his father, President of The Beach Bastards. Bear's father was a psychopathic killer, who dealt in drugs and women, but Bear still managed to have the most stable upbringing between the three of us.

"Nah, man," Preppy said, waving his hand dismissively like the question was ridiculous, but I knew he was lying. I saw it in his eyes. "Just curious is all."

I also had a very good idea of who he thought 'needed killin'.

Bear looked around and leaned in close, waving for us to lean in bring it in as well. "We got these guys, specially trained. Pops calls them 'the janitors'. You know what their job is?" he asked pausing dramatically, waiting for Preppy and me to urge him on.

"What?" Preppy asked, totally enthralled. "What do they

do?"

Bear smiled, elated that Preppy had taken the bait. "When people need killin', or get killed, they sweep in and make it so it never happened."

He made a wiping motion with his hands in the air, extending them out to his sides. He sat back, looking pleased that he could share with us something about the MC. It wasn't until he turned prospect that he'd finally gotten a glimpse of the inner workings of The Beach Bastards, and he was always excited to tell us more about the club he was raised in but didn't necessarily know a lot about before he was given a PROSPECT cut.

The kid was a born biker, but as much as he tried to get us to join, it wasn't for us.

Preppy and I never strayed from our plan.

Ever.

"You guys ever need a cleaning up, you call me. I can put a word in. Problem is, you'd owe us a favor. That's how it works. No matter when we call in that favor or no matter what that favor is, you gotta do it." Bear lit a cigarette and waved the smoke away from his face. "Nuff of that shit, boys. Preppy, you got the goods or what?"

"Goods?" I asked. I wasn't aware that we were selling to Bear today, or any other day for that matter. Since he turned Prospect, he bought his weed from the MC.

Preppy hopped up and walked over to the hall closet. He came back holding something covered with a ripped sheet. "What the fuck is that?" I asked.

"This—" Preppy waved his hand over the sheet. "—is your birthday gift, you ungrateful fuck." He set it on the floor and grabbed the sheet in the middle, lifting it off like a magician. "Voila!" He stepped back, and my eyes focused on what was in front of me. It was a cardboard box and inside of it were bits and pieces of something.

Not just something. It was a tattoo gun.

"Happy birthday, you fucking fuck! Now, let's figure out how to put this thing together, because Bear and I already picked out which tattoos we want from your sketchbook." I stared at the equipment in front of me, not believing my eyes.

"If you take any longer to get started putting it together, I'm going to request mine be put on my taint," Bear said, knocking me out of my stunned state.

"Thanks, boys." I lifted the box onto my lap and started tinkering with the parts. "And Bear?"

"Yeah, Man?"

"There is no fucking way in hell I'm ever going anywhere near your taint."

"Noted."

That day, I tattooed for the very first time. I didn't do the ones the boys had picked from my sketchbook. They were too elaborate and although I could draw, I'd never used a tattoo gun before so the full back piece Bear wanted with intertwining snakes, The Beach Bastards logo, would have to wait until I knew what the fuck I was doing.

Instead, Bear got a small shamrock behind his ear, although I'm not quite sure if he was any sort of Irish. Preppy settled for PREP on his knuckles. The lettering was thin and crooked. They were the worst tattoos in the world. Blown out edges, a bloody fucking mess. But the boys loved them, and I couldn't wait to practice on them some more.

"I'm so gangsta." Preppy said, admiring his newly tatted up knuckles.

"You're about as gangsta as my ninety year old Grandma,"

Bear said.

"Bear, doesn't your grandma have a full chest tattoo and purple hair?" I asked.

"Sure does," he replied.

"Then, I actually think she's way more gangsta then ole Preppy here," I said.

"You guys laugh now, but you'll see. King here is gonna tattoo my neck next. I'm gonna look real mean."

"Are you still gonna still wear button down shirts, bow ties and suspenders?" I asked.

"Fuck yeah. Always. That's my style."

Bear chuckled. "You may not look tough, or mean, but you might confuse the fuck out of people."

"Fuck this shit man," Preppy said, standing up. "I gotta go get the last of my shit from my stepdad's. I'll be back. Feel free to laugh at my fucking expense while I'm gone, shitheads."

"You want me to go with you?" I asked.

"Nah, I got this shit. It's past nine. Fucker's either at the bar or passed out on the couch. I'll be back in an hour."

Preppy never talked about it, but I was sure that his step-dad was still beating him up until the day he moved out. He was always slightly limping or clutching his ribs. When I asked him if he was okay, he usually told me he was working out. "Nah man, did chest today, hurts like a bitch when you do it right." He was a shit liar, but his pride was all he had besides me and Bear. Although we joked around with him, the last thing we wanted was for Preppy to be hurting at the hands of some drunken asshole.

When I hadn't heard from Preppy for two hours, I got on my bike and peddled over to the trailer park his stepdad wasted his life away in. As soon as I parked my bike, I heard a commotion inside.

"Prep?" I called out. No response.

"FUCK YOU!" I heard Prep roar from inside. His high-pitched voice cracking with his strained scream. With one kick, I knocked in the flimsy door.

What I saw beyond it would haunt my dreams for years to come.

His stepdad, Tim, had Prep bent over the end of the old corduroy couch, thrusting furiously into him while holding a pistol to his temple. When I sent the door flying into the room, he turned his attention my way, along with his pistol. Preppy turned and knocked him on his side, the gun slid across the floor. Preppy lunged for it but his jeans, which were still wrapped around his ankles, caused him to trip and fall forward against the wall.

"Get the fuck out of here, boy. You two think you're better than this place? Well, you're fucking wrong. I was teaching Samuel here a lesson. He belongs here. He ain't no better than me and needs to know it."

I kicked over empty beer cans and made my way to the gun. It was the first time in my life I remember seeing red. Seeing red isn't just a saying, I found out. My vision was tinted the color of the rage boiling inside my veins. I flexed my fingers. My joints itched with the need to release the pressure building within my bones. I wanted to hurt him, but the want was secondary to the *need* to hurt him.

"What, are you gonna do? Fucking shoot me?" Tim asked, sitting up against the kitchen cabinets. Pushing off the floor, he went to stand, but before he could, I raised the gun and knocked him in the temple with the butt. Tim went flying across the tiny kitchen, landing head first into the door of the refrigerator.

"Fucking shoot him!" Preppy called out, righting his jeans. Blood dripped from his nose. His cheek was already yellow and purple. Apparently, he'd taken one hell of a beating before Tim decided that anal rape was a more appropriate way to teach the kid a lesson.

"So, you're gonna beat me, kid? Is that it? Gonna teach me a lesson now, boy?" Tim looked up at me from the floor.

"No," I said, an eerie calm washing over me. The rage took a kind of precision-like control over my actions. "I'm not going to teach you shit."

Fear registered in Tim's beady little eyes.

"Then what, boy? You gonna call the cops? Cause I know the cops round here. They ain't gonna do shit!"

"No," I said, taking a step toward him, the gun in my still hand pointed toward the floor.

"Then, what the fuck, boy? You gonna kill me?" Tim laughed nervously until he saw the affirmative look in my face.

I raised the gun, aimed it at Tim's forehead, and fired.

"Yes."

## Doe

THE ONLY TIME KING SPOKE TO ME IN THE DAYS following Preppy's death was to ask me to go into Preppy's room to find something I thought he would like to be buried in. At least, that is what I took from the grunting and nodding that he'd been using in place of actual words. King was hurting, and I couldn't do anything to make it go away.

I'd never been in Preppy's room before, and when I opened the door, I noticed that his room was huge, much bigger than King's. Preppy had the master bedroom. The room was neat and tidy but full of random things. Shelves of books, video games, action figures, and knickknacks of all kinds.

On his dresser was a single picture. A selfie of the three of us. He'd taken it one morning when he rushed into King's room and bounced on the bed to wake us up, which he did frequently. King and I were on either side of him, tangled hair and half-asleep. King was covering his eyes.

He'd never wake us up like that again.

Preppy's closet was a large walk-in, overflowing with clothes of all kinds. One wall was lined with storage bins that were all neatly labeled. One bin was partially opened. The label read *Shit random chicks leave in my room* and was filled with women's clothing. I guess that solves the mystery as to where Preppy was getting all my clothes from.

I chose a yellow shirt and the loudest bow tie Preppy owned, a multi-colored checkered pattern, from a bin labeled *Awesome Fucking Bow Ties.*

Suddenly, holding his clothes in my hands, the final clothes he would be wearing at his funeral, it all became too much. I crumpled to the floor and held his jacket to my chest. My heart felt a million times its size. I couldn't breathe. I couldn't do much of anything except silently cry, holding onto a little piece of the only true friend I'd ever known.

I don't know how long I was down there, but I must have cried myself to sleep, because I woke with dried tears on my cheeks and Preppy's suit wrapped around me in a crumpled mess. I stood up and rehung the jacket onto a hanger and just as I was about to hang it on the back of the closet door in an attempt to dewrinkle it, I saw something taped to the back of the closet door. A small white envelope. And in Preppy's messy handwriting the words:

*OPEN ME MOTHERFUCKERS*

King insisted on taking his bike to the funeral in what I think was his way of continuing to avoid any sort of conversation. When we pulled up, there were already several bikes parked along the road that wound through the lush grounds of the cemetery as well as Gladys's old Buick.

We were the last ones to arrive. Bear and a handful of bikers, Grace, and six of the 'Growhouse Granny's' were already seated under the portable canopy covering the rectangular hole in the ground that Preppy's shiny black casket hovered above. All were dressed in black. Some of the grannies wore matching black floppy hats. King wore a black collared shirt and jeans.

I threw caution to the wind and wore a yellow sun dress. I think Preppy would have liked it.

As we took our seats on the damp plastic chairs in the front row, King grabbed my hand and set it on his lap, intertwining our fingers, bringing me as close as he could bring me without sitting me in his lap.

The preacher nodded to King, then started speaking about life and death. He even tried to say a few words about Preppy, although the two had never met. I had to stifle a laugh when he referred to him as a wholesome and well-respected member of the community. For a fraction of a second, King's stoic face gave way to reveal a hint of a smile, while Bear downright let out a blast of laughter from where he stood against one of the canopy poles. The preacher paused to collect his thoughts, then continued.

"Who has words for our dearly departed today?" His voice was mechanical, like he was reciting a manual.

I felt for the envelope in my pocket to make sure it was still there. When Bear started walking to the front of the small crowd, I stood and cut him off. King shot me a look of confusion, and Bear stopped in his tracks.

"Hi," I said, realizing my voice wasn't loud enough for everyone to hear when some of the grannies put hands to their ears to amplify the sound. I tried again, speaking a little louder this time.

"My name is Doe, and although I didn't know Preppy, er, Samuel, very long, he was my friend. A great friend. My best friend. As much as I want to say a few words about him and how much he meant to me, in typical Preppy form, he's already beat us to it."

I took the envelope from my pocket and unfolded the notebook pages with small scribbly handwriting. I'd already read it, and I didn't want to cry, so I tried to zone out while I read the final words my friend wanted his friends to hear before we laid him to rest. "So, just a warning, I know we have some…mature folks in the crowd. Because this is coming right from Preppy, it contains some, um…colorful, language."

I glanced apologetically at the preacher whose attention was already down at his cell phone, his thumb raced across the keys.

*Friends and MoFo's,*

*Like you thought I would let you have the last fucking word. Fuck that. I'm way to OCD to have you try to come up with some nice things to say about me, so I came up with them myself. I've updated this weekly since I was ten years old, thinking that because of the situation I was living in that I wasn't going to make it to see twelve and that my family, if you could bother to call them that, wouldn't expend the effort to say anything at my funeral. And the thought of that, the thought of silence when they put me into the dirt was worse than the thought of dying to me. After that, it became kind of a habit, so I kept doing it.*

*So in the event of my untimely death, this is what I need all you fuckers to hear.*

*If you're reading this to a crowd of people dressed in their funeral finest, then I've achieved a longevity I never thought I would reach. I've made it to the ripe old age of twenty six and it's been one hell of a fucking ride.*

*By now, I'm dead and will soon be rotting in the fucking ground, being eaten by worms and other random bugs and shit. But don't worry about me because I died a happy fucking man. Looking back, I never thought I would live a life where the word happy could be a fitting word so describe it, but I did And it was all because when I was eleven years old, this big fucking brute of a man-child rescued me from a bully who shall not be named, and then he became my friend. Oh fuck that, the bully's name was Tyler Nightingale and the pussy still lives with his fucking mom and works the night shift at the Stop-N-Go. Fucking twat. Go egg his fucking car on the way home.*

*Anyways, I motherfucking digress.*

*The man-child became more than my friend. He became the best fucking friend anyone could ever ask for. He became my only family. Our childhoods were complete shit, but because of him, we were able to live our lives by our own set of rules. He didn't have to befriend a skinny kid with bruises all over his body and a foul fucking mouth. He could have looked the other way. He could have ignored me when I pestered him to no end. There are a lot of things he could have done. But he chose me to be his family, and I chose him to be mine.*

*Although there were bumps in the road, a little juvie, a little jail, and whole lotta shit I can't talk about here. I don't look back at those things as poor choices. I see them as part of the highlight reel of the most epic fucking journey of my life. A journey I never thought I would see. Shit, I never thought I would live past the age of 14, and if it wasn't for my best friend, and him saving my ass one night, I wouldn't have.*

*I want to send a shout out to Bear. Big-ups to you, you big fucking animal. Go travel. Go do you. Go do all the shit you want to do before that club of yours swallows you whole and you can't see where your ideas start and their ideas end.*

*No shit. At first, I thought you were just an annoying hanger-on, but it turns out that I was capable of having more than one friend after all, and I'm fucking glad it was you, man.*

*Bear, you need to look out for King and Doe. Lord fucking knows those two will need all the help they can get. I mean, they fucking love each other, but both are too fucking stupid to see past their own crap long enough to keep their shit together.*

*I see major fuck ups in their future. Be there for them. Help them see past their ridiculous issues and preach to the about the joys of honesty and anal sex.*

*Continuing on.*

*I've done shit I'm not proud of. Thanks to all of you for not judging me. Thanks to all of you for being my friends in spite of it. Thanks for giving me a life that was worth dying for. I would do it all over again if I fucking could. So don't fucking cry for me, be happy for me. Be happy that I had friends like all of you who I loved more than fucking family, who I loved more than myself, and we all know how crazy I am about me. Be happy that I was happy and that all you fuckers were a part of that.*

*Doe, if King doesn't get his head out of his ass and marry you and impregnate you with millions of his little man-children, he is a dumb fuck and I promise I will rise from the grave to take his place. It may take me a while to figure out how, but if anyone can do it, it's gonna be me.*

*King, my brother, thanks for taking a chance on a skinny geek all those years ago. Thanks for fucking saving my ass, but you did more than that. You saved my life. You gave me a life.*

*I love you, man.*

*Be happy kids.*

*I gotta go be dead now. No after funeral bullshit. I fucking hate that shit.*

*Go get laid. That will make me happy.*

*Fuck. Party. Make merry. And know that I fucking loved all of you.*

*-Prep*

*PS-I have also written my own obituary which I would like published in all the local papers. I'm serious about this. I will haunt you if this doesn't happen.*

"Ummm, I don't know if I should read this next part out loud."

"Do it!" Bear cheered me on. Even from the other side of the tent, I could see the tears in his eyes, but now there was a smile on his face. "Let's fucking hear it!"

The crowd joined in, and I was left with no choice.

"Oh, fine," I said, taking a deep breath and speed reading through Preppy's autobiographical obituary.

*Samuel Clearwater*

*26 years old*

*Badass MoFo*

*Went out like a boss*

*Leaves behind the family he chose: King, Doe, Bear, and the GG bitches.*

*May God rest his soul...and his ten-inch cock.*

The entire group of mourners burst out laughing. Not just a few chuckles, but knee-slapping, belly laughter. As I put the note away and took my seat next to King, I realized what Preppy had done. He was the kind of guy who couldn't bear the thought of us crying over him, so he did what Preppy always did.

He made us laugh.

I looked over to King, who wasn't smiling at all. I tugged on his hand, but instead of getting his attention, he stood up.

Before the preacher said his final words, King was already long gone.

## KING

MY GIRL HAD BEEN RAPED, AND IT HAD BEEN A WEEK since we put my best friend into the ground. In that time, I didn't know where to place my anger at the person I hated most in the world.

No, not Isaac. I killed that motherfucker. Splattered his head wide open with a bullet at close range.

The person I hated most in the world was me.

After everything Doe had done for me, after everything we'd been through, she deserved better than to live a life in fear of being raped or shot. As much as I wanted out of the life, it wasn't something I could just jump out of in an instant. I need-ed to do something for her, but no matter what came to mind, it wasn't big enough to make this huge wrong, right again.

Then, it came to me.

There was one thing I could do for her.

One fucking reverse GOOGLE image search. That's all it took to find out who Doe really was. I'd uploaded a photo of her I took from my phone the first night she'd slept in my bed and pressed search and there she was, staring into the camera like she was looking right into my eyes. I wished I'd never done the search. I wished I'd never known who she really was.

I'd used the fact that I knew who she was and what that could do for me as an excuse to bring her back to me. Even though it was her I wanted since the very first moment I saw her.

I'd planned to keep her forever, and her secret even longer if need be.

Until now.

Seventeen year old Ramie Elizabeth Price.

Either the police were really shitty at their jobs, or they never really tried to find out who she was to begin with, because for the second time after searching her image, less than a second after pressing search, I was staring at multiple images of the girl I'd fallen in love with on my laptop.

There were no articles about her going missing, just pictures of her from various events. Balls, galas, fundraisers. It was her in the pictures, but it wasn't. The gowns, the makeup, the fake smile, if there was any smile at all.

The last picture of her I found was taken almost a year ago. She had a blank look on her face. Her eyes were vacant.

I knew that look. I'd regrettably put it on her face myself. It was a look that broke my fucking heart.

Indifference.

She was holding the hand of a boy who looked a little older than her, who was smiling from ear to ear.

I wanted to reach through the computer and break his fucking hand and then break every single one of his pearly white teeth.

**Senator Westmore Bigelow Price, with daughter Ramie Elizabeth and long-time beau Tanner Preston Redmond at the Heart Ball Gala to raise money for pediatric cancer.**

Even though it was my second time scanning the pictures, my blood boiled. I don't know what made me madder. The boy who was touching my girl. Or the man they listed as her father.

A senator running for president. A man who would want to avoid scandal at all cost. That's probably why they didn't even try to find their missing daughter.

Fucking asshole.

I stood from the kitchen table and threw the laptop across the room. It smashed against a cabinet and fell to the floor in a million pieces.

Bear came storming into the kitchen. "What the fuck?" he asked, looked over at the broken laptop. "You on the rag man?"

"We have to take a trip," I said, staring down at the now broken laptop as though the image of Doe or Ramie, or whatever the fuck her name was and her boyfriend were still up on the broken screen that was flashing from blue to black over and over again.

"Where we going?"

"Tell me something, Bear, and be honest. What are the chances of us getting the kind of money we need for the payoff to the senator for Max?"

My eyes met his for the first time since he came into the kitchen.

"Slim to fucking none, man" he answered honestly.

"Then, get the fucking truck. I'll drive."

"But you still haven't said why I'm getting the truck."

"Because, my friend, there is a deal with the devil that needs to be made." I looked down the hall at the closed door of my bedroom, where the girl I'd fallen in love with slept peacefully in my bed. She was mine, and I would always think of her that way. But she deserved a better life than the one I could give her, which seemed to only hurt her at every turn.

After Preppy's funeral I was thinking about giving her the truth.

Now, I was just going to give her away.

"And who is the devil in this scenario?" Bear asked, shrugging on his cut.

I was going to see the senator and offer Doe in exchange for him making sure that I had signed custody papers for Max.

The only family I had left.

I stared out the kitchen window, but couldn't see a thing. It was like I was staring into a white abyss, a place I was about to go, that I wasn't ever going to be able to come back from.

"Me."

## KING

WHEN YOU FALL IN LOVE, YOU KNOW IT'S THE REAL deal because you come to the realization you would take a bullet for that person. And when you become a parent, you realize that you would not only use your own body but the body of the person you love as a human shield to protect your child.

That is the place where I existed.

The Senator had a daughter who had a life, a boyfriend. I wasn't doing Doe any favors by keeping her with me, involved in shit she shouldn't be involved in. It got Preppy dead. I wasn't doing my daughter any favors by leaving her hanging out there in the world without protection. She needed her father. She needed her family.

She needed me.

I was going to give it all up for her. I couldn't manage the payoff, but if the senator accepted my offer of a trade, then I could keep what money I did have and that was enough to sell the house, and disappear of the radar to somewhere where nobody knew who we were.

Me and Max.

I was going be a good father to her. A good influence. A good role model. I would get us a house in a good neighborhood and send her to a good school. I would read to her at bedtime. I would make this fucking work because it *had* to fucking work. I was going to disappear because my life was going to reappear.

I lost my best friend, and that made me realize that sooner or later I was going to lose my girl, too. Because as soon as she learned that I'd known who she was from the very beginning, she would hate me forever.

I needed Max because she was all I had left, and I was bound and determine not to fuck that up. I prayed to any god who listened that if I could just be with her, I would make things right. I would give her my all.

My love.

My heart.

My daughter.

My everything.

I made a decision that broke my fucking heart and made it sing all at the same time. So what if I felt like a piece of me would always be missing? Fuck it. I would have my daughter.

And she was my heart.

In exchange for Max, I was going to give Doe, or Ramie, or

Pup, or whatever you want to call her, back to her father.

By not telling Doe about what was going to happen, I wasn't giving her an option. But there was no doubt in my mind that when she found out what I'd been hiding all along that she was going to look at me like the monster I am.

But then again, she might be grateful to me for giving her her life back.

Maybe, not.

I pretended not to care all the way to the senator's office.

I was going to have to be prepared to pretend for the rest of my life.

"Do you have an appointment?" the receptionist with curly black hair and dark freckles across her nose asked, without looking up from her computer.

"My name is Brantley King, and I don't need a fucking appointment. Let him know I'm waiting. Give him this. He'll want to see me."

I placed the folded up picture on his desk, one I took of Doe this morning while she was sleeping. I didn't wait for her to answer. I took a seat in the waiting area in a plastic chair that faced her desk. When she finally looked up from her computer, her jaw dropped. She'd probably never seen someone who looked like me waiting to see the senator. I didn't have the patience to be inconspicuous. I needed to make shit happen and make it happen before I changed my fucking mind.

The receptionist stood and walked down the hall. She emerged a few moments later and dialed a number on her phone. She held her hand up over her mouth as she whispered into the receiver.

"Senator Price will see you now," she said, with a fake smile, setting the phone back on its cradle.

She stood, and I followed her down the hall until we came to an office with a double-door entry. She opened it and stood aside to let me through. When I stepped inside, she shut it behind me. There was another click, which I'm sure meant that she locked it as well.

"I know who you are, Mr. King, and the only reason I'm even letting you in this office is because I know you had to pass through the metal detectors. So, I know you're not armed," the Senator said, standing up from behind his oversized mahogany desk, holding the picture I'd given his receptionist in his hand. He was trying to even the playing field, but he didn't seem to understand that I was the one holding all the cards.

"That's where you would be wrong, Senator." I lifted up the front of my shirt and removed the pistol from the front of my pants. I was wearing my big metal junior rodeo belt buckle trophy. The one I got for looping a sheep at the fair. "Crazy thing about those metal belt-buckles. They make the alarms go off every single fucking time."

The senator sat back down and folded his hands on the desk, gesturing to the chair in front of him. "Let's cut the shit then, shall we?"

A picture on a shelf beside his desk caught my eye. It was my Pup, several years younger than she was now, on some sort of beach, her smile bigger and brighter than I'd ever seen. She'd been happy once, and it was seeing that bit of happy that made it easier to propose my deal.

"I have your daughter. You have ten seconds to tell me why you don't know where she is and why you aren't looking for her. The truth. Not some bullshit lie either," I warned.

The senator's eyes grew wide. "You better not have harmed my daughter so help me..." He stood abruptly, his chair tipped backwards and crashed onto the floor. "What do you know?"

"Calm the fuck down. What I know is that she has big blue eyes and a tendency to talk too much when she's nervous." And then just for fun I added, "I know how her heart beats faster when she's turned on."

"What the fuck did you do to my daughter?"

"Oh, no. That's not how this works. You need to answer me first. Why haven't you reported her missing? Why haven't you looked for her?"

"Why do you think we haven't been looking?" the senator asked, settling back into his seat, nervously wringing his hands.

"Because if the senator's daughter went missing, you would think it would be kind of a big deal. All over the news and whatnot. And it isn't."

Senator Price picked his chair up off the floor and sat down, rubbing his hands over his eyes.

"We've been telling people she's studying abroad in Paris. But as you already know, that's not the truth," he admitted. "We didn't report her missing because Ramie is a troubled child. She started hanging with the wrong crowd. Disappearing for weeks at a time. This time, it's been months, and she hasn't so much as used my credit card. Her mother and I thought she was rebelling, teaching us some sort of lesson. We'd gotten into a huge fight before she stormed out. We haven't seen her since."

"So, you didn't report her missing, because she was a troubled child? Or because you were up for reelection and you were afraid the story would taint your oh-so-perfect political image?"

"Did you see what happened to Sarah Palin when they found out she had a sixteen year old who was unwed and pregnant? It killed her! I couldn't do that to my party, and I knew

Ramie wasn't really missing. She'd just run away like she'd had so many times before. So I made up excuses, lies. I told people what they wanted to hear, and her mother and I prayed every day she would at least call." He looked distraught. "Tell me she's okay."

"Yeah. She's fine."

The senator let out a relieved breath.

"Why did she never come home? Does she really hate us that much?" he asked, his fingers pressed to his temples.

"She doesn't remember. She was in some sort of accident. She woke up with no memory. She doesn't even know her own name."

"What?" He stood up again. "Take me to her. Now! I need to see her!" he demanded.

"Not so fast." I held up a hand. "Sit the fuck back down, Senator. It seems we have a little trade we need to work out."

He sat back down. "Yes, of course. What are your terms?"

"No bullshit. No money. What I'm offering is a flat trade. Ramie for Max. My daughter. Here is her information." I placed a receipt on his desk. "On the back is my daughter's name, social security number, and the address of the foster home she's been living in, as well as all my information. Be at my place. Tomorrow at noon. Bring Max and all the custody papers, giving me full rights to my daughter and then and only then, you'll get yours back." The words hurt coming out of my mouth, but they needed to be said because the trade needed to be done.

"That can be arranged, but I'll need more than a day," the senator said, nervously shuffling his thumbs one over the other over and over again. I stood and walked to the door.

"Tomorrow at noon. If you're not there, if you don't bring Max—" I turned and faced him one last time. "I'll slit your

283

girl's throat. No hesitation. If I can't have my daughter, I won't let you have yours. I don't give a shit what happens to me after that."

I waited until I was in the car and Bear was driving out of the parking lot to exhale.

"How did it go?" Bear asked.

I sighed.

"That bad?"

"It went about as good as it could have gone. It's what I did that I'm sighing about."

"What exactly is it that you did in there?"

"I just traded, Doe."

"For what?" he shouted.

"Who," I corrected.

"Okay, for who?"

"Max. I just traded Doe for Max."

"Oh. My. Fuck."

"Yeah, that about sums it up," I said, running my hand over my head. "If I wasn't sure whether I'd ever sold my soul, I'm positive I have now."

## KING

I WAS IN BED WITH DOE. IT WAS ALMOST MIDNIGHT, AND I was already counting down the hours to noon. Noon was when I would see Max for the first time since I held her in my arms the night I let my mom burn in the fire.

Noon was also the last time I would ever see my girl.

Doe was going to become the person she was supposed to be, the person she was born as, Ramie Price. She probably wouldn't bother glancing back at me in the rearview mirror after realizing the life of luxury she was heading back to. I was never good enough for her to begin with, and this was going to be both the most selfish and selfless thing I'd ever done when it came to her.

285

I was giving her back.

I was getting my daughter back.

I'd never been so miserable, and excited at the same time. A few months ago, I didn't think that if I got Max back I would be doing it all alone. I thought at least I'd have Preppy. Then, I thought Doe would be in the picture.

Now, it was down to just me.

I lifted my leg over hers. I couldn't get close enough. I'd convinced her to let go of the person she was to be with me, but unlike Preppy, her past life had risen from the grave and had been haunting me since I hit the search button.

I was tossing her back like a fish that wasn't worth keeping.

But she WAS worth keeping.

She was worth fucking everything.

Everything I couldn't give her.

There was no doubt in my mind if something like soulmates did exist that Doe was mine. The problem was that Ramie wasn't. Ramie had a boyfriend. Ramie had money. Ramie had a future that didn't include a felon with tattoos and a penchant for violence. Ramie wasn't going to have to put herself in danger, risk getting shot, or ever have to worry that either one of us was going to get hurt or end up dead.

I wanted more for her. I wanted to break her heart and mine and get it over with so we could both heal.

Her with her family.

Me with mine.

I turned her onto her back and rolled on top of her. Spreading her legs, I lowered myself until I could taste her sweetness one last time. I slowly lapped at her folds as she woke with a moan on her tongue. Water welled up in my eyes. I'd licked her into her first orgasm by the time the first tear fell.

I was glad her eyes were closed when I entered her and began thrusting fiercely into not just the greatest pussy I've ever had, and the greatest girl I'd ever known, but the greatest love I knew I'd ever have.

The only love.

If things were different, I'd put a ring on her finger. A baby in her belly. We'd have Max. We'd have Preppy. We'd be the family I always wanted but never knew could exist.

Because it didn't exist.

Preppy was fucking dead, and my girl was about to return to the life of privilege she was born into.

I told her I loved her with each thrust of my hips. I told her I was sorry. I told her that I wanted her to stay forever. I told her I wished she would have my child. I told her everything with sex that I dared not speak out loud. I told her that if things were different that we would be together forever.

*Forever.*

I'd never spoken the word in my life, but looking down at Doe, still half-asleep as I brought her to the brink of another orgasm, I saw what forever would look like.

And it was fucking beautiful.

A wayward tear dripped from my chin. I reached out and caught it in the palm of my hand before it had a chance to wake Doe from the state of sleepy ecstasy she was currently in.

Before she could find out how I really felt.

Before she was gone.

Forever.

The next morning, for the first time in my life, I made love to a woman. I didn't fuck. I didn't have sex.

I kissed her the entire time. I held her as close as two people could be. I told her she was beautiful. That I loved everything about her.

I waited until she was in the throes of her orgasm to whisper, "I love you." I don't know if she heard me, but I was saying it more for me than for her.

I needed to say those words while I still had the chance.

I think a part of me loved Doe from the first moment my eyes landed on hers. Haunted, beautiful, scared. I wanted her, body and soul.

I would only have her for a few more hours, and I was going to spend every second of that time, inside my girl.

While she still was my girl.

# Doe

Every time I woke during the night, King was touching me. It was like no matter how close we were, it wasn't close enough.

I dreamt that he told me he loved me. Once before, after finishing my tattoo, he'd told me to *shut up and let me love you*. But what I heard in my dream was the real deal.

There was something wrong. I felt it in my bones. I'd asked him what was bothering him, but he brushed me off and just kept making love to me.

For hours.

Maybe, he was lost in thoughts of Preppy, and just needed me to be there for him.

So, I was.

Our time together that morning was so unlike anything I'd experienced with him before.

I told him over again that I was okay after Isaac forced himself on me. It was a moment in life, a horrible one. But I know I'd be okay. As long as I had King, I would be okay.

It would all be okay.

I was helplessly, passionately, in love with the complicated man who touched me like I was a thin square of glass, and he was afraid I was going to shatter.

He whispered to me how gorgeous I was as he dragged his cock against my clit. He pulled out of me and rubbed against my sensitive bundle of nerves when he thrust back in.

I was alive with sensation, and full of questions.

He whispered how much he loved being inside me. How much he wished he wasn't so much of an asshole. How I deserved the world. How he wasn't good enough for me.

And then it hit me like a fucking freight train with no brakes, and my heart seized inside my chest.

King was saying goodbye.

The sun was already high in the sky by the time I woke up and got dressed. At any second, I expected King to burst through the door and tell me he wanted me gone. It was a horrible thing to be waiting for. I was going to pack, but there was nothing there that was truly ever mine.

I threw on some clothes and headed outside to find King. Rather than waiting around with my neck stretched out on the block, I went in search of the executioner. I found him outside, rocking in the swing I'd recently convinced him was the only thing missing from the porch.

"What's going on?" I asked him. "Something's wrong. Tell

me." He buried his face in his hands.

"Everything, baby. Everything is wrong," King said, looking up over the porch railing.

I walked over to him and he ran his hands up and down my arms. I sat on his lap and draped my arms around his neck. He burrowed his nose into my chest.

"Tell me. Please," I begged. "I can help."

"You can't. Nobody can."

"You're scaring me. You need to tell me what's wrong."

"My fucking heart is broken," he said, raising his raspy voice.

"Why? Who broke it?" I asked.

"You did," he said, looking up at me with tears in his eyes.

I was taken aback. What did I do to break it? Did I even have that kind of power over him?

The sound of an approaching car turned both of our heads to the driveway. A black town car with dark tinted windows pulled up in front of the house.

"Will you remember something for me?" King asked, snapping my head back around from the car to him.

"Anything," I answered. And it was true. I would do anything for him.

"Remember that I love you," he whispered.

He had said it. I didn't just imagine it.

"Why are you telling me this now?" I asked, finding it odd that King wasn't even acknowledging the approaching vehicle.

I wanted him to love me, especially because I'd known I'd been in love with him for so long, but the way he said it, and what had transpired that morning told me there was a lot more to what was going on.

"Tell me what the fuck is going on!" I leapt from his lap.

"Baby," he said, reaching for me.

"No! Don't *baby* me! Tell me what the fuck is going on!"

King finally looked toward the town car. The driver got out and walked around, opening the door of the back seat.

A boy a little older than me, with dark blonde curls stepped out of the back seat. He wore black Chucks, grey shorts, and a red batman t-shirt. It wasn't until he looked up at me when I recognized him. Or at least, his eyes.

Chestnut brown.

The eyes from my dream.

I was stunned into silence, frozen on the porch as the boy approached.

"Ray? Ray is that really you?" he asked, looking right at me.

I looked up at King whose expression had completely changed from troubled and weary to angry and vengeful. He was staring daggers at the boy. His jaw tensed so hard I swear I could hear his teeth grinding.

"Who is Ray?" I asked King.

"Don't fucking do this," Bear snapped from the doorway.

"Go the fuck back inside," King barked.

"Fine. It's your fucking life. Fuck it up more than it already is. Preppy would've kicked your fucking ass for this. I'm going to visit my sister. I can't stick around and witness this shit." Bear stepped out onto the porch and pecked me on the cheek. "Love you, pretty girl," he said before disappearing around the side of the house. A moment later, his bike whizzed by, kicking up dust in its wake.

"You," King finally answered. "You are Ramie Price."

"Ray, don't you remember me?" the boy asked. "I'm Tanner. Don't you know who I am?"

I turned to King. "What is this? Who is he? Why is he here?"

"He's your…boyfriend." He forced the words off his tongue like they were stabbing him in his mouth.

"My what?" I didn't wait for him to answer. "You knew he was coming?" Then, it hit me, and I sucked in a strangled breath. "You knew who I was?"

King didn't say anything, but most importantly, he didn't deny it.

"How long have you known?" I whispered.

King looked down at his shoes.

"How long have you fucking known?" I shouted.

"Since the very beginning," he admitted. "Since before I came for you again after you escaped."

"Escaped?" Tanner asked, reminding me of his presence.

"The entire time?" I asked, feeling as if he just stabbed me in my chest. "You knew who I was this entire *fucking* time?"

"What the fuck do you want me to say? I'm a shit person, and I do shitty things. You knew that. I fucking told you that, but you went and fell for me anyway." He ran his hand over his head in frustration. "Well, it's over now. Welcome to your new life. Or I should say your *old* life," King spat.

He lowered his eyes. "You deserve better than all this shit anyway." He waved his hand toward the house. "You deserve better than me. You've got a family. Go be with them, and forget I exist."

His eyes darted down to Tanner who stood in the front yard with confusion marring his face. He glanced back and forth between me and King.

"What's going—" Tanner started to ask.

"Shut the fuck up," King snapped, effectively silencing the

boy.

"That is NOT your decision to make," I told him. "You don't get to say where I go or who I go with."

"Actually, it is," King argued.

"What the fuck does that mean? What the fuck did you do?"

"Ray!" the boy shouted over our argument.

King looked down at him as if he were going to leap down the steps and crush his skull with his hands.

"Come down here," Tanner said in a gentle voice. "Just for a second. I just want to see you. Talk to you."

I looked back at King, and it dawned on me. It wasn't my decision to make because he was giving me away.

That's what last night and this morning were all about. He was saying his goodbyes.

King nodded to me as if to say I had his approval to go talk to Tanner. I rolled my eyes at him. I didn't need his fucking approval.

I tentatively descended the stairs one at a time. When I got to the bottom, I sat on the bottom step. "Do you know who I am?" Tanner asked, crouching down and resting his hands on his knees.

I shook my head. "I recognize your eyes, but nothing else," I admitted.

"As I said, my name is Tanner. We've known each other our entire lives. We were homecoming king and queen all four years of high school," he said with a chuckle. Then his face grew serious. "I love you. You love me. Always have." Tanner blushed and rocked back on his heels. "It feels weird to introduce myself to you when we've known each other since we were in diapers."

"Who am I?" I asked hesitantly.

Tanner took a seat on the step next to me, careful to keep some distance between us. I didn't need to look back at King to know he was watching Tanner's every move. I felt his gaze on my back as if they were rays of the sun singing my skin. Tanner smelled like the beach. His unruly hair fell into his eyes. He brushed it out of the way as he spoke. A huge smile spread across his face, revealing a dimple in his left cheek.

"You are the lovely Ramie Elizabeth Price. Daughter of Dr. Margot Price and Senator Bigelow Price. You live in East Palm Cove, about an hour from here. You were enrolled in art school, and you were supposed to start in the fall. You and I were going to backpack around Europe for the summer first, but then you disappeared."

I had a name.

Ramie. Ramie. Ramie.

"Ramie," I whispered, testing the name out on my tongue. Still nothing.

"I went to the police. They said no one was looking for me. No missing persons report. Why didn't you look for me if I was missing?" I asked.

Tanner shook his head. "I didn't want to have to be the one to tell you this, but you had this friend, and she was going through some bad stuff. She got in trouble a lot. You left a note, said you were running away. They didn't look for you because they didn't think you wanted to be found. You had just turned eighteen. You were an adult. There was no missing persons report because you weren't missing. You were just gone."

"I left?" I asked.

"Yes."

"I left you?"

"Yeah," he admitted. "You left me. And your mom. And

your dad. Everyone."

I had a mom.

"Why isn't my mom here?" I asked.

"We didn't want to overwhelm you. Your mom is at home, waiting for you to arrive, but your dad is in the car." Tanner said, pointing to the town car with the blacked out windows, still running on the driveway.

"I still don't remember. I thought I would remember if I saw someone from my past, if they told me who I was, but I don't." My head spun. If I didn't remember him face to face, would I ever remember him?

Would I ever remember anyone?

"You will, but it will take time. You just need to get back into the groove of things for a while. Your normal routine. It will come back to you. We won't rush it. Your mom's got the best doctors already on call. Specialists. You'll be back to your old self in no time," he said, nudging my shoulder.

King had already told them everything. At least enough for my mom to already have doctors at the ready.

The girl who I'd given up on might be back after all.

The back door of the car opened again, and out stepped a tall man in a sharp black suit and a solid red tie.

"Who is that?" I asked Tanner.

"Your dad," he told me. "The senator."

"Ramie," the man said. "Your mother is worried sick. Let's go. Get in the car," he said sternly, buttoning the bottom button of his suit jacket.

It was ninety degrees outside, and there wasn't one drop of sweat on his forehead. No redness on his cheeks. It's like he was too important to be affected by the heat.

From above me, King leaned forward over the railing.

With the light of the sun directly overhead, his massive frame cast a shadow onto the ground.

He really did look like a King. A force to be reckoned with. Zeus, on his perch above the world.

The senator stepped out of King's shadow as if he were too good to be standing in it. This irked me.

He wasn't better than King.

No one was.

King was a bad guy, but he was my bad guy. He was more than that. He was my world. My heart. These people may have known who I was before, but I knew who I was now, and the two versions of me were going to have to figure out how to merge before I uprooted what I had with King in search of something unknown.

"Senator," King acknowledged the man.

"Mr. King," the senator greeted, shielding his eyes from the sun with his hand.

"Where's Max?" King asked, bitterly.

"Soon, she'll be here soon. There is another car on its way here with her in it."

"Trade means trade." King said. "She isn't going anywhere until Max gets here."

Then, it hit me. King had said I didn't have a choice, and now, I knew why.

If I stayed, King wouldn't get his daughter back. The trade he mentioned was me for Max.

"There she is now," the senator said as another town car pulled up into the driveway. King bounded down the steps jumping over me as he made his way over to the car. The second it stopped, King opened the back door.

"Max?" he shouted into the car.

The driver rounded the vehicle and produced something from his jacket pocket. He slapped a metal cuff around King's wrist.

"She's not in there," King shouted, pulling at the cuff. "What the fuck is this? Where is she?"

The man I thought was the driver twisted King's other arm forward and secured the cuffs in front of him.

"What are you doing?" I shouted, running up to King. "Let him go!" A pair of strong arms grabbed me from behind and stopped me from getting any closer. "What the fuck is going on? I need to go to him!"

I kicked my feet in the air as the man I was told was my father lifted me up off the ground. King's nostrils flared as the man who'd just put King in cuffs, wrestled him into the back seat of the car.

"Mr. King, this is Detective Lyons. You're being arrested for the abduction of my daughter," the senator said, all the while maintaining his hold on me.

"But he didn't kidnap me! He didn't do anything. He saved me. He SAVED me!" I shouted, biting at his arm as I tried to break free of his grip.

And I meant it. King had saved me. In every way. He'd saved me from myself, from a life of standing still. Because of him, I was moving forward.

I wanted to move forward with him.

"You motherfucker!" King shouted. Detective Lyons closed the car door, and I lost sight of King behind the heavy tint of the windows.

"No!" I called out. The car took off and disappeared under the trees. "Let me fucking go!"

The senator turned me around to face him and grabbed

me roughly by the shoulders. "Calm down, Ramie, or you're going to scare him," he warned.

"Who? What the fuck are you talking about?"

Tanner walked over to the car and opened the door. A little boy with curls like Tanner's and hair as white as mine tumbled out of the back seat.

The little boy saw me and opened his arms. He came bounding up to me and crashed into my thigh.

The senator released his hold on me. The little boy nuzzled his face into my leg.

I looked down at him, puzzled.

Because it wasn't the way his eyes were as icy-blue as mine, or how the dimple on his chin matched mine that alarmed me the most.

It was what he shouted that made my heart stop.

"Mommy!"

To be continued in the next book, **TYRANT**, available now.

Read on for a glimpse at the Prologue.

# PROLOGUE

## KING

THE AVERAGE TIME SPENT BETWEEN INCARCERATIONS for a career criminal is six months.

I'd only been out three.

I'd expected to find Max in that car. Instead, cold metal clinked around my wrists, and the asshole pig had the audacity to laugh when he tightened the cuffs to the point of pain.

I didn't wince though. I wouldn't give him the satisfaction. He pressed down on my head roughly and shoved me hard into back of the old police cruiser. I landed on my side, and my cheek slammed against the sticky seat. It smelled like vomit and bad decisions. My hands tingled from the loss of blood flow.

The motherfucker was lucky I was in cuffs.

Three years. They already had me for three fucking years,

and now they were going to have me for a whole lot longer.

Kidnapping wasn't exactly rewarded with a light slap on the wrist, especially for someone whose record was as long as mine. I promised I was never going back, but keeping my promises is just another thing I was never very good at.

I was all out of fucks to give though. The system could have me. I belonged to them now, but they didn't fucking own me. They would NEVER fucking own me.

*She* owned me.

Heart and black fucking soul.

I will walk to the fucking chow line with a shit-eating grin on my face wearing my scratchy orange jumpsuit every motherfucking day. I will play cards with the worst of the worst and make nice with the guards who were willing to cut me some slack. At night, when I'm alone in my windowless cell with my dick in my hand, I will remember what it was like to have her in my bed; how her innocent wide eyes stared up at me as I moved inside her, the way she arched her back into me as I made her come over and over again.

I kept telling myself that I didn't have anything to offer her, but that wasn't true.

I had *love.*

Pup. Doe. Ray. Whatever the fuck her name was. I loved her more than what was normal, rational, or sane, and I would gladly rot in fucking prison with a smile on my face if I knew my girl was going to be okay.

But I didn't know that. I couldn't know that.

I should have known that motherfucker was going to fucking cross me.

"The notorious Brantley King," the pig said with a smirk as he got into the front seat. The plastic-like leather squeaked against his belt as he closed his door and started the engine. "You'd think you'd have learned your lesson by now, boy."

He laughed and shook his head. It was obvious that this guy was getting some sort of sick pleasure out of being the one to put me in cuffs.

"King," I corrected him defiantly. Nobody called me Brantley but *her*.

"Excuse me?" he asked, raising an eyebrow at me through the mirror.

I sat up straight, meeting his gaze with mine as if I were staring straight through to his pussy-ass soul. "They call me King, mother fucker."

The rage inside me grew to epic proportions. That's when I noticed the detective didn't turn onto the main road but instead drove straight onto the path through the woods.

This guy was no fucking cop. I spotted his gun; he'd set it on the dash. It was a Judge, not the kind of gun that was standard police-issue. This guy wasn't taking to me jail.

He was taking me to ground.

There was no time to waste.

My girls needed me.

More than that, I needed them.

The moron had cuffed me in front. That should've been my first sign that something was off. A real cop would've never done that unless he was transporting a nonviolent criminal.

Which wasn't me.

Using the chain that connected my cuffs, I trapped the fake detective's neck against the headrest and yanked back with all my might until I felt like my biceps were going to explode.

His hands left the wheel and flailed about as he tried to connect with my head, but I dodged him by lowering myself behind the seat.

The car veered off the path and bounced from side to side as it ran over a patch of knee-high roots.

The pressure mounted behind my eyes as I tugged back on the cuffs, squeezing tighter and tighter. I didn't release my hold until the car came crashing to stop and every inch of life had drained from his body.

The fake cop was right. I would never be anything more than the notorious Brantley King.

That was fine by me because the senator had a lesson to learn. You did not take what was mine and not expect to pay in blood, sweat, or pussy.

He took my girl. He wanted to take my life.

His payment would be in blood.

# Other Books by T.M. Frazier

**KING SERIES:**
KING
TYRANT
LAWLESS
SOULLESS
PREPPY, PART ONE

STANDALONES:

THE DARK LIGHT OF DAY, A KING SERIES PREQUEL
ALL THE RAGE, A KING SERIES SPIN OFF

# ABOUT THE AUTHOR

T.M. Frazier is a *USA TODAY* BESTSELLING AUTHOR best known for her *KING SERIES*. She was born on Long Island, NY. When she was eight years old she moved with her mom, dad, and older sister to sunny Southwest Florida where she still lives today with her husband and daughter.

When she was in middle school she was in a club called AUTHORS CLUB with a group of other young girls interested in creative writing. Little did she know that years later life would come full circle.

After graduating high school, she attended Florida Gulf Coast University and had every intention of becoming a news reporter when she got sucked into real estate where she worked in sales for over ten years.

Throughout the years T.M. never gave up the dream of writing and with her husband's encouragement, and a lot of sleepless nights, she realized her dream and released her first novel, The Dark Light of Day, in 2013.

She's never looked back.

For more information on books and appearances please visit her website www.tmfrazierbooks.com

FOLLOW T.M. FRAZIER ON SOCIAL MEDIA
FACEBOOK: www.facebook.com/tmfrazierbooks
INSTAGRAM: www.instagram.com/t.m.frazier
TWITTER: www.twitter.com/tm_frazier

For business inquiries please contact Kimberly Brower of Brower Literary & Management. www.browerliterary.com

11745565R00197

Made in the USA
San Bernardino, CA
07 December 2018